PRESENTED TO

PRESENTED BY

ON THIS DAY

COURAGEOUS IN SPIRIT

COMPASSIONATE IN SERVICE

SEA OF GLORY

KEN WALES & DAVID POLING

A NOVEL

SEA
OF GLORY

BASED ON THE TRUE WW II STORY OF THE
FOUR CHAPLAINS AND THE U.S.A.T. DORCHESTER

BROADMAN
&HOLMAN
PUBLISHERS

NASHVILLE, TN

Ten-digit ISBN: 0-8054-4380-0
Thirteen-digit ISBN: 978-0-8054-4380-6

Published by Broadman & Holman Publishers,
Nashville, Tennessee

Original hardback version published by Broadman & Holman Publishers
under the same title in 2001. The hardback version is now out of print.

Dewey Decimal Classification: 813
Subject Heading: HISTORICAL FICTION

Back cover photo courtesy of The Mariners' Museum, Newport News, VA.
Shipbuilding plans courtesy of Newport News Shipbuilding,
Newport News, VA.

1 2 3 4 5 6 7 8 9 10   10 09 08 07 06

To all who served their country with valor, and
fought with courage, so that good would
triumph over evil . . .

. . . to those who braved the Atlantic on the
Dorchester . . .

. . . And to the men and women whose lives were
given so that we, in Freedom, might live . . .

"Greater love hath no man than this, that a man
lay down his life for his friends" (John 15:13).

CONTENTS

CHAPTER 1

RENDEZVOUS

The sea was gray and calm, lapping the rocks along the beach with a steady, regular motion. There was no wave curl to crash and melt onto the land, only irregular patches of white foam moving up and down rhythmically on top of the quiet water, dotting the surface from shoreline to horizon where the steely ocean met the somber sky.

"I'm getting cold, Poppy. Can we go back inside now, please?"

Wesley Adams looked down at his grandson. As he spoke, the boy put an arm around Adams's waist and buried his head in the front of his coat. His blond hair blew in the wind, and he closed his eyes tight against the sudden blast of sea air tinged with salt spray.

"In a minute, Alex. Just one more minute." Adams spoke softly without looking away from the water.

The two stood alone on the rocky beach. Behind them, lights from the windows of the Arctic Hotel shone in the twilight, projecting their bright rectangles in precise formation across the sloping, pebble-strewn lawn that ran between the building and the shore. Above the sound of the wind they could hear the animated murmur of conversation and laughter coming from inside. There were fewer of them every time, Wesley thought. The longer they could keep this up, the better. The more it meant. The more Alex and the rest of the world might understand.

"Poppy?"

Adams didn't answer, didn't look away from the quiet gray sea and the misty line that fused it with the sky above.

"Is this where it happened?" Alex waited a long moment. He knew his grandfather had heard him.

"Yes, Alex. Here."

"I wish I'd been here too."

Did he really? Wesley didn't know if that was a good thing or a bad thing. He'd spent the last fifty years turning that question over in his mind one way or another. He could hardly explain how he felt about this place to his wife, or his best friends, or anybody who hadn't seen and felt and done what he had here once. How could he explain it to a ten-year-old boy? He longed to explain it, though; it was the main reason he had brought the lad with him. Every other trip here over the years he had made alone.

"Poppy?"

The old man broke from his gaze and looked down at his grandson. "You go ahead, Alex. I'll be there in a little bit."

Wesley watched as the boy bounded over the rocks, up across the lawn, and into the front door of the hotel. Alex was doing well, he thought. Picking up a sense of this place and the occasion that brought them here was a pretty fair accomplishment for a kid his age. And it was cold, Wesley had to admit. Spring in Greenland must be quite a jolt to a youngster who had spent all of his springtimes up to now in Indianapolis.

Alone, Wesley walked a few yards over to where The Rune waited, gray like everything else, looming over the other rocks nearby. Somebody had named it after the stones prehistoric settlers had put up on the island: tall rocks sort of like he'd seen in pictures of Easter Island. This jutting slab was the landmark he remembered from the day he came ashore; this was the spot he and the others always came back to, standing at the base of The Rune to look out over the water and let the memories come cascading over them like a waterfall.

He pulled off one glove and fished inside his pocket for the envelope. It was crisp and new, about half the size of a regular manila envelope but white, capturing and holding the last of the daylight as he ran his fingers across it, looking first at it and then at the empty seascape in front of him.

He reached inside and pulled out a thin sheaf of lined paper that had been folded and folded again so many times the pages looked like they might spontaneously separate into quarters any minute. He put the envelope back in his pocket, and held the pages tightly, protectively, against the gusts. Shielding them with his body, he unfolded them carefully and, finding the best angle for catching the faint dusk that remained, he began reading to himself, sometimes pausing to look up at the water.

If I made it to the lifeboat, it would be a miracle.

I'd waited as long as I could to jump, to the point where it was more like stepping off the front porch of the house in Springfield, Illinois, where I grew up than it was jumping off the rail of a ship swarming with desperate men. As the icy deck inched steadily under the water on its way to the bottom of the dark North Atlantic, the area where men could stand grew smaller, driving the remaining soldiers and sailors into one another in an ever tighter and more frantic huddle. Once in a while one of them would separate from the cluster and jump into the swells, like a kernel of popcorn from a skillet.

I heard other soldiers shouting and screaming all around me, some of them still on deck and others already in the water. The noise seemed muffled and distant even though several of them were so close their life jackets bumped against mine. I felt their hot breath as they bellowed curses, prayers, and the names of their buddies out into the Arctic darkness.

I felt my own legs and other legs nearby churning up the icy water, instinctively trying to stay afloat and keep the circulation going. Every other sensation was shut out by an all-powerful coldness. Below decks in my bunk twenty minutes ago I'd been about to roast. Even though the temperature hovered around zero outside, it was sti-fling and miserable down there. Now the water was like a thousand needles sticking in me from every direction.

At the first shock of it I couldn't breathe for a minute; my whole chest was paralyzed until a crest rolled me on my face and gave me a snootful of water mixed with fuel oil. I didn't know then that the oil insulated me in the water and probably saved my life. I gagged and heaved for a while, finally got a couple of clear gulps of air, then looked around to try to figure out what to do next.

Only two or three lifeboats had been launched. Some dangled useless because of the list angle of the ship as she sank, but most of them were jammed in the davits. It hadn't been above freezing since we left St. John's almost four days ago, and the sleet and saltwater spray had gradually encased the pulleys in smooth, translucent spheres of ice harder than steel. These frozen globes had withstood the onslaught of axes and knife blades until the brittle steel snapped, of frantic fists until they were bloodied and broken. The men who had wielded those axes and knives were in the water with me now. Fear made their eyes flash brilliant in the red light of the emergency beacons that began shining from the corner of every life jacket.

After a few minutes the eyes began losing their brilliance, gradually transforming two by two into milky, vacant circles on faces frozen in hideous variations of agony and disbelief.

I don't know how far away the lifeboat was when I first saw it. Forty or fifty yards maybe, headed away from the ship. As I watched, it came about and stopped. One or two guys in the water started swimming for it; the rest I guess didn't see it or didn't care anymore. I made it to the side of the boat and grabbed for the gunwale. Hands came down over the edge and took hold of my wrists, then my arms and shoulders. I couldn't tell when I was all the way out of the water because I was so numb. I sat down and somebody gave me a blanket.

Around us in the dark I could see red locator lights from the life jackets, bobbing on the swells, spread out in every direction like roses on velvet. I knew for every light there were probably two more men who had gone overboard without life jackets. Nobody had wanted to wear them down below as hot as it was, even though we were ordered to keep them on twenty-four hours a day, including sack time. By the time they'd run up to the deck without them, it was too late to go back; the gangways were already full to the ceiling with seawater. Sitting on a bench in the lifeboat, I couldn't imagine being hot again as long as I lived.

The sky and the ocean were the same jet black color. I could hardly see due to the faint light of the languid moon, and when I first looked over at the Dorchester, *it seemed like it was hovering in midair. The bow was already underwater; crests lapped at the foot of the superstructure amidships. That was when I saw the four lieutenants standing on the exposed hull near the fantail in the dim light, accented by a dozen or so flashlights, some red, some white, waving around in the void. I'd only met them a couple of weeks before, but sitting there in that pitching, freezing boat I knew that because of them my life—however much longer it lasted—would never be the same.*

In spite of everything going on, they stood there almost like friends at a picnic, casual and relaxed. They had their coats on, but none of them now had a life jacket. As I watched, they locked arms in a circle and lifted their heads up to the dark sky. I could see their mouths moving but heard nothing at first; then, straining, I caught snatches of their voices interspersed among gusts of wind, the slap of waves on the sides of the lifeboat, and the cries of dying men in the water.

Music. They were singing.

Eternal Father, strong to save,

Whose arm doth bind the restless wave . . .

It was faint, but what I heard was lusty and confident. Not typical of the sounds men make when they're obviously minutes from death. But nothing had been typical about that bunch.

*I forgot about those thousand needles in my flesh as
I watched the circle of men settle lower toward the surface of the sea. The ship was sinking fast enough now
that every wave crest lapped closer to where . . .*

The bottom of the page below the crease was still in
the envelope in his coat pocket. That was all right; he
knew the rest of it by heart. The pages ended up in
smaller pieces every year. Here was another quarter of
a page that had to be taped.

The sun had been down for a while now, but it was
still light. Darkness came slowly this time of year to a
place less than four hundred miles from the Arctic
Circle. Wesley looked out at the North Atlantic. As he
glanced down again at the dog-eared sheets in his
hand, a tear ran down his cheek and dropped onto the
paper. He thought it was a good thing he'd written in
pencil. If it had been ink, the pages would have washed
clean years ago.

He transferred the pages to his gloved hand and
reached into another pocket. After fishing around a
few seconds, he pulled out an old-fashioned watch
chain. On the end of it dangled a delicate and beautiful pocket watch. Any passerby walking to the hotel
just then would have thought it a mighty odd thing
to have on a rock-strewn beach in Greenland. The
watch and chain were both made of old rose gold that
glinted and flashed even on a gray day like this one.

The beautifully engraved case seemed almost to glow with a warmth of its own.

He held it up so it caught the light from the hotel windows. There was a shell design—a family coat of arms and, Wesley always reminded himself, a symbol of baptism. He looked at it carefully, running his thumb across the surface to feel every familiar nick and imperfection. Slowly he lowered the watch back into his pocket and dropped the chain in afterward.

Wesley Adams was still rather handsome to be more than seventy years old. Taut and wiry, he had fared better over the years than some of the men back up at the hotel, those who were left to meet here to mark another anniversary of the night they had shared and survived together unlike any other night of their lives.

He didn't know how long he stood there with the cold wind coming off the water and whipping his hair around his face. Every sensation from the first time he had stood there on that beach came forward from some distant recess. The confusion and shock. Too exhausted to be hungry. Too cold to think about anything but the cold. Helped ashore by strangers from the Coast Guard cutter that had picked them up six hours before in Arctic blackness.

He could see the old night again as clearly as he saw his hand before him, feel the freezing needles, replay the sight of that wedge of the rear deck of an old coastal steamer hovering between sea and sky, yielding steadily to the waves. The weakening cries of dying men. And the triumphant sound of that strange impromptu quartet of lieutenants, all chaplains, cast across the water and debris and pockets of burning fuel oil, folding the night itself into a strangely comforting embrace.

Who bidd'st the mighty ocean deep
Its own appointed limits keep . . .

He turned back toward the Arctic Hotel. It was the biggest building here in Narssarssuaq, near Cape Farewell on the southern tip of Greenland. Now a modest tourist attraction, it had been built as one of the most important top secret Allied installations of the war. Sergeant Adams had been on his way to this place that night.

"Blue West One," he said softly to himself looking up at the building. Then he smiled and put his tattered pages away.

"Poppy?"

Wesley started. He had neither seen nor heard Alex come down over the rocks to the water's edge.

Alex stared at his grandfather's eyes. "Are you OK?"

"I'm fine."

"Your eyes look sad."

"Sorry." The two stood together, and the boy put his arm around the man again. Wesley swallowed, cleared his throat, and spoke. "Really, I'm OK. I feel good, actually." Another pause. "I'm glad you're here."

Alex looked around. "I've heard about Blue West One for years. Since I was a little kid," he said.

Wesley Adams chuckled. "Years, huh? Well, we'll see if this trip won't tell you a little more.

"Still cold?" the man asked.

"I'm better now."

Wesley squeezed his grandson's shoulder. The two stood looking out to sea again, squinting into the wind. Now he could barely make out the line separating sea and sky. As he stared northward along the beach, he thought he saw four figures in the distance walking toward him. What would four guys be doing that far from the hotel this time in the afternoon? Was it some kind of illusion? Temperature inversion? An old man's imagination agitated with thoughts of times and things past?

He was mesmerized by the sight. He didn't know whether Alex saw it too; he didn't ask but looked on silently as four images came closer. Soon the four seemed close enough for him to recognize, as plain to the old man as if the four chaplains were walking there on the beach and coming over to greet him. He could see they were talking and laughing among themselves, though all he heard was the sea breeze and the water lapping up on the rocks of the beach. He recognized them by their walks even before he could see their faces: friendly, easygoing Father John Washington; calm, confident Reverend Clark Poling; experienced, knowledgeable Pastor George Fox; and last but never least, athletic, enthusiastic Rabbi Alex Goode.

There they were, friends ambling along the beach and looking around nonchalantly at the shore they were destined never to reach in life. Adams stood with his back to The Rune, watching them. His eyes met Washington's; in them he saw the answering gleam of recognition.

O hear us when we cry to Thee
For those in peril on the sea.

"Thank you," the old man said, not realizing he had spoken aloud. Alex hugged him tight, and his grandfather looked down in reply. The boy saw tears streaking down his grandfather's face.

"I love you, Poppy."

"I love you, Alex."

Arms around each other's waist, the two stood for a moment together.

"Go on back inside if you like," Wesley Adams said. "I'll be right there."

CHAPTER 2

THE
VETERAN RETURNS

Before George Lansing Fox had any idea he was heading toward the Methodist ministry, he knew he had to get out of the boxy old duplex in Altoona, Pennsylvania, where he grew up. His father worked at the Altoona railroad shop—the largest in the world—and spent his evenings with fellow Sicilians on the South Side. His German mother kept her daughter and four sons in line and out of their father's way. She was an organized, no-nonsense woman whose steadfast faith and regular church attendance helped her cope with her husband's hair-trigger temper; she was sure it was caused by the constant pain in the stump of his amputated leg.

George shared an attic room with his three brothers. With its low ceiling and windows, the room was stale, hot, and miserable all summer. Trying to fall asleep in the heat, George thought of stories he read in books borrowed from the Kruezpointers, an old, kindly, childless couple down the street who had turned their living room into a library for neighborhood children. Imagine what it would be like to be free of the household routine and his father's stifling rules!

George was seventeen when America declared war against Germany in 1917. He could hardly wait every morning to read the newspaper accounts of all the action and study the maps of troop movements and campaigns. Young men from Altoona flocked to recruiting offices to volunteer, and George ached to join them, but he was a year too young. He thought perhaps his mother would give her consent, which would allow him to enlist now. But what if she refused? What if she told his father? He was already thinking about moving the family to the country and starting a farm, where he would be in iron control all day every day, and where he would insist that all the boys pitch in to help.

A few days later George stood on the sidewalk in front of the recruiting center wondering if he should go in. He paced back and forth for a while, then stopped and stood a little longer. Finally, chin up, eyes straight ahead, he stepped confidently inside. The sergeant on duty had a gruff voice, but his eyes seemed friendly and kind.

"What's your name, son?"

"George Lansing Fox."

"When were you born?"

George was quick with the answer. "Eighteen ninety-eight," he lied.

"Where's your birth certificate?"

"Didn't know I'd need it, sergeant."

The sergeant paused a moment and sized up his young applicant. George was muscular and well-developed for his age. He looked twenty.

"OK. I'll ship you out to Columbus Barracks. You can send for it from there. Be here tomorrow at eight o'clock sharp to board the 8:09 with the rest of the recruits. Congratulations, soldier."

"Yes sir, sergeant!" George's smile lit up his whole face. "Thank you!"

Back home that night, George decided to keep his plans to himself. His brother John had already run off and started a new life on his own, and now it was George's turn. When he heard his father's wooden leg tap-tapping on the sidewalk, he thought, *This is the last night I will ever sit at the kitchen table in this miserable house dreading that sound.* He wouldn't miss his sister or his other brothers. Certainly he had to admit he would miss his mother, but he had confidence that her faith would protect her and keep her safe. George would get in touch later to tell her he was all right.

After a sleepless night—the sleeplessness of excitement and anticipation, not of fear or indecision—George got up and dressed for school as usual. In his pockets he put a toothbrush, a clean handkerchief, and what little money he had. That and the clothes he wore were all he would take with him. After breakfast and the usual cursory good-byes, George walked out the door, down the ramshackle front steps, and headed for the train station. He never looked back.

Most recruits chafed at army discipline, but to George it was heaven compared with the oppressive atmosphere of home. And because he was in top physical shape, the marches were a piece of cake. He particularly enjoyed the time between duties when he was free to do whatever he wanted. All his life he had watched his mother faithfully reading her Bible and going to church; now he started filling some of his off hours by reading from a little khaki-covered New Testament small enough to carry into the field.

He was assigned to the ambulance corps. That was God's providence, he thought: he'd be healing wounds instead of causing them. It would be a dangerous assignment, though, one of the most dangerous in the army. But if God could keep track of sparrows as they fell, he knew God would protect him, unarmed and exposed to cross fire on the battlefields of France.

He went to Camp Baker, Texas, to learn to drive an ambulance. Hardly anybody back at school in Altoona knew how to drive, and here he was learning how and getting paid thirty dollars a month for it! This was a new sort of job for the army; it was the first war where there were motorized ambulances. Up until now the dead and wounded had been evacuated in horse-drawn wagons.

George and the other soldiers spent weeks practicing first aid on each other, setting up treatment stations in the field, and learning the teamwork that would enable them to work as fast as possible under enemy fire. According to established rules of war, ambulances were supposed to be protected from attack. But in the modern era, their instructors warned, it seemed like whatever rules of war there were had been all but abandoned. Even though ambulance crews were unarmed, they were fair game.

Late in the fall Private Fox was transferred to Camp Merritt, New Jersey, in preparation for shipping out to France. He was there for only a few days but still had time to enjoy a twelve-hour pass to New York City, where the young man got a glimpse of a life he had only imagined: the excitement of Forty-Second Street, lined with nightclubs and packed with excited, thrill-seeking servicemen; magnificent Grand Central Station, where the trains came in under the ground, right up into the basement; the skyscrapers, capped by the Gothic grandeur of the Woolworth Building, the tallest building in the world. He wondered if he'd ever be back.

December 3, 1917, Private George Fox shipped out for Europe aboard the *Huron,* traveling in a convoy and zigzagging through the water to avoid German submarines. By the time he arrived at Brest he had survived debilitating seasickness and a flu epidemic on board. Two men had died en route and were buried at sea. Fox thought the chaplain who conducted the service seemed tentative and a little unsure of himself. Maybe it was that the chaplain was sick too. No doubt the stench of sickness on board, which nobody could get away from, distracted him as much as it did everybody else. After all, chaplains were only human.

After a season of cold, wet duty in field hospitals well behind the lines, Fox was transferred to the front. What he had seen already made him grieve at the horror of war, but it was tame compared with the carnage that arrived at the field hospital in Ventri, near the American headquarters at Chaumont. The wounded there were like something from a nightmare: faces blown away, arms and legs shredded and mangled. Blood, pus, gangrene, agonized screams, and the smell of death ran together in one constant presence.

Fox could scarcely stop to think about any of it. It took all his concentration to hold his stretcher level and run across the cratered, muddy ground with yet another wounded soldier hour after hour, week after week. Off duty, exhausted, cold, and covered with mud, he would try to find a quiet corner to sleep. But he always found time to read his New Testament—by now dirty and dog-eared—that had worn its shape in the left shirt pocket where he always carried it.

Rumors of an armistice were as thick as the sodden winter air as Private Fox helped set up a new field treatment station at Giraucourt. It was November 10, 1918. One moment Fox was hammering tacks in a wall. The next instant, there was an ear-splitting roar followed by a terrific crash as a 200-mm "Jack Johnson" artillery shell hit the building. A collapsing wall showered the medical team with bricks; Fox saw a flash as the roof of the building split open and was flooded with light. There was no sound.

Then there was a whiteness all around him, and Private Fox was surprised to realize he was in a bed made up with clean white sheets. He tried to sit upright, but his muscles failed to respond. Instead he felt a sensation like a thousand hot rivets from the Altoona yard pounding into his back at once, pain so sudden and hideous he couldn't even take in a breath to scream.

His back had been nearly broken in the hail of bricks. It was months before Fox could walk again. Like so many soldiers, he spent a lot of time wondering what the whole experience meant. He had a nice box with a Silver Star in it and a Purple Heart. But what would he do? As he recuperated, Private Fox thought about the future. He had reconciled with his family by mail. But they had moved to a farm, just as he thought they would, and he had no interest in joining them there.

At nineteen, with certified 29 percent disability because of his back injury, no high school diploma, and no family he wanted to claim, he was on his own.

He began to think about preaching. Leading the lost to the living waters of Christ's salvation was the only way he knew to put an end to war and the suffering he had seen. The cries of dying men desperate for God haunted him. More and more he felt called to devote his career and his life to Christian service.

Returning to the States in August 1919, George Fox took a job with Guarantee Title & Trust Company in Brooklyn, New York. There he worked his way up to the position of auditor while finishing high school with night classes. As the months passed, the call to ministry not only continued, it intensified. George decided that if he was going to preach, he needed an education. After he earned his high school diploma, he thought about where he should go from there, what place would best prepare him to do the Lord's work.

He came across a brochure from the Moody Bible Institute in Chicago. Founded by a former shoe salesman named Dwight L. Moody, the Institute stressed a simple, literal interpretation of the Bible and was one of the most respected and successful schools of its kind. Even though it was a long way off, Fox felt in his heart that it was where he would learn the approach to Christian teaching that the soldiers he served with and his old neighbors in Altoona could understand. This was the training that would prepare him for the ministry.

George Fox enrolled at Moody in 1923. There he met Isadora Hurlbut, a star student from a well-to-do farming family in Vermont. They married and moved to her home state, where George became a circuit rider, preaching at several small churches along the Canadian border. It was beautiful country, quiet, covered with lush hardwood forests, and a world away from the hot attic room and smoky skies that had shaped his early life.

After two fulfilling years in Vermont, George wanted to know more about preaching and teaching the Word of God. And so he gave up his picturesque country parishes to continue his education, earning first a bachelor of arts degree at Illinois Wesleyan, then a seminary degree from the Boston University School of Theology.

Over the next ten years, George and Isadora had two children, Wyatt and Mary Louise, and George served as pastor in a series of Vermont communities. George also was appointed state chaplain of the American Legion and the Legion's state historian. He enjoyed getting to know the men of his Legion post. They were from many different religious backgrounds. But regardless of their beliefs, George Fox took pleasure in spending time at the Legion Hall with them, visiting them in Veteran's Hospital, even lobbying the bureaucrats in Montpelier to increase their pensions. Though the Legionnaires wondered at first whether they wanted a preacher in their midst, he won them over with a kindness and concern that cut across all denominational and theological lines.

George was dismayed at the increasingly troubling news from Europe. Germany had rearmed and was threatening her neighbors in every direction. After Pearl Harbor, Reverend Fox was torn between his duty to his family and his congregation and duty to his country. Understanding the teachings of Jesus, he knew, was the only way to keep men from killing one another.

The First World War had robbed him of his perfect health, and no one expected him to go to war again at the age of forty-one. There was the very real question whether the injury sustained in one war would keep him out of another. He was elated when the doctor at Fort Ethan Allen gave him medical approval.

"You're in, padre," he said. "I'll certify you fit for any duty."

Fox was assigned to the chaplain school at Harvard, then to the 411th Coast Artillery Battalion. As much as he relished being back in uniform, he felt disappointed at the thought that he would sit out the war watching for German bombers along the Atlantic coast—which was fully and absolutely protected by two thousand miles of water that no aircraft on earth or on the drawing board could cross.

Before long his prayers to be back in the action were answered. One morning he arrived at his office on the post to see an official-looking envelope on his desk. Opening it, he read:

"CLASSIFIED—EYES ONLY

"You are hereby ordered to report to Camp Myles Standish, Taunton, Massachusetts, for special assignment NLT 0700 HRS 3 January 1943. This is a classified order under the authority of the Secretary of War. Transportation instructions to follow."

CHAPTER 3

SCHOLAR
AND
PATRIOT

Alexander David Goode was the son of a rabbi, the oldest of four children. His home in Brooklyn was a refuge of warmth and love, shaped by the historic, timeless rituals of the Jewish faith. His earliest memories were of candles and Sabbath prayers.

Devout though they were, the family enjoyed outings in the neighborhood and the occasional trip to Coney Island. One day Mama Goode had taken the children to the beach when a storm threatened. As hundreds of merrymakers headed to the subway, little

Alex got lost. His mother took the rest of the children home and waited anxiously for her firstborn. About seven o'clock he came in.

"Mama got lost in the subway," he explained to his father. "I knew she'd make it home safely, so I waited in the nickelodeon for the rain to stop."

"I'm proud of you," the rabbi answered. "But remember, as the oldest son, you are responsible for your mother's safety. You must try to stay with her next time."

"Yes, Papa," Alex nodded seriously.

When Alex was in school, his father accepted an invitation from the synagogue in Georgetown to be their rabbi, and the family moved to Washington. Accustomed to the tolerance of their Brooklyn neighborhood, Alex and his younger brother Joe were surprised to be confronted one morning on the way to school by some young black toughs.

"Give us your lunch money," one of them demanded. The boys complied, and their assailants disappeared.

After the same thing happened on two other days, the brothers decided they had to have a plan of action. The next time a confrontation took place, Alex and Joe started to put their hands in their pockets, then took off running as fast as they could. After a block or so, the two turned as one to face their foes. Alex sent the biggest opponent reeling with a solid right to the jaw; Joe bloodied another one's nose. The whole batch of bullies vanished as quickly as they had appeared, and that was the last time the Goode brothers had anybody challenge them for their lunch money.

Alex felt obliged to tell his father what had happened and feared he might be rebuked for fighting. He was relieved when his father reacted with a soft chuckle. "As long as you don't start it, it's all right," he said. "A man has got to stand up for his rights, or he won't have them long."

Alex grew into a serious, successful adolescent. He had a profitable paper route, was the best boxer and fastest runner in the neighborhood, and was first in his class at school. He especially loved mathematics and anything mechanical. Like his father, Alex was a staunch patriot and cherished the words of the Declaration of Independence, eagerly reading about the lives of Washington, Lincoln, and other great figures in American history. As much as he loved his country, he couldn't understand why, even as a native-born American, his classmates at school insisted on taunting him sometimes, making fun of his kosher lunches and calling him "Jew boy."

If he ever wondered whether he was "all-American," the question was settled in his own mind the day the Tomb of the Unknown Soldier was dedicated at Arlington Cemetery on Armistice Day, November 11, 1921. The pride that welled up inside him was too much to put into words: it required action. To show his respect for America's brave soldiers and the country they defended, Alex resolved to walk from his home in Georgetown all the way to Arlington. Leaving the bicycle he had earned with his paper route leaning on the porch, he made the trip on foot, alone—a solitary pilgrim on his own personal mission of honor.

Not long afterwards another important ceremony marked a milestone in Alex's life. The first Sabbath after his thirteenth birthday he celebrated his *bar mitzvah*. He wore his new fringed tallith and sat in the synagogue with the other men. There was so much to learn about God, and yet he was eager for it, always wanting to know more.

In high school Alex discovered his gift for oratory and also discovered a pretty girl in French class named Theresa Flax. Their acquaintance began when he forgot his book one day and the teacher suggested he look on with the student beside him. Their friendship grew: he taught her to play tennis; she taught him how to dance. As he soon learned, dancing ran in the family. Theresa's uncle was Al Jolson, one of the biggest stars on Broadway and in Hollywood, whose movie *The Jazz Singer* revolutionized the entertainment business by combining motion pictures with sound.

In his senior year Alex won a gold medal in track and a strong second in oratory. He began looking ahead to the future and a career, always thinking he might be an engineer. He continued to excel in math and mechanics, and his father relished the idea of his son being a builder of skyscrapers and great bridges.

He also joined the National Guard in the summer between his junior and senior years. The long marches and hours of drill instruction were tough, but Alex relished the camaraderie, discipline, and tradition. He also enjoyed the opportunity to express his patriotism in a concrete way that was genuinely useful to his country. Alex returned to camp the summer after graduation and prepared to start at Hebrew Union College on a scholarship in the fall. The biggest question about his future, though, was not school or military drill but whether Theresa would wait for him until he could support them.

It was too soon to make a commitment like that, they decided. Besides, it was the spring of 1930, and the economy seemed caught in a downward spiral. Alex was afraid he would never get a job. Saving every penny, he hitchhiked to Cincinnati and was soon caught up in the wonderful discoveries and opportunities of college life at Hebrew Union.

The dormitory there was comfortable, the gym was well-equipped, and the library was the third-largest Jewish library in the world. As always, Alex excelled as a scholar, and this time his experience was especially sweet, since he was among other scholars who shared his background and interests. No longer was he on the outside looking in.

Month after month, year after year, Alex asked Theresa to marry him. "Wait a little," she always said. "I don't want family responsibilities to stand in the way of your education. Besides, there's a depression going on." By 1935, the Great Depression had done its worst, and the economy began slowly improving. Alex was only two years away from finishing his studies. And Theresa Flax at last gave him her hand.

After their wedding at Theresa's house, the couple went to Virginia Beach in Alex's decrepit Oldsmobile, then returned to Cincinnati, where his last two years passed in a blissful blur. He completed his thesis examination with honors and was ordained a rabbi with the ancient words, *Yora Yora. Yadin Yadin*—"He may teach, he may teach. He may judge, he may judge." After a round of family celebrations in Washington, Rabbi Goode assumed his duties at Temple Beth Israel in York, Pennsylvania, only forty miles from Johns Hopkins in Baltimore, where he could begin work on his doctorate.

Energetic, young, and friendly, the Goodes threw themselves into becoming part of the community. Theresa entertained constantly; Rabbi Goode joined the Elks Lodge, the Rotary Club, the YMCA, and volunteered as a Boy Scout leader. He liked the fact that these organizations put him in contact with people from a wide range of interests and backgrounds. He knew firsthand the importance of being accepted as a part of a community rather than being perceived as an outsider. Clubs were an effective way of building bridges to every type of person. Goode enrolled at Johns Hopkins and began working on his Ph.D. two days a week, played squash or handball at the Y almost every afternoon, and devoted himself day and night to teaching and spiritually guiding his congregation.

The young rabbi had a deep interest in cooperating with other religious groups. He had the opportunity to demonstrate his views the first winter after he arrived, when a fire burned the neighborhood Lutheran church to the ground. On the spot, Goode offered his synagogue to the church for their worship services. (They respectfully declined.) Alex also worked with the school district to recommend books on human relations and to help bring an end to segregation and racial bias in the night classes. The more people knew about one another, he thought, the more understanding and compassionate they would be toward people who were different from them. Knowledge and truth made fear and prejudice melt away. "The best cure against religious hatred," he was proud of saying, "is information." During the Feast of Pentecost, he invited Catholics, Protestants, and black and Chinese congregations to share the celebration with them—all of whom accepted with enthusiastic thanks.

Goode also hosted dinner parties at the Hotel Yorktown where teachers, seminary professors, ministers, priests, and rabbis shared bread at the same tables, listened to one another's triumphs and challenges, and laughed at one another's jokes. As Alex reminded them, "Laughter is the best medicine for prejudice."

In the fall of 1939, a host of changes began in Rabbi Goode's life. Always a joiner, he stepped up his activities in the name of faith after hearing the first tragic reports from Poland after it was overrun by the Nazis, becoming a member of the Jewish Organized Charities, United Jewish Appeal, and other groups. In December his daughter, Rosalie, was born. By January Alex was going to school three days a week instead of two and received his doctorate later in the year. He began writing articles for the *National Jewish Monthly*.

Alex was convinced he should join the army. Some people called this a European war and none of America's business. But it was a war against the freedom America stood for. Moreover, it was war against the Jews. Every Jew had a stake in turning back the Nazi tide. His brother Joseph had already signed up, and Alex ached to serve his country. But what about his wife and daughter? His congregation? The friends and neighbors who had contributed so generously to his scholarship?

At last Rabbi Goode decided to join the navy as a chaplain. He volunteered in the first weeks of 1941, but there were no vacancies. Alex responded by throwing himself into his work more aggressively than ever, visiting the camps near York as a civilian chaplain volunteer, studying Braille, and working on a book about the spirit of democracy.

After the shock of Pearl Harbor, Rabbi Goode applied for a post in the army chaplain corps. After what seemed ages, the letter of acceptance arrived. Grateful at his chance to serve, Goode went first to Washington, where his brother Joseph pinned the Hebrew chaplain's insignia to his uniform, then reported to the chaplain school at Harvard. He loved the first aid courses, the sports, and the drill; they reminded him of his seven summers in the National Guard. But most of all he enjoyed the close relationships among the Presbyterians, Catholics, Jews, Baptists, Methodists, and other denominations all thrown into close contact. They soon recognized they could work together without compromising their distinctive religious convictions.

Alex's first duty assignment was to the army air force base at Goldsboro, North Carolina. Theresa and Rosalie came to be with him, and his father was nearby in Winston-Salem. It was a satisfying situation—too satisfying for a patriotic man of God who felt a burden to be where the action was. Alex wrote to everyone he knew, trying to get a transfer to a battlefield unit.

As he had waited so impatiently before, he waited again, pacing back and forth in the small bungalow Theresa had transformed into a remarkably homey place, especially with the warmth of the Hanukkah decorations as that holy season approached. One day an official-looking envelope arrived. Goode eagerly ripped it open, only to find a free membership card to the YMCA in York, courtesy of his friends there. In acknowledging their kind expression, the rabbi wrote

33

of the power he saw in the combination of patriotism and faith. "Our soldiers are more serious minded than in other wars; they seem to know the high religious purpose for which they are training and fighting, and as a result chapel attendance reaches unheard-of figures. In my personal contacts with these men, it is also apparent that a deep religious feeling underlies their patriotism and idealism."

A few days later another important-looking envelope arrived. Rabbi Goode held his breath as he tore it open:

"CLASSIFIED—EYES ONLY

"You are hereby ordered to report to Camp Myles Standish, Taunton, Massachusetts, for special assignment NLT 0700 HRS 3 January 1943. This is a classified order under the authority of the Secretary of War. Transportation instructions to follow."

CHAPTER 4

ONE CHRISTMAS MORE

The first question in the life of Clark Poling was whether he would have much of a life at all. As a newborn in Columbus, Ohio, he was seized by fits of whooping cough that the doctors could not control; they warned that the condition might be fatal. He surprised everyone by surviving the ordeal. Two years later, when it was time for the Poling family to return to Auburndale, Massachusetts, little Clark's spasms were nothing but distant memories.

Clark was born into a family rich in church tradition with six unbroken generations of clergy. His father Daniel had risen to national prominence as a preacher, writer, and visionary, and his mother Susan was active in church life. Clark and his brother, Dan, and sisters, Mary and Jane, loved their big old house in

Auburndale with its wide, welcoming fireplace and
beautiful views overlooking oaks and chestnuts and the
Charles River. Their earliest memories were of that
house and the fine old church which their family
attended, its cool stone walls washed in colored sunlight from the stained glass.

Preachers' kids though they were, the Poling children knew how to have fun, not only climbing trees
and swimming in the river, but festooning the house
with toilet paper to make it into an ocean liner. And
Clark revealed his love of poetry at a tender age with a
poem, inspired by the German kaiser, that he recited in
front of his Sunday school class, and which none of
them ever forgot:

Kaiser Bill went up the hill
To take a look at France;
Kaiser Bill came down the hill
With bullets in his pants.

He was attracted to all kinds of poetry, especially the
works of Robert Frost. And he also wrote his own,
sometimes inspired by the quiet dignity of his invalid
mother, who was often bedridden and in pain. Susan
died during a flu epidemic when Clark was just eight,
and he and his siblings went to live with their grandparents in Pennsylvania for a year. When they moved
to New York, their new mother, Lillian Diebold, an old
family friend, brought love and guidance to the children. Soon their father became international president
of Christian Endeavor. In 1920, he was also pastor of

the historic Marble Collegiate Church and editor of the *Christian Herald.*

After his first year of high school, Clark attended Mt. Hermon in Massachusetts for two semesters, then went on to Oakwood, a prestigious Quaker school in Poughkeepsie. He loved the peace of the place and the intensity and dedication of the students. Clark admired the spiritual strength of his classmates and formed fast friendships with a number of boys, many of whom shared his passion for football. In 1928, Clark started at halfback on the team, and Oakwood went undefeated—and unscored upon until the last game.

One summer Clark brought his friend Tubby Painter home to Long House, the Poling summer home, a gracious pre-Revolutionary residence in New Hampshire. They spent their time working on a neighbor's farm, looking after the milk cows and learning to plow with horses. And Clark continued reading and writing poetry, including a touching verse in memory of his mother Susan:

> By Mother's knee
>   in twilight time
> I prayed to thee.
> My mother taught me so
>   in childhood days
>   not long ago.
> Strange one above,
>   from her I learned
>   of your great love.

After graduating, Clark and Tubby enrolled at Hope College, a Dutch Reformed school in Holland, Michigan, where Dr. Poling was a member of the board of trustees. Clark continued with his interest in sports and literature, but his football career was cut short his sophomore year by a broken wrist. He joined the literary society, began writing for the school newspaper, and continued with his poetry, but he seemed restless and unfulfilled. He needed direction, guidance, a purpose; it was during these months of searching that he began to consider the ministry.

Hope College was a conservative, highly disciplined place, and by the end of his second year there, Clark decided he would be better off preparing for his career at a school where religion was offered more as a challenge to be met or a calling to embraced, rather than a requirement to be fulfilled. Furthermore, exercising his sense of artistic freedom to the limit, he criticized the administration for overemphasizing sports, and found himself in trouble several times for minor infractions of campus rules.

These incidents convinced Clark that as his career path became more clear, it took him more clearly away from Hope. His junior year he transferred to Rutgers College, in New Jersey, which was not only better suited to his personality, but closer to his family as well.

When he finished his undergraduate work at Rutgers, Clark enrolled at Yale Divinity School. Although he had a great passion for learning, he was an indifferent student; so many classes seemed boring or simply irrelevant to his activist nature. Before his last year at Yale, he spent the summer touring England by bicycle with his friend Roy McCorkle, ever alert for poetic inspiration, as if preparing for a cause to employ his spiritual energy.

That cause came little more than a year later, just after his ordination, in the form of a call to the pulpit of First Reformed Church in Schenectady, New York. Clark arrived to a festive welcome but soon realized the church, dating from the French and Indian War, was living in the past. Its history was a proud one, but history alone was not enough to sustain a vibrant church body. Attendance had dwindled over the years to fewer than thirty-five at Sunday worship, barely twenty-five in Sunday school. On snowy Sundays the choir outnumbered the congregation. The situation wasn't just difficult; it was more like desperate if Clark were to admit his innermost feelings.

The young pastor sprang into action, venturing out into the community on a series of unannounced, informal visits. His neighbors, church faithful, lapsed members, and potential prospects were pleased when they recovered from the shock of his initiative—and his appearance. They weren't used to a preacher in a sport coat and slacks with the athletic gait of a tennis player who bounded up the steps two at a time. With his flashing smile and easy laughter, he didn't look or sound like a Dutch Reformed "domine"—black suit, clerical collar, matching homburg. He was like one of them. And they found it appealing, even amazing.

Soon First Reformed Church began to fill up on Sunday mornings, with people who came not just to hear this new Reverend Poling preach, but clearly because they were attracted by his friendly, giving, unpious personality. He treated his listeners as equals, partners on the same spiritual journey filled with love and laughter. He preached in a conversational style, compelling and persuasive.

He wove his ministry into the fabric of the city, resuscitating the Boys Club, starting discussion groups, and building bridges with the business community. He encouraged religious tolerance as well. When word first began breaking about Nazi atrocities in Germany, Clark Poling didn't rant about it from the pulpit; he said the same seeds of intolerance were in all of us and invited a rabbi to address the church. The rabbi's comments were well received by members of his church.

About the time he got comfortably settled, Pastor Poling began a whirlwind courtship of Betty Jung, his sister Treva's friend at Temple University in Philadelphia, next door to Baptist Temple where Clark's father was pastor. At the wedding the groom seemed constantly in motion—first dashing off to get Betty's flowers (which he had forgotten), then to get the ushers' boutonnieres (also forgotten). They left for their honeymoon without Betty's suitcase, and she somehow ended up with a black eye in all the confusion.

With his new wife and helpmate at his side, Clark saw his ministry thrive as never before. Within a few months Sunday school enrollment doubled after having been stalled at the same low attendance for decades, and parents took a new interest in their children's spiritual development. When their own child, Clark Jr., was born, the Polings moved into a fine old antebellum home with a big backyard, its grassy slope shaded by ancient elm trees and stretching all the way to the Mohawk River.

Because Poling was a man of peace, the attack on Pearl Harbor was especially wrenching for him. How could a man of peace kill? But on the other hand, how could a man of faith refuse to defend the freedom God had so graciously provided? He himself had encouraged his congregation to create "personal sanctuaries which cannot be stormed by the forces of adversity, in which things of the mind can be cultivated and in which love, a modicum of physical comfort, and a measure of spiritual tranquillity can be enjoyed." These sanctuaries, he went on, were built by "returning to the fundamental pleasures of home and family, of good books, and, most important, to the joy of worshiping God. If our happiness is dependent upon these, the outside world can tumble about us, and we can still have peace."

History, as it unfolded before him, was proving otherwise. And if Hitler and Tojo were out to destroy his sanctuary—his church, his family, his freedom—he had to defend it.

He decided to enlist as an infantryman and asked his father for advice.

"Not go as a chaplain?" his father asked.

"No, as a soldier, to fight."

"What's the matter? Are you afraid?"

The question startled Clark. "What do you mean?"

Daniel Poling had served in the First World War. "Chaplains had a higher mortality rate than any other unit," he said deliberately. "They're unarmed—men of peace, love, and reconciliation in the middle of a battlefield."

Clark took his father's words to heart. He would become a chaplain if he could get an assignment. When his commission came through, he went before his congregation to resign as pastor, but they wouldn't hear of it. "We'll save your spot for you," they said. "When you're done with Hitler and Tojo, we want you right back here."

His first assignment was to Camp Shelby in Hattiesburg, Mississippi, a world away from Rutgers and Yale and summers at Long House. Chaplain Poling had never seen so much drinking, smoking, swearing, fighting, card playing, and general misery in one place in his life. He soon found out, though, that under the surface these were lonesome, frightened young men who longed for companionship, assurance, and spiritual comfort, even if they didn't call it that. The amazing thing, he decided, was not how bad they were, but how good they could be in spite of the peer pressure, loneliness, and empty hearts that conspired to assail them from all sides.

It wasn't what he had expected, but, as he wrote in a letter home, "The worse the situation becomes, the more I am needed." He sat with enlisted men at meals, played horseshoes with them, and used the same friendliness to lure people into chapel that had been so successful with his congregation in Schenectady.

Five months later he was reassigned to a Massachusetts advanced training unit close enough that he could visit home. That meant he would have the blessing of being with his family and his congregation for at least one Christmas more.

As the big day came nearer, Betty Poling had more and more of a challenge getting three-year-old Corky into bed. He was enough of a wiggle-worm every night of the year; the last few days before Christmas he was on the verge of spontaneous combustion.

"Is Santa coming tonight?" little Corky piped merrily, "Tonight?"

"Two more days, sweetheart," his mother answered with a smile.

Clark's rich, resonant voice coming from the hall interrupted them. "How can it be two more days?

Surely it must be Christmas by now! How long does a fellow have to wait for Christmas these days anyhow?"

Seeing his father enter the room, Corky lifted both his hands and wiggled his stubby fingers. "Daddy!" he chirped. His father walked to the bed and stood beside his wife as the two of them beamed down on their young son.

"Say your prayers now, Corky, and go to sleep," his father said gently but firmly. With a radiant smile the youngster complied.

As a married minister and a father, Clark Poling was as safe from the draft as any healthy young man could be. But safety wasn't what interested him; he felt a call to serve the cause of freedom.

"How do you feel tonight, dear?" Clark asked softly, brushing a curl off Betty's forehead.

"For a girl who's been on her feet all day, I'm in pretty good shape," his wife answered. "I made another batch of star cookies. Corky ate the last of the others this morning. And I baked a couple of loaves of bread. And I'd forgotten about your father's jam cake until today, so I put that in after the bread was done. Then—"

"Whoa, whoa," Clark interrupted. "One moment, please. I thought you were going to take it easy this year." She smiled up at him. He loved it when she smiled like that. "What does Thumper have to say about all this?"

Betty put her hand on her apron and felt a smooth little bump through the printed cotton. Though it wasn't yet obvious and they hadn't shared the news with anyone, she had just found out she was expecting their second child.

"Thumper seems happy with whatever the lady of the house decides," she answered.

"For all we know Thumper may *be* the lady of the house," answered Clark with a chuckle.

They had seated themselves on the couch in front of the fire. "Let's sit on the hearth," said Betty, moving to the floor and gently pulling her husband's hand after her. "The fire feels so good down here. And before long Thumper will be too big for me to get down here, 'cause if I did I couldn't get back up."

They sat quietly, leaning against each other and staring into the fire. "Wonder where we'll be next Christmas?" Clark said after a moment. "Together here with Corky and Thumper? Some musty castle in Europe? A cathedral in London? Berlin?"

"We'll be where God wants us," Betty replied evenly. "At least that's what my husband keeps telling me."

Clark turned to face her and caught her chin delicately with the side of his bent index finger. Her face was even more beautiful in the firelight. "I love you, you know that?" he said.

"Yeah," she answered, closing her eyes. "I know that."

On Christmas Day, after all the presents were opened, Betty excused herself and went to the kitchen to get dinner on the table. The tantalizing aromas of cinnamon, nutmeg, rosemary, fresh-ground pepper, bay laurel, chocolate, and more had drifted around them as they sat beneath the tree. Though breakfast had not been all that long before, the excitement of the day and the bouquet of smells had given everyone a hearty appetite.

Dr. Poling arrived just in time to sit down to a feast in the family tradition. The first course was steaming leek and potato soup; next came fresh oysters on the half shell. The main event was an enormous ham, scored in a diamond pattern, dotted with cloves and covered with pineapple rings, the whole a rich, golden brown and glistening with succulent glaze. Clark carried the large serving platter into the dining room from the kitchen, to the delight of Dr. Poling and little Corky alike. Between the two of them, he and Betty ferried into the room carrots with parsley, rice casserole, green beans, yellow squash, pickled beets, and a fresh loaf of bread.

"Dad, would you do the honors?" Clark asked, when the whole family was seated.

"With pleasure," Dr. Poling answered, surveying the feast that lay before him on the crisp damask table-cloth. The group held hands around the table and bowed their heads, Corky's (by special dispensation)

still surmounted by the fire chief's hat that had beckoned him from under the Christmas tree.

"Lord, we can never thank you enough for your love.
It is the great miracle of our lives," Dr. Poling began.
"But even greater is the miracle of your son, Jesus,
whose birth we celebrate today. Thank you for sending
him to us. Thank you for all the blessings you have
showered on us, unworthy as we are.

"Thank you for our freedom. Help us rise to the
challenge we face today in protecting it. Help us have
the courage, in your name, to do whatever is necessary
to defend our nation and our families from evil. We
fear no evil, for you are with us. Our help is in the
name of the Lord.

"Thank you also for this family—the joys of home
and hearth, the laughter of a child, the sweet memories
of our sainted loved ones and others you have called
home to be with you. Bless Lillian and the Jungs in
Philadelphia. Make this a day of peace and hope all
over the world. Wherever soldiers face danger or suffering or want, be with them. Comfort them. Bring
them home safely. May this be the last Christmas they
ever spend at war."

After the prayer, the three of them stared silently
into the fire for a moment. "Wherever any of us are,"
Dr. Poling concluded, "it's where God wants us to be."
Betty and Clark looked at each other and smiled as
they recalled their own conclusion the night before.

"One of the best comments I've ever heard on that particular topic," Dr. Poling continued as the meal began, "was a Christmas message written a few years ago by a minister I've grown to admire very much. I've even committed it to memory. It goes: 'Let us be reminded during the joyous season of Christmas that the choicest gifts of God are not always labeled as such, that his holiest Son was the lowliest child born in a manger. The wise men found a king because they sought a king. We may find God in unexpected places. Miracle, wonder, and beauty may be present unnoticed at our feet.'"

As he heard his father quoting his own words, tears welled up in Clark Poling's eyes. Nothing made him feel so honored as to have this great preacher and servant of God think his ideas were worthy of such attention.

"Wherever he sends us," Clark said at last, "it will be an honor to follow where he leads."

In that moment the lieutenant remembered the time back in the summer, just before he went on active duty, when his father asked to pray for him. "Don't pray for my safe return," Clark had answered. "That wouldn't be fair. Just pray that I shall do my duty, never be a coward, and have the strength, courage, and understanding of men. Just pray that I will be adequate."

Three days after Christmas, arriving at his duty station early in the morning, Clark was surprised and puzzled to receive a specially marked white envelope. He opened it immediately and read:

"CLASSIFIED—EYES ONLY

"You are hereby ordered to report to Camp Myles Standish, Taunton, Massachusetts, for special assignment NLT 0700 HRS 3 January 1943. This is a classified order under the authority of the Secretary of War. Transportation instructions to follow."

CHAPTER 5

SAVED FOR
A REASON

On Twelfth Street in the Irish section of Newark, New Jersey, nobody was rich and nobody was poor. The men had blue-collar jobs, and the women stayed home with the children. There were lots of children in the neighborhood, and that was one of the reasons the families knew one another so well. Kids grew up playing together and visiting in each other's houses; their mothers gossiped over the back fences as they hung out the wash, and their fathers played cards together in the evenings after work. Twelfth Street took care of its own. If somebody got sick, or lost a loved one, or was temporarily out of work, neighbors would pitch in to help without being asked. Nobody formed a committee; it just got done.

In one of the long rows of brick houses that filled the middle of one of the blocks, Frank and Mary Washington lived with their seven stair-step children. John was the oldest, and so he was the first to do everything: climb a fence, jump out of a tree, win a fight, lose a fight, and first to go to school at St. Rose's. He loved school from the beginning. Home had been wonderful—presided over by his reliable, predictable mother and his fun-loving father who loved telling stories about his native Ireland—but school was even better. John was a quick study, and he was impressed by the quiet, contemplative nuns who served as his teachers. He appreciated the respectful order of the place and enjoyed hearing the beautiful hymns sung in chapel every morning.

Enthusiastic though he was, John revealed a quick temper at school. He hated making mistakes in front of the class, and he had no patience for other boys— Germans and Poles—who called him names and who swore when the teachers were out of earshot. "Boys who talk like that can't be the friends of God," his father told him. "A man talks like a man, not in words that are fit for the animals." John took his father's words to heart, but they didn't keep him from sometimes answering his classmates' taunts with his fists.

As he grew older, John thought more about his faith. Learning the catechism was hard but rewarding: now he could claim its truth in his own life. He solemnly attended his first confession and first communion.

That first communion service made John feel peace and confidence unlike he had ever felt before, and the breakfast feast that followed was one of the most joyful days of his young life, with all his brothers and sisters fussing over him and making him feel like a king.

Not long afterward John and some friends were pretending they were big game hunters in Africa, sneaking up on elephants and zebras at a water hole. His friend Harvey carried what looked like an ordinary BB gun, but to them it was the finest Holland & Holland elephant rifle, destined to save the village from wild animals on the rampage.

As the boys moved cautiously forward on all fours, the trigger of the BB gun caught on a twig. John heard a pop, then felt a searing pain in his right eye. In an instant the eye filled with blood; John screamed in pain and fear. Concerned faces appeared in windows of apartments overlooking the field where he and his friends were playing, and in less than a minute a doctor, a policeman, and John's father arrived. Frank Washington picked up his son and carried him inside, where the doctor did what he could. John didn't lose his eye, but it was weak from then on, and the vision in it was cloudy. He started wearing glasses, which he hated at first but eventually learned to accept.

Soon the Africa of the boys' imagination became the fields of Flanders and the forests of France, as headlines brought news of the kaiser's conquests in Europe. The great British liner *Lusitania* was sunk by a German submarine off the Irish coast, with more than a thousand innocent lives lost. When America entered the war in 1917, the neighborhood was draped in bunting, and the streets echoed with cheers as the young men of Twelfth Street went off to war. John watched the send-off parades with a mixture of excitement and envy—if only he were old enough to go!

Irish pride ran strong up and down Twelfth Street, and Saint Patrick's Day rivaled Christmas as the most festive holiday of the year. For a month beforehand, the nuns at St. Rose's taught children in every grade Irish songs and dances. Some years John's father would drive their old Buick into New York just to buy special Irish bacon for the occasion, and his mother would send for shamrocks from her family back in Roscommom near Lough Derg.

Other than Christmas and Easter, Saint Patrick's Day was the only day in the year that Father McKeever wore his white vestments. *Why*, John wondered, *didn't he wear green?* "Patrick was a great confessor," Frank Washington explained, "and the liturgy says the priest will wear white for a confessor." John wasn't sure he understood entirely, but he enjoyed learning about it just the same. And he relished the traditional story-telling time on the steps of the church after mass on that special day—stories of Irish kings and despised English aggressors, Cork and Killarney, cool streams and rugged mountains, heather-hued pastures and moss-covered stone fences. It made John long for a place he had never even seen.

When summer came around, John's thoughts turned to baseball. It was a great way to release the tension that built up inside him from time to time, a more productive way to let off steam than fighting, and the catcher's mask he wore hid his glasses. So for at least as long as he was on the field, he was like everybody else. His parents watched his progress on the diamond with approval, but his mother wanted him to take piano lessons too. She noticed how much he enjoyed the music at mass and thought he had a natural gift for it.

"Music lessons are for sissies," John announced when his mother made the suggestion.

"Paderewski's a concert pianist, and he's the premier of Poland," his mother answered.

Mary Washington didn't press the point, but in time John came around and not only took lessons but excelled in them. Like baseball, music was a way to control the tension he sometimes felt welling up inside. At the piano he could express himself productively, even beautifully, rather than letting his feelings fester inside until he snapped over some little thing like a wisecrack from a classmate.

John also became an altar boy, learning the Latin prayers and plainsongs that were so much a part of the Catholic heritage. Participating in the mass, he sometimes felt a presence of God that awed and excited him.

Before he was out of high school, he felt God was calling him to be a priest.

He confided in Sister Anna Clarita and asked her to keep his plans a secret. She agreed. "But you must be especially good, John, if you want to be a priest," she warned him. He would have to be a man of learning and a man of God.

John hoped to prepare for the seminary by attending Seton Hall, but his plans were shattered when a sore throat turned into quinsy—a serious infection of the tonsils—and threatened to take his life. The doctor couldn't get his fever down, and after two days the boy fell into a coma. Desperate, Mary Washington sent for a priest to pray for a miracle of healing for her dying son. The next day his fever broke. Once he understood what happened, John said, "I guess I nearly put on my wings. But God must have kept me for something. I'll try to figure out what it is."

Almost miraculously John recovered in time to begin the academic year at Seton Hall in nearby Orange, close enough that he could live at home and take the bus to school every day. He knew he wanted to be a priest, but he also knew he wanted to be a regular guy. So along with Latin and history and psychology, John learned how to smoke and shoot pool. As one classmate put it, he had "intellectual powers but not intellectual taste." He didn't want to be known as a scholar; he'd rather be famous as a catcher or a pool shark.

Another pastime John and his friends enjoyed was dancing. On Saturday and Sunday nights they went down to the Irish-American Dance Hall, where Irish men and women, boys and girls from all over town came to dance to traditional Irish music, catch up on gossip, and exchange stories and memories about the Emerald Isle. The boys even secretly took dancing lessons so they could impress the girls right from the beginning. John paid for his with money saved from his paper route.

The one sad memory of his high school years was the death of his sister Mary at fifteen. She had been pale and sickly all her life, and her death was not unexpected. Even so, it brought home the realization of how fragile life was. After she was gone, John liked to think of Mary in heaven with angels watching over him and encouraging him on.

After finishing at Seton Hall, John Washington enrolled at Darlington Seminary, only an hour from Newark but a world away in surroundings and atmosphere. The campus was surrounded by fourteen hundred acres of picturesque woodlands, sparsely settled by dirt-poor farmers. John had spent all his life in the city, surrounded by Irish Catholics like himself. Darlington was his first taste of how much variety God had put in the world.

The main hall was a magnificent castlelike mansion designed by the great New York architect Stanford White and built originally for a California millionaire.

John lived in a more modest caretaker's house nearby, easing quickly into the strict routine of the place: Up at five-thirty, half an hour of morning meditation followed by mass, a fifteen-minute service of thanksgiving, then breakfast. From the morning meal the students hurried back to make their beds and clean their rooms in time for the first class of the day at nine o'clock.

At the seminary he wore his black cassock day and night and attended prayers, mass, and meditation every morning. Like all the other students, he had to keep his shoes shined, his room neat, and take his turn serving in the dining hall. His academic schedule was formidable: moral and dogmatic theology, canon law, church history, plainchant, and other similarly weighty classes.

Most of the reading and many of the lectures were in Latin, which kept John constantly on his toes. His schoolbook Latin had scarcely prepared him to understand presentations in the language on complicated and deeply theological points. Still he persevered. Through it all he saw that he really had two goals. The first was to conform himself as much as he was able to the example of Christ. The second was acquiring the knowledge and strength of will to understand and follow that example. These were the tools he was convinced he needed to live a Christlike life.

There were times when John wanted to go even deeper in his search for spiritual truths. He thought about entering a monastery, but the one that appealed to him was full. God had saved him from death for a reason, he thought. Was it to serve in the priesthood? To be a monk? A missionary? He was more eager than ever to figure out what it was.

In his free time John kept up his interest in baseball—he was first on the diamond almost every afternoon—and also enjoyed golf and hunting. A lot of his friends liked to swim, but try as he might, John could never seem to get the hang of it. After dog-paddling across the river one time on a dare, he declared, "Swimming is for fish. From now on I'm staying on shore with the rest of the high-level primates."

Washington fell in with a group of fun-loving, sports-minded young men like himself known as the Sunny Corner Gang for the spot on the seminary grounds where they always met during breaks from the classroom. They joked about their professors, argued about sports, and wrestled with theological questions all in the same earthy, high-energy conversational tone.

Outwardly John tried to make sure he still fit in. Inside he knew he was drawing closer to God, deepening in his commitment to be more Christlike, and preparing for a life of service to the church.

On June 15, 1935, John Washington was ordained, and said his first mass only a few days later at St. Rose's, where the first stirrings of faith had come to him so many years before. Exhausted as he was when his first service as a priest was over, he felt an assurance at last that this was what God had called him to do. After a year in Elizabeth, New Jersey, and a year in Orange, Father Washington was assigned to St. Stephen's parish in Arlington, New Jersey, where the cornerstone had just been laid for a beautiful new church.

His four fruitful years there were marred only by his father's death in 1938. Summoned in the middle of the night, Father Washington ran from the bus stop down Twelfth Street to his old home. Death rites had already begun, and Frank Washington had only a few minutes left to live. His last words were, "Now John's here. Everything will be all right."

A little over three years later, John had taken his mother to dinner and a movie on the afternoon of December 7, 1941. On the way home he flipped on the car radio and heard the tragic news about Pearl Harbor. He resolved to enlist on the spot.

The navy wouldn't take him because of his bad eye. It shook his confidence and made him hate his glasses more than ever. But he decided to try the army, and after an interminable wait his acceptance came in the mail. Sad as he was to leave his mother and the rest of the family, he never doubted it was the right thing to do.

He was ordered to Fort Benjamin Harrison in Indiana for training. The rough life of camp invigorated him and made him wish he were fighting on the front with the infantry squads. In time, though, he came to see how critical his mission was and what a fight a man of God had in front of him.

With Christmas approaching his training came to an end. He scarcely had time to think about what would happen next when he received a white envelope from the War Department. Opening it, he read:

"CLASSIFIED—EYES ONLY

"You are hereby ordered to report to Camp Myles Standish, Taunton, Massachusetts, for special assignment NLT 0700 HRS 3 January 1943. This is a classified order under the authority of the Secretary of War. Transportation instructions to follow."

Chapter 6

MAYBE A QUARTET

I t came as no surprise that January 3, 1943, was a raw, cold, miserable day at Camp Myles Standish, Massachusetts. Sleet hammered the tin roofs of the Quonset buildings and ricocheted off the muddy slush that covered the parking lot. Their teeth clenched, sentries stood at parade rest on either side of the entrance gates, rifles slung upside down to keep water out of the barrels.

They stood to attention as a military bus pulled up. The vehicle stopped, and one of the sentries shined a portable spotlight on the upper center of the front bumper. Seeing the green decal with a wide horizontal yellow stripe, the young guard decided it was unnecessary to order the driver to slide open his window and show his orders which, in better weather, he would have been inclined to do in order to relieve the boredom.

Lieutenant George Fox watched through the window as the bus lurched past the gate and headed toward the in-processing center. No matter how miserable Camp Myles Standish was, it had to be better than his previous assignment in the Coast Artillery. The likelihood of German bombers appearing over the beaches of North Carolina was slim to none, and everybody there knew it. At least now he'd feel like he was doing something.

Though Fox was handsome and healthy-looking, he was almost old enough to be the father of some of the men riding with him. A fellow passenger would have been forgiven for thinking, *Hey, this guy's kinda old to be a lieutenant,* not seeing he was a decorated veteran who'd been wounded in action when half the soldiers on the bus were in diapers. The dim light filtering through the frosted panes of the windows shown on a face with only the first hints of age creases here and there around the mouth and eyes, a face that bespoke intelligence and compassion. His thick, dark hair was cut and combed with military precision.

The bus squealed to a stop at the entrance of a drab one-story building with a large barren flagpole in the middle of the snow-blanketed front lawn. Fox walked across the driveway toward the light coming through the window of the gray-painted front door. The lieutenant looked around him. Everything in sight seemed as gray and drab as that door. He wondered why the same cold and snow back in Vermont felt so different. He had always enjoyed the winter there—actually looked forward to the Christmas card-like scenes of snow on the white clapboard village churches and town halls, skating on the ponds, boiling maple sap for syrup and candy. Except for the sizzle of sleet on the bus and on the roof of the porch in front of him, this weather was almost the same. But to George Fox that night it could hardly have felt more different.

A rush of warm air greeted him and the other passengers as they opened the door and went inside. They stomped the snow off their boots on a big rubber mat covering the linoleum by the entrance, stacked their duffel bags, and shuffled along in front of two folding metal tables where several sergeants pushed paperwork forward for them to sign. None of the officers read any of it. They weren't given the time, and if they had been, they wouldn't have understood most of it. Besides, they had to sign it anyway, so whether they read it didn't really matter.

Turning from the last stack of forms at the end of the table, Lieutenant Fox suddenly felt tired. He had boarded the bus in Vermont hours ago, and now here it was who-knows-what time of night in Massachusetts. At least he'd been able to get home for a little while before this next duty assignment.

Fox knew from experience that being tired wouldn't necessarily mean he could get to sleep. Riding all day had aggravated his back; he took a couple of aspirin, downing them without water as he had taught himself to do over the years, but it would be a while before they kicked in. Meanwhile he'd take his coat off and read a little.

Unfastening his duffel bag, he took out one of several books he had packed on top, relatched the bag and walked across the room to where several round tables were placed. The room was a large one; the in-processing station had been set up near the door. The rest of the area contained couches, tables, chairs, and a small kitchen for preparing coffee and snacks— a dayroom for officers as they waited to be shipped from one duty assignment to another, usually overseas.

Settling into a chair, he glanced over at another lieutenant who had been sitting quietly reading when the new arrivals came in. The second man had looked up from time to time but hadn't spoken as the officers sidled along signing their paperwork. Now he looked up at Lieutenant Fox and smiled.

"Welcome to the club," said the stranger.

"Thanks," replied Fox. "It feels good to get off that bus."

The man who addressed Fox had almost delicate features punctuated by dark, heavy eyebrows and dark eyes that shone with surprising intensity. Fox looked at him more closely, a glimmer of recognition taking shape as he pondered for an instant.

"Seems like I know you from somewhere," said Fox.

The stranger nodded in agreement. "Same here." He paused. "School, I think."

"Did you go to seminary at Boston U?"

"I don't think that was it," said the stranger with a soft chuckle. "Chaplain's School."

"Chaplain's School! Harvard! You're absolutely right!"

"I'm Alex Goode," said the young lieutenant as he rose and walked the few steps to where Fox was seated. Fox rose and energetically shook Lieutenant Goode's outstretched hand, his weariness forgotten.

"Of course, Rabbi. It's great to see you again. Who'd ever have thought we'd end up together in a place like this?"

"On the other hand, you could say if we ever did meet again, it was bound to be in a place like this—or worse!" Both men laughed as Goode took a seat on the couch across from Fox's chair.

Sitting together in the large, dimly lit room, the two soldiers were a study in contrast. Fox was trim and raw-boned like his mother's Teutonic ancestors. At forty-two he was graying at the temples, yet his wife insisted he still had the square jaw and clear eye of the Arrow Shirt man, the idyllic advertising figure of a generation past. Alexander Goode was ten years younger, his agile outdoor look complemented by the studious countenance of the intellectual and scholar that he was. Son of a rabbi, he enjoyed a world where education was prized, family bonds were strong, and God was worshiped freely and joyfully as a part of everyday life.

"So what are you in for?" asked Goode in his best Cagney impersonation, scrunching his face up and cocking one bushy eyebrow.

Fox laughed. "Twenty to life. Actually I'm not sure what's going on, but it's great to be doing something besides getting neck strain in North Carolina looking for German bombers. Still, you never know—we might be here for the rest of the war, waiting for somebody to find the right rubber stamp or something. By the time they dig it out of the drawer, we'll have Hitler cooling his heels in Alcatraz, and the whole thing'll be over."

"We can only hope," answered Goode.

Fox began to feel weary again. Pain pulsed around his waist and down his left leg like an electric shock. The aspirins weren't going to do the trick tonight.

Goode saw him wince as he shifted in his chair.

"That back of yours still acting up?" he asked.

"Most of the time it's not a problem," the older man replied. "This ride's gotten it kinda shaken up, that's all."

"Maybe all those damaged vertebrae smell revenge in the air! They're just so excited about evening the score with the Germans that they can't settle down."

Fox laughed again. "Who needs a doctor with you around!"

"Exactly," Goode replied. "And as your doctor I advise you to head to your quarters on the double and get some shut-eye."

"In a minute," said Fox. "If I'm good and sleepy when I lie down, it improves the chance I'll sleep through the night."

"Sounds like you've got the routine down." Fox nodded. There was a short pause. "So how's the family?" Goode continued after a moment. "You've got a couple of kids, I think."

"Good memory, Alex," Fox said with a smile. "Mary Louise is fifteen now. Quite a lady."

"Good for you all the guys are out fighting," Goode offered.

"Including Wyatt," answered Fox with a tinge of pride in his voice. Goode sat staring, uncomprehending.

"My son Wyatt and I went down to the recruitment office the same day. He joined the Marine Corps, and I talked my way back into the army."

Goode's eyes widened. "You and your son enlisted on the same day? What a blessing to you both! Congratulations!"

"Thanks. So while the ladies keep the home fires burning, Wyatt and I will be filling der Führer's jodhpurs with buckshot. What about you? How's the wife? And you have a little one if I remember."

"Theresa is fine," Goode answered, picturing her before him in his imagination with her broad smile and sparkling eyes. "Rosalie just had her fourth birthday. We couldn't be happier, except for this little inconvenience." He gestured around the room. The sergeants had folded their in-processing tables and left; Lieutenant Fox's fellow passengers had gathered up their duffel bags and gone off to their assigned quarters. Fox and Goode were left alone in the room. In the silence they could hear the sleet buzzing against the windows.

"Well, shall we call it a night?" asked Goode after a moment.

"Might as well," said his friend. "I'm in OQ-15."

"Same here," Goode observed. With a few more words the two men climbed into their heavy military overcoats, picked up their luggage, and walked out into the gray night, across the frozen parade ground toward the row of officers' barracks that shone dimly in the streetlights.

After breakfast the next morning the lieutenants returned to the dayroom and soon found themselves discussing an article on the sports page.

"Since all his players are being drafted, William Wrigley wants to start a baseball league for women," said Goode with a note of surprise.

"Not a bad idea," declared Fox after a moment. "I guess the Cubs might as well have women on the team."

"Spoken like a true Red Sox fan," Goode responded. "This would be a league for women only. Regular hardball, though."

"I don't see any reason they shouldn't give it a try. Women are ready for it. As a matter of fact, Isadora preaches in my place once in a while, and I think some of the congregation like her sermons better than mine. They're just too polite to tell me." Fox's wife, who had a seminary degree, did in fact preach from the pulpit of her husband's Methodist church in rural Vermont several times a year.

"Thank God I don't have to worry about such competition," deadpanned Goode, who could hardly fathom the upheaval at his own congregation in conservative York, Pennsylvania—even if it was Reformed—should a woman consider assuming the role of rabbi.

As they talked, a green army bus pulled up at the door and men began piling out, duffels on their shoulders, and entering the room where the sergeants from the night before had reprised their duties as clerks, setting up the two metal tables and piling them high with stacks of forms.

They watched with interest as the newcomers filed along the tables, stooping to sign papers. They could see the face of each man as he turned away from the last stack of paper on the left-hand side and walked to reclaim his luggage.

"Look, there's another chaplain. And another one," said Fox, identifying their lapel insignia. "I wonder if they know each other?"

As the new arrival bent over to pick up his luggage, he glanced across the drab room and saw a pair of intense blue eyes looking at him. Goode rose from his chair and walked over to meet him halfway. "Welcome to the party, Chaplain. I'm Alex Goode."

"John Washington," said the other, reaching for the rabbi's outstretched hand.

"Meet Chaplain George Fox," said Goode by way of introduction, turning and gesturing toward the older officer. "Lieutenant, Chaplain John Washington." The men shook hands. "Looks like we've got a trio."

"Or maybe a quartet," interjected the second new-comer. They turned to face a tall, elegant looking young man with soft, curly hair and blue-gray eyes. The shoulders of his army greatcoat were dark with melting sleet. "Clark Poling," he said simply. The men shook hands again all round.

"Well," Fox said, "my guess is that you all are as beat as Lieutenant Goode and I were when we got here last night. We'll walk you across the way and show you your new digs."

"Thanks," Lieutenant Washington said, as Poling nodded in assent.

The four men gathered up the luggage of the new arrivals and walked outside. As weak as it was, the wan winter sun seemed inviting after the miserable conditions of the past few days. The group walked diagonally across the frozen quadrangle to building 15 in the officers' quarters. The chaplains all had rooms in the building, each one identical to the others. Every one was furnished with a metal bed, metal chair, metal locker, and a sink. Doors to the rooms opened onto a long center hallway that led to the washroom and showers at one end.

After the new arrivals unpacked their luggage, the men gravitated to Fox's room, carrying the chairs from their own rooms with them and crowding them into the small bare space.

Fox was their host and obviously the oldest. His easy manner made everyone feel comfortable from the first moment.

"So, Fox, you were watching for the Jerries coming to bomb the beach in Wilmington?" asked Poling. "Where are you headed now?"

Fox furrowed his brow. The motion lasted only a fraction of a second, but it seemed so out of character it caught Washington's attention. "The truth is, I have no idea," Fox answered with a can-you-believe-this grin. "I'm reporting for some kind of special assignment."

"What are you talking?" Lieutenant Goode said under his breath.

The small room fell instantly silent. The chaplains looked at one another with questioning eyes.

"Sounds like I've got the same orders!" said Washington.

"Same here," followed Goode.

They all looked at Lieutenant Poling. He paused a moment for maximum effect.

"Hey, there's no way something like a war is going to break up this quartet so soon. I'm in the same boat all of you are."

"You think it's a boat? We're *sailing* somewhere?" Washington asked with a tinge of uneasiness.

"Purely a figure of speech," Poling answered lightly. "We could be headed out to preach on the Times Square Shuttle for all I know."

★ ★ ★ ★

In the days that followed, the chaplains got to know each other. They were very different men, but together they complemented one another like the pieces of a jigsaw puzzle. Fox's experience and stability, Goode's sharp intellect, Poling's sensitivity to the needs of others, and Washington's refreshing directness somehow played off each other and made them all better: steel sharpening steel.

Their routine was interrupted just after breakfast one morning by orders to report to a special briefing. They had been informed separately, and so every chaplain was surprised and pleased to see the others in the small briefing room.

It was then that they learned Chaplain Poling's offhand remark had been truer than they ever imagined.

They were shipping out, sailing on the army transport *Dorchester*.

"That doesn't tell us much," Washington said. The others nodded.

"Finally we'll be out of here and heading toward the action. At least we hope that's where we'll be heading," Goode noted.

Two days later the chaplains all received twenty-four-hour passes to go into New York City. "Must mean we're shipping out soon," Poling suggested. "They're giving us our last night on the town."

Chaplain Fox recalled his last military pass there with mixed emotions. "It's one heck of a way to see New York," he said after a moment, his thoughts far away.

CHAPTER 7

HAPPY NEW YEAR

Times Square was still dressed in its Christmas and New Year's finery, almost like there was some special unspoken dispensation extending the holidays in honor of the soldiers and sailors who packed the streets searching for excitement and a place to escape from thoughts of war. It was a different place entirely from the year before, the first Christmas after Pearl Harbor, when the Pacific fleet lay in ruins on one side of the world and the Nazis were gobbling up Europe on the other. That was a season of shock and desperation. The year had seen the largest surrender of Americans in history on the island of Bataan, and the threat of domination on a massive scale as Hitler initiated a two-front war against the Allies in the West and Russians in the East. But by the end of the summer, Americans had defeated the Japanese at Midway and

Guadalcanal. By Thanksgiving the Germans had fought to a weary, winless stalemate in their attack on Stalingrad.

To the cluster of soldiers walking down Broadway, soaking up all the sights and excitement, the constant stream of war news was a mixed blessing. Every newspaper on the street, every radio on the air was peppered with reminders to buy war bonds or save your old tires. Front pages were filled with maps of North Africa and the Dutch East Indies. Network broadcasts were filled with crackly voices from London or Casablanca crisply reporting the latest updates.

The fact that the news was generally good made the young men in their military overcoats optimistic about what lay ahead of them. Balancing this convivial feeling was the fact that the hours were ticking away until they expected they would face armed and dedicated fellow soldiers as determined to kill them as they were determined not to be killed.

Of the seven or eight men walking together, only Chaplain John Washington seemed unimpressed at the sweeping vista of theater lights, taxis, street vendors, and shoppers looking for after-Christmas bargains, all covered with a light dusting of snow. He had heard that to some of the guys indoor plumbing was a novelty; the lights of Broadway must be unimaginable to them. Though in some ways midtown Manhattan was as alien to him as it was to a Mississippi farm boy, Chaplain Washington had grown up only a thirty-minute bus ride away.

Twelfth Street in Newark was just across the Hudson River from where he was walking now, but that quiet avenue of tidy brick townhouses standing shoulder to shoulder, front lawns lined with elm trees, was a world away from the pulse of activity and brilliant lights where Washington ambled easily with the cluster of enlisted men who had come into town, grateful for his offer of a guided tour.

"Hey, they got anything to eat around here?" asked Sergeant. Mike Patterson hopefully. "A person could starve to death."

"I don't think you're in any danger, buddy," replied Tim Ketchum, a sergeant himself, sinking his gloved finger into the ample midsection of Patterson's green army overcoat. "Army chow seems to agree with you." Patterson and Ketchum had enlisted on the same day in Stillwater, Oklahoma. Their instant friendship was testament to the notion that opposites attract: Patterson's rotund shape and effervescent personality were the exact opposite of Ketchum's lanky build and slow midwestern drawl.

"Any of you guys ever been to a deli before?" the chaplain asked.

"I knew a girl back home named Deli," offered Captain Tommy Simmons with a grin.

"What's a deli?" inquired Matt Overton, a newly minted corporal staring at the Lionel electric trains running in endless circles in a toy store window stenciled with sale prices.

"Is deli good for the belly?" wondered Sergeant Patterson, patting his midsection expectantly.

"A deli," explained Washington with mock disdain, "is a restaurant such as you unfortunate types have never seen in your lives, filled with the most exquisite and delightful delicacies this side of heaven."

"Do they have fried chicken?" wondered Sergeant Ketchum, who had frequently bemoaned the lack of his favorite dish in the company chow line.

"Better," affirmed Washington.

"What could be better than fried chicken and biscuits with milk gravy, corn on the cob . . ." Ketchum was gathering momentum as the memory of his mother's Sunday dinners came flooding back, so bountifully laid out on the kitchen table that a visitor couldn't even see the color of the oilcloth.

Chaplain Washington held up his hand. "Wait. Put that poor old fried chicken out of your head. I'm talking top-of-the-heap here."

All the men gathered around in anticipation, the circle of breaths vaporizing into the brittle January night.

"I'm talking smoked salmon, boiled tongue, gefelte fish." He smiled in anticipation of the response. A chorus of groans burst out from the group.

"Geez, you're making me sick."

"I thought you were Irish, not Jewish."

"People really eat that stuff? We slop the hogs with it!"

"I ate gefelte fish once on a dare—tasted like cat food."

"You'd know!"

"Guys! Guys!" Washington yelled above the commotion, arms outstretched, gloved hands extended palms down. "Are we going to stand here on the street and starve, or are we going to deli discovery hour?"

"Lead on, Padre," said Sergeant Patterson with a regal wave. "We put our trust entirely in you." Amidst a cordial rumble of agreement, Washington led the way to the Stage & Screen Deli, a block off the bustling thoroughfare.

Patterson's remark was the first mention anyone had made all evening of Washington's being a chaplain, and that was the way the young lieutenant liked it. He always tried to avoid standing out in the crowd more than any other college-educated officer would stand out in a company of soldiers. He acknowledged his role as a leader; still John Washington liked to be one of the guys. It was his personality to prefer that. Besides, he was convinced he could counsel men better if they thought of him as a friend and equal, not as a priest or an officer.

The men piled into the Stage & Screen and sat down around two adjacent tables by the window. The room was warm and filled with an exotic mix of smells—fresh bread, smoked fish, capers, anise, horseradish mustard. Seeing the soldiers enter, the waitress rolled her eyes, wiped her hands on a clean dish towel, and picked up her order pad. As the men took off their overcoats, she dealt out menus, simple sheets of laminated paper with long columns mimeographed both sides. The soldiers studied the purple words intently, plowing slowly through the unfamiliar fare.

"What's a knish?" asked Corporal Overton cautiously, as though he didn't really want to know the answer.

"Fish guts," replied Sergeant Ketchum seriously.

Overton looked up, his face white.

Washington burst out laughing, his voice ringing across the room. "You chowderhead! It's potatoes! Just like your momma used to make only better."

The two tables of young men exploded with laughter and a smattering of applause.

The waitress had stood with good-natured impatience in her white uniform. Now she took the pencil out from behind her ear with a flourish and addressed her audience. "Are youse guys gonna spend the night making fun of the food around here or are ya gonna order something?"

"Yes, sir, Captain, right away," said Ketchum with a snappy salute. A chorus of affirmations followed accompanied by ragged salutes all around. "Corned beef for me," offered Washington, raising his voice above the melee, "a fine Irish meal by the way, with slaw and"—he stared at Corporal Overton, wide-eyed— "a knish." Overton blushed at the good-natured jibe.

The others ordered turkey, pastrami, and other reasonably familiar items.

"As long as it *looks* like a sandwich, I'll eat it!"

As the waitress sauntered back toward the counter, Sergeant Ketchum tapped Washington on the arm. "What we gonna do after dinner? A Broadway show maybe?"

"The shows all start at eight o'clock. We missed our shot tonight," Washington said, turning away from the window where he had been watching the people walk back and forth and looking at his pocket watch.

"Hey, will you get a load of that!" said Ketchum, snatching the watch from Washington's hand and holding it up to the light. The watch chain, clipped securely to Washington's belt loop, pulled taut and arrested the sergeant's movement.

"Easy there, Ketch. You're gonna rip Uncle Sam's britches," said the chaplain, shifting in his chair to relieve the strain on the chain but making no move to recover the object of the sergeant's interest. It was always a good conversation starter.

A little more carefully, Ketchum examined the watch in the glare of the overhead fixtures. It was small for a man's. The chain and case were both of a rose-tinted gold that seemed almost to generate its own glowing warmth. The face was white enamel with black Roman numerals and black hands. Just above the pivot point where the hands were attached was small flowing script that read "J. Wells & Co., Ltd., Dublin." Ketchum turned the watch over, this time gingerly, and discovered an elegantly engraved cluster of initials on the back, centered in a seashell design.

"My grandmother gave it to my grandfather on their wedding day," Washington said after a moment. "It was one of the few things my father brought over from Ireland, and when I left for the army, he said he wanted me to have it. I told him it was too valuable to take off to war who-knows-where. He said, 'If you're afraid to use something for the purpose it was intended, it isn't worth a nickel. If the Japs or the Germans capture you, at least you'll know what time it is.' I promised him I'd take it with me, so here it is."

The waitress reappeared with a mounded-over tray in each hand. Setting one of them on the empty table beside the men, she began placing plates of sandwiches, crocks of pickles, raw vegetables, side dishes, and other delights before her eager customers. Having forgotten all their complaints about the unfamiliar food, the men tucked eagerly into their meals, appetites sharpened by the cold, the wait, and the comforting smells that continued wafting over from the counter.

As they ate, the door opened, and in walked Chaplain Alex Goode. Washington signaled with half a sandwich in his hand. "Chaplain Goode!"

Goode looked over at the table and smiled broadly. "Well, Chaplain Washington, what a pleasure. I admire your taste in restaurants."

Washington chuckled. "Thanks."

Goode quickly scanned the two tables. "Men, you know you've absolutely got to try the gefelte fish while you're here. Every Jewish kid in New York comes here for it. It's the best there is!"

The enlisted soldiers sat frozen in their seats, not knowing for an instant what to do or say. Then Goode winked broadly, and the tables rocked with laughter.

"Say," Washington said as the noise died down and the men returned to their meals, "we're heading out to the movies a little later. Want to come along?"

"Thanks," Goode answered, "but I think I'll call it a night early. You know our pass is just for twenty-four hours, and besides, I want to get my beauty rest. Remember, we're heading out on the *S. S. You-Know-What* tomorrow."

"How could I forget?" Washington replied. "I'm showing these guys the town"—he gestured to the two tables of soldiers still packing away their meals—"and I think we'll take in a movie or something."

"Good idea. I know they'll appreciate it."

"Seen anything of Fox or Poling?"

"I think Chaplain Poling went to visit Marble Collegiate Church where his dad used to be the pastor." Washington nodded. "And Chaplain Fox went off by himself to a Broadway show. Said he wasn't going to be here on the government's nickel a second time and still miss seeing the Great White Way."

They shook hands, and Chaplain Goode took a seat at an empty table as Washington and his companions made their way to the cash register to settle up. Rebundled in their coats, the men stepped out into the bracing wind, leaving the warmth and the lingering fragrances of dinner behind.

Only a few doors down from the deli was a USO. "That's a hoppin' joint," Corporal Overton observed. In the time it took the group to walk there, the door opened two or three times as soldiers entered and left. Pausing on the sidewalk, they could hear music coming from inside. When the door opened again, a rush of warm air and cigarette smoke came out to invite them in. The music was suddenly louder. They got a glimpse of men and women inside dancing, sitting at tables listening to the band, and standing around the bandstand in animated conversation. Whirling couples moved in and out of their field of vision through the doorway. The door pulled shut; the music got quiet again.

"What do you say, guys?" Overton asked expectantly.

"Suit yourself," Chaplain Washington said. "As for me,"—here he affected his father's Irish brogue—"I've got dancing in me blood. But laddies, I'm going to sit this one out!"

The group smiled as Overton deliberated briefly. "I'm with you, Chaplain," he said finally. The group continued on. It started snowing again lightly, filling the air with a silvery sheen of streetlights and marquees.

"What about that new Cagney movie?" suggested Sergeant Ketchum, breaking the momentary silence. "I hear it's a corker."

"Nah, the last thing I'm in the mood for is some kind of gangster picture," answered Sergeant Patterson. "Hey, look at this." He stopped at a movie poster in a big frame outside the movie theater they were walking past. The others stopped with him. "What about Judy Garland?"

For Me and My Gal? Thanks, but no thanks. I want some action. Not a bunch of women dancing around the OK Corral or whatever. Besides, we've got to find something that starts a little earlier. Remember, we're on government time and we've got to be back at camp by the time our leave is up. Or else our taxi turns into a pumpkin."

"So we don't want Judy Garland dancing around. How about Jimmy Cagney dancing around?"

"You're puttin' me on. Tough-guy Cagney with a straw boater and cane?"

"I'm telling you, it's something. *Yankee Doodle Dandy.*" He pointed to a marquee halfway down the block with Cagney's name and the name of the movie in huge lights. "About George M. Cohan. If that doesn't make you feel good, you better see a doctor."

"Hey, wasn't he Irish?" asked Washington with mock seriousness.

"Yeah, I think he was," Ketchum said. "Faith and begorrah, whatever that means."

"Sold!" exclaimed Washington.

The men walked down Broadway to Forty-seventh Street. The stage show at the Strand Theater was just

ending, and the men each paid their fifty cents and
went inside. The Strand was a huge, elegant theater
befitting its location on the Great White Way. Stepping
into the vast Edwardian foyer, the men turned right
and headed for the concession stand, their recent
dinner notwithstanding.

"Hey, look who's here," a voice called from the
refreshment line as the smell of freshly made popcorn
wafted around the new arrivals. Washington and his
friends were surprised to see three other chaplains in
the line. The voice was Alex Goode's, standing between
Fox and Poling.

"What's the occasion?" Washington asked with a
smile.

"I got finished at the deli, changed my mind about
the movie, and just wandered over," Chaplain Goode
explained.

"My show down the street was lousy, and I decided
to find something better to do," Fox spoke up. "Been
meaning to catch this movie for a while anyway."

"The secretary at the church told me this was a great
show and that nobody should miss it, especially us boys
in uniform," Poling said in turn. "So here I am. Now
here we all are!"

Juggling wax-paper bags glossy with melted butter,
the group filed into the hall and was escorted by a
uniformed usher to their seats in the mezzanine.
Stagehands were removing the last of the chairs and
music stands from the stage in front of the screen

where Jerry Wald and his orchestra had been playing only moments before. The same ticket would have admitted the soldiers to the earlier live performance plus a comedy routine by Jack Gifford. This was still a good deal, though—a classy Broadway theater, fresh, hot popcorn on top of an adventurous and satisfying dinner, and the anticipation of a new musical picture the newspapers were giving rave reviews.

As the house lights dimmed, ushers seated last-minute arrivals guided by flashlights shielded with red translucent cones. The heavy purple velvet drape at the front of the theater parted silently, sweeping across the arc of the stage in delicate twin curves.

A feature film would be the last and grandest of a series of screen presentations that typically began with a cartoon or two, moved on to previews of coming attractions, then to a short subject, and finally the film itself. But tonight, of course, there'd also be the latest war newsreel, both to help fill the insatiable public demand for information from the front and to keep the country's spirits high.

As the brass fanfare sounded from the speakers, the screen filled with a scene from a New York street. A crowd of soldiers was in the center of the shot with a large group of people milling around them. The announcer intoned, *"Beautiful Ginger Rogers reminds America's fighting men what they're fighting for and reminds movie fans everywhere to buy war bonds."*

The clip continued with other stars, some accompanied by comedians like Red Skelton and Bob Hope. Then, with an abrupt change in music, the image of General Eisenhower appeared, chatting with British officers, and then another quick cut to grainy footage of tanks plowing through North African sand as the narrator continued in a booming, confident voice:

"Lt. Gen. Dwight D. Eisenhower commanded the British fortress of Gibraltar during the first days of Allied North African operations beginning December 5, 1942. Top secret until recently, this event marks the first time in two centuries that the British Empire has relinquished control of its Mediterranean fortress to a foreign power. Allied tanks are now on the offensive in Africa, and the Axis powers are going to be looking for another sandbox."

The soldiers stared uncomfortably at the screen. Three hundred others in the darkened theater cheered at the announcer's words. There was another change in scene, and the narrator went on:

"Hitler has pushed the Russian Colossus as far as he will go. Hopelessly bogged down in their offensive against Stalingrad, the Germans are learning, as Napoleon did, that the Russians' best ally is Old Man Winter."

Now the jumpy, grainy image showed long lines of German infantry, bundled against relentless wind and blowing snow, burdened with packs, rifles, and bedrolls on their backs stacked higher than their helmets, slogging through waist-high drifts. They were dirty and unshaven. Their faces showed the strain and exhaustion of their ordeal. They stumbled and rose, stumbled and rose again, struggling slowly into the Arctic wind toward the front where they knew, if they made it, Russian lead would be awaiting them.

Then another quick change. Newspaper headlines splashed across the screen, followed by the sight of a convoy at sea intercut with sinister footage of a German submarine. The announcer went on:

"Eight more Allied ships were sunk in recent weeks as convoys seek ways to outmaneuver the U-boat menace. The Atlantic Ocean east of Newfoundland has become a Nazi shooting gallery for troop transports and cargo vessels on their way to resupply British and Free French forces. The U-boat wolf packs are everywhere!"

Aerial photography showed a merchant ship on fire and sinking.

"But American sea dogs have big plans for Jerry. The navy brass is keeping everything under wraps for now, but remember, the bigger they come, the harder they fall!"

The screen showed a U-boat hit by Allied fire and bursting into flames. The theater audience cheered wildly. Chaplain Washington looked over at Corporal Overton and saw a somber expression in the reflected light of the screen. His mood darkened even further as he watched the next segment.

Another grainy image showed an army transport ship dead in the water and enveloped in flames. Men were jumping into the ocean, which was covered in places with flaming fuel. As the scene continued, explosions flashed, and clouds of black oil smoke billowed upward. There were a few lifeboats scattered around, but many men held onto bits of floating debris.

Watching the scene, the audience heard the announcer: "*The latest victim of German atrocities, the army transport* Harrowgate, *was torpedoed and sunk in broad daylight two hundred miles east of Newfoundland.*"

Stunned, Sergeant Ketchum and Corporal Simmons whispered between themselves as the voice-over continued.

"Are you up for this?"

"I'm not sure."

Sergeant Patterson elbowed Chaplain Washington lightly. "Chaplain, I suddenly don't feel much like a movie any more."

"I'm with you, Sarge."

After a few more whispered words, the soldiers rose from their seats and walked up the aisle to the lobby.

"I don't know about you men, but I think it's time I headed back to camp," Washington said.

"I'm with you, Chaplain," Corporal Overton said quickly.

"Besides," Sergeant Ketchum observed, "we've gotta keep an eye on the time."

"But," Patterson said with a hint of a grin, "we still got our popcorn."

"Right you are, Sergeant," Washington answered.

With that, the men buttoned their overcoats and headed outside to find a couple of taxis. Turning onto the sidewalk, the wind hit them square in the face. It was a cold enough night, and the relentless breeze that had come up while they were inside made it seem even colder.

Their twenty-four-hour pass was over.

CHAPTER 8

SEALED ORDERS

The four chaplains returned to Camp Myles Standish that night. After a restless sleep interrupted repeatedly by the disturbing war images they'd seen on the screen, the men awoke the next morning and packed their duffel bags. They assembled in the hallway, then walked single file across the frozen parade ground to the mess hall where they had a satisfying breakfast of eggs, corned beef hash, buttered toast with jelly, and thick, heavy mugs of strong coffee.

After a short wait, the four chaplains were escorted with another group of men to a railroad platform in an out-of-the-way sector of the camp. A train was waiting for them, smoke pouring from its stack, steam hissing expectantly around its wheels, and they all climbed aboard. Some of the seats were already filled, and the new passengers navigated around the coats and luggage of the others to get themselves settled. Seeing the rising tide of duffel bags in one corner, Alex Goode called out to no one in particular, "Obviously they're getting us conditioned for life on the high seas. How thoughtful." The men nearest him broke out into chuckles, with others joining in as the commentary was repeated.

It wasn't until Lieutenant Fox had gotten his coat off, hung it on a hook, and settled in his seat that he turned to look out the window. The sun had been high in the sky when he walked to breakfast but now it looked pitch black outside. It took a minute for Fox to realize his window was painted over. Looking up and down the car on both sides of the aisle, he saw that every window had been obscured.

Seated next to him, Father Washington had noticed the same thing at the same moment. Uncharacteristically stunned into silence, the priest thought back through the information he had been given and orders received, trying to remember any scrap of information that might have prepared him for such an unexpected situation. Painted out windows. If he already knew where he was going—for a ride on a troop transport called the *Dorchester*—what difference did it make if he looked out at the stark, snow-covered countryside? At least he thought he knew where he was going.

With a confident chuff of its drive wheels, the locomotive began moving slowly away from the platform, through the camp, past a large gate in the perimeter fence, and then through the town of Taunton. Chaplain Poling expected the trip to be a short one; if they were going to sea, he figured they'd depart from Boston. But as the minutes passed and the train picked up speed, it seemed that whoever was in charge had something else in mind. There was a secret here bigger than anything a trainload of surprised and curious soldiers had expected.

There was little chatter aboard. Some men figured it didn't much matter where they went, since they didn't know what they would be doing when they got there anyway. Others were overcome by the combination of their heavy breakfasts and the monotonous rumbling of the engine and nodded off to sleep.

For hours they rolled along. Once the door at the end of the car opened, and an MP in fatigues stood in the doorway, a machine gun hanging across his back on a sling. His appearance generated a buzz of low whispers throughout the car. Chaplain Fox thought to himself, *This sure isn't like any other troop transportation I've ever been on before.* After standing at the end of the car with a perfectly neutral expression on his face for a minute or two, the sentry silently left the car, closing the door behind him.

Had they been able to see the view, it would have been impressive even in the weak winter light. They were in New Jersey now, across the Hudson from the Manhattan skyline. The Empire State Building and the Chrysler Building thrust their spires into the low clouds.

White billows of steam and water vapor roiled upward from other buildings here and there.

At the foot of the skyscrapers on the far side of the river was a long row of piers. This was where the great, elegant passenger liners—*Queen Mary, Normandie, Rex, Nieuw Amsterdam*—had called until recently, carrying passengers to and from the distant corners of the world. Countless partings and homecomings had taken place on that quayside among the noise and bustle of ships being loaded, unloaded, and reprovisioned. Now all was quiet and still, and all the ships but one were gone, transformed from luxury liners into troopships carrying soldiers to exotic battle theaters in Europe, Africa, and the Pacific, their mahogany dining halls and smoking lounges filled with soldiers and supplies.

The one ship remaining at the passenger terminal was a vivid reminder of the waste of war. Lying half submerged on its port side between Piers 88 and 90, the burned-out hulk of the *Normandie* wallowed in the icy water of the Hudson. The first thousand-foot liner and the fastest passenger ship in the world, she'd been the pride of France when she was launched in 1935. Stranded in New York at the outbreak of the war, she was too tempting a target for German subs to sail her home. During refitting as a troopship, she'd caught fire and foundered at the pier almost a year ago. And there she lay, beyond repair, with too much else going on in the world even to spare the time and resources to haul her away for scrap. Anyone standing on the New Jersey shore who knew where to look could see the low mass of its superstructure and three sleek funnels on their sides, half under water.

To pass the time on the train, Chaplain Poling had decided to write a letter to his wife. He found himself thinking about her a thousand times a day, wondering how she and Corky were, what they were doing at that moment, imagining what the latest news might be from Thumper.

"My Darling Betty," he wrote, "We're on our way to sea at last. I still don't know where we're going exactly, but the whole adventure gets more interesting by the minute. I'm on a train with three other chaplains and a company of men on what I thought would be a ten-minute ride to the harbor. We've been going along for hours now, and I have no idea where we're headed because the windows have all been painted out."

He stopped to look over the page. It was a genuine challenge to follow the lines as they wove up and down with the rocking of the coach. That would be fun for her to decipher, he decided, and she'd certainly point out Daddy's hilarious writing to Corky. He wrote only a few more lines before the train slowed to a stop. The door at the end of the car clanked open. Chaplain Poling put his half-finished letter away and looked up.

A tall soldier stepped smartly into the coach—another MP, but this one in dress greens. Over his right shoulder was slung a rifle. Around the upper left sleeve of his coat was a black armband with "MP" in large white capitals. Instead of the customary dress cap, the soldier wore a steel combat helmet, emblazoned with the same two capital letters.

"Gentlemen," he said briskly as the wind blowing through the open door whipped at his collar, "welcome to your next duty station. We will be boarding your transport vessel, the *U.S.A.T. Dorchester,* immediately. Please bring all your belongings and follow me."

The soldiers exchanged curious looks, some tinged with alarm, then repeated the cumbersome ballet they had performed upon entering the coach as they wrestled into their coats and gathered up their gear. Shuffling down the steps and onto the platform, the soldiers were directed by the MP to a gate in a chain-link fence topped with barbed wire. On the other side was a row of piers, and in the distance ships of all types and sizes were sailing in and out of New York Harbor. The sky had cleared, and the sun was just setting, bathing the harbor and the ships in a golden glow.

The train had stopped on Staten Island, where the track ended in a maze of loading docks, warehouses, and freight yards. "Staten Island. If I'd known this is where I was going to end up, I could have stayed for another movie," Chaplain Washington said, looking around him. "And I could have had another bagel," added Rabbi Goode with a grin. "So they were bringing us to New York after all."

In contrast to the ghostly calm at the passenger piers along the Hudson, the Staten Island docks were roaring with activity: cranes lifting cargo high into the air and down into holds, stevedores scurrying around yelling to one another, quartermasters barking orders and consulting their clipboards, and lines and knots of uniformed men everywhere waiting for news of why they were here and what they were supposed to be doing.

"We're looking for the *Dorchester*," Lieutenant Fox said to a steely-eyed sergeant manning the guardhouse.

The sergeant snapped a salute, but his crisp military manner couldn't completely hide the trace of a grin. "That way, sir." He pointed and nodded toward the dockside.

"Wonder what was so funny?" Fox asked to no one in particular as they resumed walking, amused at the stern young guard's reaction.

The chaplains continued in a cluster of men down to the first ship in the line. Not seeing a name on the vessel right away, Chaplain Goode asked an official-looking man in civilian clothes, "Is this the *Dorchester?*"

The man chuckled, showing a row of fine, even teeth. "The *Dorchester?* Right down there, gentlemen, third gangplank on the right. Watch your step when coming aboard. And have a wonderful voyage." As he spoke, he gestured grandly down the line of ships, each with its gangplank monitored by a personnel officer checking passengers off his ever-present clipboard.

The group walked past long lines of soldiers waiting to board the other ships. There was the feeling of forced calm common to every soldier who ever shipped out to the front, as if everyone were nervous and scared but would do whatever it took to appear outwardly confident. Lots of banter. Lots of jokes, sharing of cigarettes, even a few knots of soldiers singing. But to a seasoned observer like George Fox, the tight lines around the mouth and the far-away look in the eyes revealed their true feelings.

The sun was down now, and the dock was bathed in the harsh glare of arc lights. The men could read *Dorchester* on the bow of the next ship as they approached it.

"I'm no expert," Father Washington declared, "but I'd say we got the runt of the litter."

"Amen to that," Chaplain Poling replied.

Without a doubt, the *Dorchester* was the shortest, smallest, least impressive looking vessel of the bunch. She was 368 feet long, 52 feet abeam, and 5,649 gross tons. Clearly not built for extended travel on the high seas, she looked even smaller surrounded by the other ships. There was, however, an undeniable touch of class in the *Dorchester.* Her trim silhouette and teak railings were evidence of a pedigree beyond the usual mongrel troop transport. The vessels to its bow and stern loomed over it like overgrown brothers, even though the stalled line of soldiers waiting to get aboard her seemed as long as for any of the others.

There was one line for enlisted men and a second for officers. Looking down the line as they walked by, the chaplains saw almost every human emotion registered: fear, arrogance, boredom, curiosity, excitement. Two privates were in the midst of an animated discussion.

"What makes you so sure there's anything to be worried about?" said a lanky young man with a shock of red hair. "You wouldn't know a spy if he tripped over your chow table."

"I'm telling you," his stocky, sandy-haired companion was saying, "this is nothing to make jokes about." Suddenly his eyes flashed. "How do I know you're not a spy?"

"Carlson, you've been reading too many comic books!"

"Yeah, well loose lips sink ships!"

Walking on, the four chaplains took their places at the end of the officers' queue, had their names checked off the clipboard, and stepped aboard.

They followed a line of men across a section of deck. The cables along the railing and the lines running overhead were drooping with icicles. A thin film of ice seemed to cover every surface, though sand had been sprinkled along the officers' path to give them some footing.

The parade of men disappeared through a doorway. Lowering their heads, the chaplains clambered down a short staircase to a narrow gangway. Their first impression was that this was going to be a cozy voyage. What had obviously been reasonably spacious quarters had extra beds and lockers in every available foot of space.

Following the personnel officer's instructions, they found their way to the cabin the four of them would share.

"Pretty toasty down here, don't you think, gentlemen?" observed Rabbi Goode. He smiled impishly. "A place this hot in the middle of a New York winter is a worthy reminder for us to be good little boys." The others laughed, accompanied by guffaws from nearby men who'd heard the comment.

They found their room, B-14 on the promenade deck. The door was open, and the men stepped inside. "Not a wasted inch," said Chaplain Washington, eyeing the cramped, crowded space. "We're going to leave here as best friends—or sworn enemies." His roommates nodded their assent and smiled.

Obviously the stateroom had seen better days. The door and its frame were teak, and the waist-high paneling was of good quality but shop-worn and neglected. There was a mirror, a four-drawer dresser, and a nightstand, all artfully designed yet showing signs of heavy use. Everything was overshadowed by the two pairs of bunk beds that had been shoehorned into the room. Two metal lockers had been wedged in as well. The remaining floor space barely left room for all four men to stand at the same time. The outside wall contained a large porthole fitted with a window set in a metal ring, hinged on one side and with a locking handle on the other.

"So, who gets the lowers?" Washington asked lightly, throwing his duffel bag on one of the lower beds.

"Age before beauty," Fox answered jovially, tossing his bag on the other lower.

"I hear possession is nine-tenths of the law," Goode said, looking at Washington.

"I'll flip you for it," the priest replied.

"Nah, it's yours. Who wants to get airsick and seasick at the same time?" Goode slung his bag up onto the bed above.

"Guess that leaves me this one," said Poling, heaving his duffel onto the bed above Fox's. "Goode and I are closer to heaven than you guys anyway."

"Right," Goode continued. "And we'll have more time to bail if this luxury liner springs a leak." More laughter all around.

As they stowed their gear as best they could, a man in an unfamiliar uniform poked his head through the doorway. "Good morning, men. I'm Dereck Hardaway, part of the crew that'll be manning the ship. Just thought I'd stop in and say welcome aboard."

"Thanks," Goode replied, eyeing him briefly. "You're not navy."

"Merchant marine. Fact is, I sailed on the *Dorchester* five years as a civilian. Several of us joined the merchant marine to help out the war effort. The navy needs ships, and we know how to sail this one. She's been chartered by the navy and commissioned as a

United States army transport for military duty. I'm here to make sure she behaves herself."

"So where'd she come from?" Fox asked. "She looks serviceable, but my guess is there's no warship in her pedigree."

"Good guess." Hardaway leaned into the doorway, evidently in no hurry to move along, positioning himself out of the way of the steady stream of soldiers passing behind him, lugging their gear and looking for their quarters.

"The *Dorchester* was laid down at Newport News in '26 as a coastal steamer, running between Atlantic ports like Boston, New York, and Charleston. We carried 325 passengers or so and a crew of about 100. Passengers would be on board for a couple of days at the most. We also made the Bermuda run.

"Come on and I'll show you around."

Glancing at one another in agreement, the four lieutenants followed their impromptu guide down the narrow, dimly lit gangway, inundated with the noise of men walking in every direction shouting questions, dragging luggage, looking for their assigned quarters. The little ship seemed to be getting more stuffed by the minute, which indeed she was.

"Fifty-six hundred tons, twelve-knot service speed," Hardaway was saying, "though the extra passengers on these trips cost us a couple of knots." The chaplains bunched up around him as they walked in order to hear him over the din. "One oil-burning triple expansion steam engine that'll make 80 RPM all day—plain but reliable power. She holds more than nine hundred passengers now."

"So you're at more than twice regular capacity?" Washington asked, surprised.

"About that," Hardaway affirmed. "But if we can squeeze 'em on here, we can carry 'em. And these days it seems like Uncle Sam needs everything afloat to keep one step ahead of the Jerries."

"It's been a tough year for shipping," Poling said.

"And this year's gonna be tougher," Hardaway shot back. "U-boats are all over, and they've got some bloody good marksmen. Now the scuttlebutt is that there's a new long-range model that can make longer sorties. That means more enemy subs in the water every day of the week. At least we ran them off from New Orleans, for crying out loud."

Early in the war, as everyone who read a newspaper that year knew, U-boats had actually penetrated to the mouth of the Mississippi, where they waited to ambush oceangoing traffic as it moved into the Gulf of Mexico. Decimated by the Pearl Harbor debacle, American shipping tonnage and firepower had been so completely concentrated on the Pacific that the eastern seaboard was left relatively unprotected. Now, slowly, the defenses were being rebuilt; there were no longer German subs west of the Straits of Florida, and they were steadily being driven north and east toward the North Atlantic. That still left plenty to worry about.

"We're building ships faster than the Jerries can sink them," Hardaway continued, "but we've got to rely on civilian shipping to help us out right now."

"So the *Dorchester* isn't an oceangoing ship," Washington said, half as a question, half as a statement.

"Not a North Atlantic ship," Hardaway admitted. "That's the most unpredictable, most treacherous ocean in the world. But she's oceangoing just the same. This'll be my sixth taxi jaunt across the pond, and I don't expect it'll be the last. Too bad for all of us the *Normandie* burned. It would have been nice to kick back with a cigar on the fantail of the sleekest ship afloat. Besides, it'll take us a dozen trips to carry the number of troops she could have taken in one."

As he talked, Hardaway led his audience through a doorway into a relatively large room on the main deck. It was in fact the largest on the ship, though still with a low ceiling, still dim, and still unnaturally hot and stuffy.

"This was the dining saloon. Now it's the mess hall. No difference really except that the seating's a lot more crowded than it used to be." There was the same feeling here as in their room: original furnishings—simple but sturdy mahogany tables and chairs—bearing marks of hard use, and supplemented with huge numbers of temporary tables, shelves, dish racks, and other necessities to feed three times the number of passengers the space was designed to serve.

The four followed Hardaway up two elegant flights of stairs to the promenade deck. "In here is the day-room, known once upon a time as the smoking lounge. Think of it as your living room on the high seas."

This was the most elegant room they'd seen so far, with carpet on the floor, glittering wall sconces, and old but serviceable stuffed chairs, couches, and felt-covered card tables. These were supplemented by a quantity of plain metal chairs and small square tables with a decidedly military appearance.

Along with inexpensive framed landscapes and photos of the *Dorchester's* old ports of call, there was a poster taped to the wall. There was a cartoonish drawing of a sailor whispering something to his perky and attractive girlfriend, and in the background was a sly eavesdropper with a Hitler moustache. Across the top in big letters, the headline read, "Loose Lips Sink Ships!"

Looking around the room as they passed through, the chaplains instinctively took note of the men sitting around, talking in groups, looking out the porthole windows, or sitting silently. Were there any loose lips in this room? At some level it was a question everybody asked. Would any of the men aboard suspect someone else on the *Dorchester* wasn't playing on the same team?

Who was that grizzled top sergeant in the corner? What were the two fuzzy-cheeked privates at the table near the door having such an animated conversation about? What was the dark-haired army captain thinking of, staring into space with his pencil poised over a sheet of paper. It would be their burden and joy to get to know these men and the others on board, to share their fears and victories, to laugh with them, and pray with them, perhaps to watch some of them die. God only knew.

In a few minutes the group made their way back to B-14. "Thanks for the tour," Fox said.

"Don't mention it," Hardaway replied. "Before it's all over, you'll see these rooms enough to last you the rest of your life." With a wave he was gone.

The chaplains stowed their belongings, then waited for whatever was happening next. Finally word came that departure had been delayed. After evening chow the men collapsed into bed early. Whatever was in store for them tomorrow, they figured they might as well be rested.

The next morning the four lieutenants had scarcely returned from breakfast when a chisel-jawed MP appeared in the doorway.

"Sirs. Captain Danielsen requests the presence of all officers in his office in five minutes."

"Thank you, Sergeant," Fox said.

The soldier disappeared as quickly as he'd come.

As the chaplains went down the passageway and up the stairs, they heard and felt the *Dorchester*'s "plain but reliable" engine come to life. There was no sense of motion as yet, but clearly they were on the verge of casting off.

Like every other room they had seen on board, the captain's office was too small for its job. It was jammed with twenty or more men—army officers, a few navy brass, and a handful of Coast Guard. As the officers sat, they felt the room sway gently. The *Dorchester* was moving away from the pier, turning slowly to starboard until her bow pointed east toward the foreboding Atlantic.

A moment later a side door opened. The room rose as one as Captain Hans J. Danielsen entered. His piercing, sky-blue eyes scanned his audience for a split second.

"Gentlemen, take your seats." His curly, iron-gray hair was brushed straight back on top, close-cropped on the sides. Danielsen had Viking blood in his veins, but he was every inch an American citizen. This was his first voyage as master of the *Dorchester.* In spite of the clammy heat in the room, he, like most of his audience sitting shoulder to shoulder, was in full winter uniform including wool jacket.

"You already know this voyage is something out of the ordinary," Captain Danielsen continued. "The windows of your train were painted out. The section of pier you were admitted to was surrounded by electric fences topped by concertina wire. This vessel—though I can tell you myself she's as seaworthy as they come—is not your typical transport. In short, there's nothing routine about this voyage.

"Everyone on this ship has been chosen for a mission that is vital to the interests of the United States and her allies." He held up a large manila envelope. "What is the mission? Even I don't know. Our orders are here, sealed in Washington and delivered to me by special courier. My instructions were not to open them until we were approaching the convoy rendezvous. We're assembling ten nautical miles east of Sandy Hook. As soon as we get there, I will exercise my authority to open this envelope"—he waved it once, then set it on the table beside him that served as a lectern—"and we'll all learn about this from the horse's mouth. That way there will be no misinformation and no rumors. Information about our mission is not to leave this room. The personnel officers know everyone here. If there's an information leak, we'll find you. As the sign says, gentlemen, 'Loose Lips *Do* Sink Ships!'"

There was a ripple of nervous laughter in the crowded room as the *Dorchester* increased power and built her speed. The dull throb of the engine coming from deep in the center of the ship grew more intense, though still no louder than a hum.

"Here's what I do know," said the captain. "We have just over nine hundred souls on board. More than half of them are soldiers. We've got sailors manning our guns—four 20-millimeter antiaircraft guns plus a 50-caliber gun forward and a four-inch 40 aft. Not your average pleasure cruise armaments." Again, a few chuckles. "We've also got some Coast Guard personnel traveling as passengers and 171 civilians, two of them female." A couple of quick wolf whistles pierced the air amidst a murmur of voices that soon died down again. "Sixteen of those civilians are Danish. And I expect to take especially good care of them, even if I am from New Jersey."

The chuckles came more easily now; the captain was forging his bond with officers who, only a few minutes ago, had been complete strangers to him.

"The *Dorchester* has made five transatlantic runs in the past year. She won't win any beauty contests, but she's proven herself in every way. We're fueled and provisioned for an Atlantic crossing, so my best guess is that our mission will take us across the pond.

"The weather this time of year is no picnic. But the weather's not our biggest enemy. U-boats are, especially in wolf packs. The long-range models coming on line now allow Hitler to put more firepower in mid-ocean. Land-based bombers can keep them offshore over here, and British bombers take care of them in the East. But in the middle of the Atlantic, it's a shooting gallery, and we've got a big bull's-eye painted on our flank. Convoys help. Evasive maneuvers help. Our guns may help us too. But when it gets down to brass tacks, if the North Atlantic is where we're headed, only God can help us."

The chaplains exchanged glances. Captain Danielsen went on.

"One classified piece of information I do know is that we have some electronic gear on board designed to help us find U-boats before they find us. Everybody in the Axis knows we're working on it, but it's still classified. It's the latest version of a rig that sends out underwater sound waves, then listens to see if any of them bounce back. Sort of a subsea radar. If the sound echoes back, it means there's somebody out there that shouldn't be."

As ship's officers in the room already knew, the system, named for the committee in Britain that developed it, was ASDIC, for Anti-Submarine Detection Investigation Committee. It was based on principles that had been under development all the way back to World War I, generally referred to as SONAR, itself an acronym for Sound Navigation And Ranging.

"It's an experimental system. It's temperamental. It breaks down. It doesn't know a U-boat from a codfish. It doesn't always know whether the target is coming or going. And it's only accurate to between a quarter and half a mile. But it's the best thing out there."

A young officer entered the room and walked briskly to the captain. They exchanged a few quiet words, and the messenger left as quickly as he had come.

"We've passed Sandy Hook. For you newcomers, that means we're in open ocean. Time to have a look at our game plan."

Captain Danielsen picked up the envelope, broke the seal, and pulled out a single, crisp, unfolded piece of paper. He read aloud.

"To the *U.S.A.T. Dorchester,* Captain Hans J. Danielsen commanding. You and your command are ordered as follows:

> • Take previously assigned position in Convoy SG-19 off Sandy Hook at 0900 hrs 23 January 1943. There will be fifty vessels in formation.

> • Maintain standard separation. Execute standard avoidance maneuvers.

> • All ships are to maintain absolute radio silence. No exceptions.

> • Should any ship be hit or otherwise incapacitated, no other ship is to break formation. No ship is to break formation for any reason whatever. No exceptions.

> • Specified components of Convoy SG-19 will proceed to St. John's, Newfoundland, by way of navigational coordinates detailed below.

> • Further orders upon arrival at St. John's."

Instead of solving the mystery of their mission, the sealed orders had only deepened it. Newfoundland? It was a vital shipping and resupply point for transatlantic traffic, particularly aircraft. Positioned just over a thousand air miles from New York and seventeen hundred from Ireland, it was the only safe, civilized place the flyboys could gas up. Did they suddenly need nine hundred pump jockeys?

Try as he might, Captain Danielsen couldn't completely hide the astonishment on his face. "Gentlemen," he said slowly and with precision, "you know as much as I do." By the time his audience could rise to their feet, he was through the door and gone.

CHAPTER 9

AN ADMIRAL'S PREROGATIVE

Clusters of officers moved out of the room and up and down to various parts of the ship. The chaplains had hardly returned to their cabin when a crewman appeared in the doorway and knocked on the jamb. "Chaplains, a message from the captain." He offered a small blue envelope. Washington took it from the messenger's outstretched hand, thanked him, and the man disappeared.

"It's to all of us," Father Washington announced, pulling out and unfolding a slip of paper, holding it at an angle close to his good eye in order to read in the dim light. "The captain wants to see us in his quarters in five minutes."

Gripping the handrails, they staggered back to the main staircase as the ship rocked in the troughs between the mountainous waves and asked a passing crewman for directions to the captain's stateroom. As the four assembled in front of the doorway indicated, Chaplain Poling knocked briskly on the polished wood.

"Come in," a voice answered from inside.

The chaplains found themselves in a room that, though small like all the rest of the rooms they'd seen, for once didn't seem overwhelmed with people and furniture. The space was immaculately clean and organized with the efficiency of a man long accustomed to fitting his belongings into tight places. Captain Danielsen had spent twenty-two years at sea and had every expectation of spending at least twenty-two more.

The four lieutenants stood respectfully at attention. "At ease, gentlemen," the captain said. "Please have a seat. Thanks for coming up on such short notice."

There were a couch and two chairs in the room. The chaplains found their seats while Captain Danielsen wheeled his chair around from its accustomed place at his desk facing the wall and sat with his callers, the five of them making a circle that almost filled the room.

"This is the *Dorchester*'s sixth voyage as a troop ship," he began. "But it's my first on the *Dorchester*, and it's the first time I've sailed under sealed orders. I've never weighed anchor without knowing where in the Sam Hill we're going.

"But you chaplains need to know that even a trip up to St. John's is going to be a rough ride. Gonna hit some chop, I'm afraid. And those wolf packs are going to be everywhere."

"Question, Captain." Fox spoke quietly but with a sense of confidence that came from being a veteran.

"Shoot."

"The Atlantic's a big place. What makes you think the Jerries will be waiting for us in the western ocean when they're supposed to be after ships on their way to England? It ought to be clear to them that we're not carrying anything to the front."

Captain Danielsen smiled. "Do you know what we're carrying?"

Fox smiled back. "No, sir, I don't."

"Neither do they. You're right that, strategically, the transatlantic convoys are a lot more important, but let me show you something."

He pivoted his chair around to the desk, opened the lap drawer, and took out a rolled piece of paper. He unrolled it on a small table in the middle of the room. Along the left margin was the Atlantic coastline of the central and northern U.S. and southern Canada.

"Here's our course," he said, his finger tracing a dashed line that ran in an arc northeast from New York Harbor then northwest and west into the harbor at St. John's. "As stated in my briefing earlier, we've finally run the Germans out of the Gulf of Mexico, and the bombers keep them well off the East Coast. Now that's both good and bad. Good because it keeps them away from U.S. soil, cities, and coastal shipping. Bad because intelligence reports indicate there are actually more U-boats in the western Atlantic than there were a year ago, but in an area north of the Caribbean and east of the mainland—out of bomber range—that keeps getting smaller. That means the concentration of enemy firepower in this region is greater than ever—and getting meaner all the time."

His thick finger described a circle on the map. The *Dorchester* was on a course that would take it deep into that circle, then out again as the convoy headed westward.

"The safer the protected zones are, the more dangerous this area is," he went on. "On top of that, the new Series 3 U-boats can stay over here ten to fifteen days longer than the older units. But the most powerful enemy we have is Kraut bragging rights."

"Bragging rights?" Fox repeated it as a question.

"If one commander sinks fifty thousand tons of shipping, the next one wants sixty. And the next one seventy. Admiral Dönitz has encouraged this in a big way. His U-boat captains get one another all stoked up, so he doesn't have to worry about lighting a fire under anybody. We're points in a game."

Captain Danielsen paused to let it all sink in.

"What I'm saying here, gentlemen, is that this voyage is important, it's different, and it's dangerous. We haven't carried chaplains with us before, and I don't know any more than you do why we're carrying four of them this time out of the blue. What we do know is that, wherever you're going and whatever you're doing, the men on this ship need you here and now.

"Look around you the next couple of days. You'll see men who believe in what they're fighting for. No question. But they're young and lonesome and scared. Man, I'm scared. These are good men. They'll go up against anything. But this time we're asking them to go up against the unknown. We don't know what they're facing any more than they do.

"And that's the most terrifying enemy there is."

The chaplains nodded in agreement.

"We don't know where we're going or what we're doing. We don't know where the U-boats are, even though we know they're watching every move we make. The weather's going to be dicey. We know we've had spies on board ships in other convoys, and I'd say there's always a chance we've got one in our midst here.

"Though this first jump to St. John's ought to be safe, the anticipation—just knowing the Jerries are out there and we're sitting ducks for them—can eat away at a man's mind. Make him less effective. Make him worry about things that aren't even there. You men have your work cut out for you.

"You have the run of the ship. You have unlimited access to me day and night. Help us get through this."

"We're honored to do everything we can," Chaplain Fox responded firmly.

"Thank you." Captain Danielsen rose, indicating the meeting was over.

"Captain," Rabbi Goode said as the men stood to leave, "could we pray for you now? Here?"

The captain's steel-blue eyes wavered for an instant. Then there was the hint of a smile. "Shoot."

The five men stood in a circle and bowed their heads. After a beat or two of silence, Goode spoke out in a confident, resonant voice. "God of our fathers and of all the earth, you are both master of the seas and master of our hearts. I ask your special blessing on Captain Danielsen, the *Dorchester,* and everyone on board. Keep us from fear of anything except your power. Give us the resolve and the courage to meet whatever challenge lies ahead. Give us the calm that comes from knowing everything we do is for your glory.

"Give Captain Danielsen the assurance every day that he is guided and protected by your all-powerful hand. We lift him up to you. Amen."

By the end of their first day at sea, it was clear to the chaplains that conditions on board were every bit as bad as the captain had predicted. By dinner on the first day out the sky disappeared, the gray sea churned mercilessly, and rain and sleet cascaded down in sheets once more. Singly and in groups, passengers occasionally ventured out on deck for a little exercise or a breath of fresh air.

Nobody stayed for long. The precipitation and salt spray were frozen into a sheet of ice that covered every surface. Footing on deck was treacherous. The lines and rigging were all encased in ice built up a fraction of an inch at a time—clear as crystal and hard as iron.

Yet for all the discomfort on the deck, a constant flow of men braved the ice and wind to get away from equally miserable conditions below—trading one form of misery for another just for the sake of variety. In spite of the bitter cold outside, the air in the living quarters of the *Dorchester* was hot, stale, and becoming more unpleasant every hour.

With windows and portholes shut tight against the high seas and sleet, there was precious little air circulating inside. Except for little electric fans here and there and exhaust ventilation shafts for the kitchen and engine room, there was nothing to move the air and nothing at all to bring cool, fresh air in from outside.

The bad air was made even more inhospitable by a constant nauseating combination of smells: marine fuel oil, freshly painted metal, kitchen grease, and the bodies of 902 passengers packed into an area designed for less than half as many. It was enough to make practically everyone on board very seasick. And it did.

And hanging over everything, as palpable as the stale atmosphere, was the knowledge that German submarines would soon be able to draw a bead on them—

where and when, they wouldn't know—and there was nothing they could do about it.

In their cabin after dinner, the chaplains' discussion turned to developing a plan of action for the next few days.

"Seems the best way to get to know the guys is just to spend time with them," Chaplain Poling began. "I don't expect a call for heavy ideological debates, even though they're a specialty of mine." He grinned in a self-deprecating way, then went on. "These men are going to want somebody to talk to, pure and simple."

"You're right," Fox answered. "Let's chat some people up. A few will come to us, but not many, at least not at first. We'll go to them one-on-one during the day, then get together and compare notes every night. If one of us has a situation he thinks another one could handle better, ask for help."

"It won't take long for word to get around," Father Washington predicted. "As soon as the men know we're here, we won't have to go looking for trouble; it'll find us wherever we are."

The four nodded in agreement.

"One thing we forgot," said Rabbi Goode.

"What?" Fox asked.

"Us. Who's going to listen to us? Pray for us? Hold us accountable to God? To one another? To ourselves?"

No one spoke.

"I say we use the buddy system," Goode went on. "Each of us agrees to pray for another chaplain—be his sounding board. Help him if he needs it. I'll pray for Washington here, Washington prays for Poling, Poling prays for Fox, and Fox prays for me. What do you say?"

A hearty chorus of agreement filled the small room. As the noise died down, an unfamiliar face leaned into the open doorway.

"What are *you* so happy about?" The tone was half legitimate question and half sarcastic taunt. It came from a uniform with three stripes on it, a sergeant.

"Ah," the stranger exclaimed, spying the chaplain insignia on their uniforms. "Chaplains. That explains it, I guess." Before any of the chaplains could speak to him, he was gone.

"One of our first customers, I predict," Washington said.

"No argument there," Poling replied.

★ ★ ★ ★

The chaplains arrived for breakfast the next morning five minutes apart, thinking that if they were alone other passengers would be more likely to speak. Chaplain Washington went first, making his way through the serving line, his metal tray being filled with eggs, potatoes, and the old navy standby, chipped beef on toast. He filled a cup with fresh, steaming hot coffee and trolled for a spot at one of the long tables that filled the room.

Unlike the great Atlantic liners, whose legendary dining rooms represented the pinnacle of luxury and spaciousness (the main dining room on the *Queen Mary* could hold all three of Columbus's ships with room to spare), coastal vessels like the *Dorchester* had serviceable but unpretentious dining salons. Another difference was that on the North Atlantic run, looking out the window was not necessarily good for the appetite; dining room windows were small or nonexistent. The mess hall aboard the *Dorchester* had a row of windows on both long sides of the rectangular room, in a horizontal line just above the wainscoting that encircled the space. The original tables for two, four, and six were gone, replaced by long metal tables and benches to make room for all the extra people. Passengers had to eat in shifts anyway. Even with the added table space, only a third of them could sit down at once.

Scanning the room, Washington saw that the tables immediately in front of him were all full or nearly so. To encourage visitors, he started a new table, taking the first seat at an empty table with room for eight or ten.

To his surprise he found himself eating his entire meal alone. He'd arrived at the peak of the breakfast hour and watched over the next few minutes as the room gradually emptied, leaving only a few groups and isolated individuals scattered around.

The time to himself gave Washington the unexpected opportunity to take a good look at the people who came and went. Reinforcing the impression he got as he waited to board the day before, he saw what seemed to be every kind of man on God's earth sitting at those rows of metal tables: old salts and soldiers who didn't look old enough to drive, easygoing types and others clearly more animated and aggressive, the quiet and the boisterous, the handsome and the homely.

He thought back to Captain Danielsen's remark about the spies discovered on other ships. Was it even possible that one of these people could be working for the Nazis? He laughed softly to himself. What a crazy idea. It struck him that every person in the room would have a part to play in the mysterious drama that was beginning to unfold. "Wonder what part I'll have?" he said aloud, to no one in particular.

"Beats me," boomed a voice unexpectedly from behind him. Washington turned to see a huge black man, dressed in white pants, white T-shirt, and a stained white apron. He had a white paper cook's cap covering his close-cropped hair, and held a cigarette between the first two fingers of his left hand.

"How you doin', Chaplain?" The black giant stuck his hand out in greeting. Washington shook hands; he had the sensation he was grabbing a piece of steak rather than another hand. "Morris Jones. I'm the cook. How you like my work so far?"

Washington stood, then motioned to the long metal bench at the table. "Morris, I'm Chaplain Washington. Pleasure to meet you. I've got to say I like your work just fine." Jones waved off the offer of a seat and took a drag on his cigarette.

127

This was true. The food on board, though plain, had been fresh, hot, plentiful, and tasty. In fact, Washington had noticed it was a lot better than he'd expected.

"I just wish there was a little nicer place to enjoy it." Jones laughed, his teeth brilliant white against his black skin. Washington laughed too. "Where'd you learn to cook like this?"

"My momma taught me. She cooked for the railroad men at the car plant in Pascagoula."

"Pasca-what?" Washington smiled.

"Pascagoula. Near Biloxi. Surely you heard of Biloxi."

"Heard of it, yeah, I think so." Technically, it was the truth.

"I always wanted to be a fighter. Wanted to box. Make me some money and take care of my momma. I did OK, but it drove Momma crazy. I told her I couldn't make as good a living doing anything else. And she said, 'People got to eat. You cook for 'em. I'll show you how.' And so I been in the kitchen eight years now, three of 'em here on the *Dorchester*."

"I'd say by the quality of your work that you're pretty happy with it."

"Cooking is one of the best jobs a colored man can have. And I like the *Dorchester* just fine. I will say this: I'll be glad to get back to business as usual when this is all over."

"You and me both, Jones."

★　★　★　★

Sitting at breakfast, Chaplain Fox had received a note requesting his presence in the captain's stateroom in half an hour. He knocked at the appointed time and was admitted to the same small, tidy room he and the other chaplains had been in the morning before.

The captain stood in front of his desk chair. Seated on the couch were two women, both around thirty, Fox guessed, Scandinavian, big-boned. The one on the left had hair so blond it was almost white. The other had straw-colored hair lightly tinged with a strawberry red.

"Ladies, I'd like you to meet Chaplain Fox. Chaplain Fox, Helge Thomasen and Kristen Sorensen—Danish citizens, civil engineers, and volunteers on this little enterprise." Greetings were exchanged, and the men took their seats.

"We are pleased to meet you, Chaplain Fox," Helge, the light blond, said slowly with a thick accent.

"With so many men out fighting, these two have offered their engineering expertise to the Allies. They're both electronics experts, experienced civil engineers, and ready to do whatever they can to spring Scandinavia from the Nazis."

"You may know how Denmark has suffered under the Nazis," Kristen said. "We will do anything to stop Hitler."

"I'm sure you will," Fox answered, both surprised and encouraged by her intensity.

"Chaplain, I hope you'll keep an eye on these young ladies as long as they're with us. There are nine hundred men aboard and two women. Even so, I'd say the odds are long that anything would happen, but I promised their king myself that I'd take good care of them. Their quarters are off-limits, and there's a sentry on duty twenty-four hours. Still, if they need you, I want them to know you're available."

Fox, thinking of his own son in the Marine Corps, smiled a fatherly smile. "Yes, sir. Ladies, I am yours to command." The captain left his three visitors to get acquainted while he departed to see to other business.

Chaplain Goode spent the morning in the dayroom getting to know as many of the soldiers and sailors on board as he could. Coming off watch and ready for a sandwich and a smoke, Dereck Hardaway took a seat at a card table next to where the chaplain sat.

"Interesting breakfast," Goode observed, looking at the thick ham sandwich Hardaway was wolfing down.

"The cook keeps sandwiches and coffee out twenty-four hours for the watches. It may be the middle of the morning to you, but it's dinnertime for me." He gestured with his sandwich, then took another huge bite.

"What brings you to the *Dorchester?*" Goode asked.

"Merchant marine, remember?" Hardaway answered with his mouth full. "Doing my part for Uncle Sam and freedom and all like that. Besides, the navy chartered us lock, stock, and barrel. And crew."

"Where's your family?"

"Nashville. Parents still live there. Two brothers, two sisters—all of 'em married but me. Just never had the time for a wife, I guess. It's just as well."

At that moment a soldier walked in one door of the room, crossed through without a word to anybody, and went out a door at the other end. It was the sergeant who'd poked his head in the chaplains' quarters the night before.

"Who's that?" Goode asked, as Hardaway swallowed the last bite of sandwich and fished a pack of Luckies from his shirt pocket.

"Adams," Hardaway answered, lighting up. "He's only a sergeant, but he's a *major* pain in the rump." He laughed at his own joke, exhaling a cloud of smoke.

Goode smiled, then asked, "What's his beef?"

"Beats me. But he's one to stay away from. Been busted twice in four years for fighting. Keeps to himself. I wouldn't bother if I were you."

"Thanks for the tip," Goode answered, staring at the closed door where Adams had been.

★ ★ ★ ★

Since the captain's first briefing for the senior officers, Chaplain Poling had been fascinated by the idea of ASDIC. The fact that the system was on board was an open secret. After some discreet inquiries, the chaplain secured permission to visit the system control center, in a converted closet next to the radio room.

Passing through a security checkpoint, Poling was introduced to Lieutenant Aubrey Burch, communications officer in charge of the ASDIC setup. "Squeeze in here and have a look, chaplain," Lieutenant Burch offered. "This is a new high-performance British version of SONAR. Very secret. Very good."

Poling found himself in a tiny, windowless room with banks of mysterious electronic instruments on three sides. In the center of it all was a large speaker that looked like it had come from a console radio. An operator sat before it, his hands endlessly adjusting a row of dials on the surface immediately in front of him. Poling could hear the "boop" of an outgoing signal at regular intervals. If by any wild chance there was a spy on board, Poling thought to himself, this was no doubt his objective.

"That's the sound ASDIC sends out," Burch continued. "When it comes back, we know there's something out there for the sound wave to bounce off of. This new version has an enhanced response over current systems, though we've still got a long way to go. Operators work in four-hour shifts around the clock listening for signals. The minute they hear something, they call me, and we decide whether it's fish or Führer."

"How do you tell the difference?"

"At this stage we're not always sure. It's all so new and experimental. Signal strength is mostly what we have to go on. Anything suspicious we treat as hostile."

A few minutes later Burch and Poling were having a cup of coffee in the dayroom.

"The idea of 'hearing' the Germans through the water is fascinating," Poling said. "I'd think it would give everybody a lot more peace of mind."

"It's a mixed bag," Burch replied. "It's prone to false signals, but you never know until an identified target starts to move. A school of fish moves different from a U-boat taking a bead on you. There are times when I'd almost rather not know and not get that horrible feeling in my stomach when those boops start coming back.

"Besides, what in heaven's name can we do anyway?" Poling was surprised by Burch's sudden intensity. "We can't contact other ships in the convoy. They couldn't break formation to help us even if they knew we were hit. The water's thirty-six degrees out of St. John's, and nobody can live in that more than twenty minutes. All the boop tells you is that you've got less than an hour to live."

After a couple of minutes, Chaplain Poling broke the silence. "Tell me this: why are the U-boats running the show here? We're pounding the Japs in the Pacific, building ships faster than the bad guys on both sides of the world can sink them, and yet we're so outnumbered in the Atlantic. What gives?"

"Admiral's prerogative."

"Come again?"

"Admiral's prerogative. Fleet Admiral Ernest J. King, to be exact, who has a bee in his bonnet for the Japs. Commanders in the Atlantic have been screaming for months that we need more protection for convoys headed to England. Here we got the Cadillac factory in Detroit turning out tanks to do a dance on Hitler's Mercedes-Benz. But those tanks don't do us any good at the bottom of the ocean. Same with ammunition, food, arms, and soldiers. If we're not willing to protect them in transit, we may as well not spend all the time and effort to produce them in the first place."

"So what's with Admiral King?"

"He insists we need to save our naval firepower for the Pacific Theater. No doubt we started turning the tide at Midway. But ever since then, he's concentrated everything on island-hopping his way back to Tokyo. Every plane, every ship he sees as part of the victory. No doubt he'd have the *Dorchester* in the Philippines if he thought she'd hold together across the Pacific.

"We get support from coastal bombers as far out as they can fly, and we get escort vessels from the Coast Guard. But King has his mind made up. We send in the reports of tonnage lost to the Germans, and he sends back word that we need to do the best we can with what we've got, and that only the senior command has the knowledge and perspective to decide where to commit resources—that's the admiral's prerogative."

Poling made a mental note to pray for Admiral King. The admiral was in a position to make things happen, and Poling would see whether God might give him a nudge in the right direction.

As the conversation continued, the *Dorchester* plowed gamely ahead through the Atlantic swells, maintaining the prescribed one mile separation from the other ships in the convoy. Fanned out over the surface of the Atlantic, they stretched as far in every direction as the eye could see. Fifty ships, loaded with thousands of troops and thousands of tons of food and supplies for the battle-weary Allies holding out against the Nazi machine.

As the slowest of the ships, the *Dorchester* set the cruising speed for the voyage—eleven knots. Submerged and on the attack, U-boats averaged eight knots on electric motors. On the surface with diesels in action—their typical cruise mode and always the way they ran at night—they made fourteen.

If there was a U-boat out there on the prowl, the *Dorchester* was a sitting duck.

CHAPTER 10

SERGEANT ADAMS

By the second day out, life on the *Dorchester* had settled into a routine—as much of a routine as possible considering no one aboard knew where they were going or what they would do when they got there. If they got there.

The rain and sleet had stopped, but the wind and high seas continued as strong as ever, and the sun remained hidden behind clouds as gray and impenetrable as the ocean. The mercury hung stubbornly under twenty degrees—out of the wind. And in its small box with a hinged lid on the bridge deck, the thermometer was the only thing that was out of the wind. Taking the icy arctic gusts into account, the sailors aboard figured the temperature at zero or below. But they were quick to add, there was no telling how cold it really was.

Despite the harsh conditions, men continued to brave the elements for a little exercise, fresh air, and relief from the crowded conditions and squalid atmosphere below. Singly and in small groups, bracing themselves against the gusts, hearty passengers gingerly picked their way along the frozen decks, every handrail and line encased in a layer of ice thickened by each crash of salt spray.

The convoy sailed northeast, past Georges Bank and off the Continental Shelf into the deep Atlantic, where the surface heaved and rolled more than three thousand fathoms—almost three and a half miles—above the still, silent, pitch-black ocean floor.

Though it was nothing but an imaginary line on the page, Captain Danielsen was relieved when the convoy sailed east of 60° west longitude. That marked approximately the halfway point between New York and St. John's. Many miles to the north and invisible far over the horizon, the coast of Nova Scotia was off his port quarter. After Nova Scotia came Newfoundland and safety. Another two days and they'd be there. Then the next part of the mystery would be solved.

Sixty degrees west also meant the *Dorchester* and a few other ships separated themselves from the rest of the convoy. According to private orders he had received along with the instructions to proceed to St. John's, Captain Danielsen was to alter course along with two freighters, the Norwegian vessel *Biscaya* and the Panamanian-flagged *Lutz.* As they executed the change in heading, three Coast Guard cutters broke off from the main convoy, as planned, to escort them. Where the rest of the ships were headed, the captain had no idea.

The cutters maneuvered smoothly into position. In the lead as senior escort was the *Tampa,* formerly stationed in Mobile Bay. Flanking the formation were two smaller ships with icebreaker bows, the *Comanche* to port and the *Escanaba* to starboard.

Now all that stood between the captain and a hot bath and soda in St. John's—maybe—was a German U-boat captain looking for another hide to nail to his trophy wall. In the pilot house, on the boat deck, in his office, or lying in his bunk waiting to fall asleep, he wondered who was out there. Maybe nobody, though that was unlikely. Maybe a commanding officer—a family man like himself—dedicated to doing his duty like any other military professional. Only his duty was to sink the convoy the *Dorchester* traveled in—not disable it, or turn it back, but to send the men and supplies it carried on a three-and-a-half-mile voyage straight down—the better to keep all those men and supplies from harming him and his family, his country, his Führer.

Competition, he knew, was keen among U-boat captains. The more tonnage they could claim sunk, the more hardware they'd have pinned to their uniforms. The thought of an Iron Cross hanging around their necks made those men plenty brave. It was up to the

Allies to make getting that prize more trouble than it was worth.

To Captain Danielsen, it all boiled down to Torpedo Junction. That was the spot south and east of Newfoundland that marked the boundary of the U.S. and Gander-based submarine reconnaissance and bombing squadrons. Just beyond where the airplanes turned around, the U-boats hovered like jackals outside a fence, waiting. It wasn't a long trip from the edge of the safety zone to the shelter of the submarine nets in St. John's harbor. But it was across that expanse of ocean, between 58° and 51° west longitude, that the invisible German force lurked, watching, torpedoes at the ready.

Approaching the junction, the convoy would begin a prearranged zigzag maneuver designed to present a smaller target to the wolf packs for a shorter time than sailing dead on. The lead ship would begin a turn every thirty minutes. The *Dorchester* and the freighters, following half a mile behind, would coordinate their turns accordingly. Then the flanking escorts, which stayed astern of the ships they were protecting, made a third rank, also turning to maintain their position in the formation. Since radio contact and even semaphore signals were forbidden, turns were precisely timed using the ships' chronometers.

After breakfast the third morning out, Chaplain Poling walked into the dayroom and scanned the faces.

One foursome was engrossed in a lively game of gin rummy. Others sat talking or reading. The sailors and merchant marines had watches and other duties to perform, but the army soldiers that made up the majority of the passengers had no official duties on board.

Every morning they had inspection and roll call, and daily morning reports were prepared to turn in once the *Dorchester* reached St. John's. Morning reports, the same in all corners of the army world, were the bane of every company clerk's existence, reporting the condition and whereabouts of every soldier in uniform—present for duty, sick, on leave, missing, captured, deserted, wounded, or dead. Aboard the *Dorchester* there weren't many options beyond the first two, but that didn't keep regulations from requiring the clerk to type up a new form every day. It was the army way.

Poling's eye fell on one young soldier sitting at a card table, pencil in hand, staring at a little disheveled pile of blank paper on the table in front of him. He gazed straight ahead, lost in thought.

The chaplain walked up and stood beside him. "Mind if I sit down?" he asked. His voice startled the young soldier out of his daze.

"No, Chaplain, pull up a chair."

It didn't seem possible that this young soldier could be old enough to enlist. Chaplain Poling knew some boys couldn't wait to join the war effort and that recruiters weren't above taking an eager youngster's word he was of legal age when the truth was right before his eyes.

"I'm Chaplain Poling."

"Sam Nelson. Private Sam Nelson."

The two shook hands. Young as he was, Private Sam Nelson had an older man's hand—strong, square, and callused with manual work.

"Where's your home, Nelson, when you're not cruising the seven seas in luxury?"

Private Nelson smiled. "Bluefield, West Virginia."

"Beautiful place, huh?"

"Most beautiful place I know."

"And what do you do in Bluefield?"

"Little bit of everything, I guess. Pop has a store there. We do some farming, blacksmithing. Most people round about work in the mine. Both my granddaddies did, but Pop said he'd rather starve. He's kept me and my brothers away from there."

"How many brothers have you got?"

"Two brothers, one big and one little. And two sisters, one big and one little. I'm right in the middle.

"My cousin's in the air corps. Flies B-17s in England. I couldn't wait to join. The air force wouldn't take me, but the army said, 'Come on!'"

"You look awfully young to be a pilot. I might say you look awfully young to be a soldier."

Nelson broke into a conspiratorial smile. "No birth certificates out there in the hollers. If you think you're too young to do something, you are. If you think you're old enough, you're old enough."

The two sat silent for a moment. They felt the ever present vibration of the engine through the soles of their feet. The room rolled with the gray Atlantic waves.

There was a question in Private Nelson's eyes. Chaplain Poling waited for him to speak.

"Chaplain . . ."

"What is it, Nelson?"

"I wonder if you could help me."

"Sure. Whatever I can."

"I want to write a letter to my family. I miss them so bad." Suddenly his eyes welled with tears.

"I think that's a great idea. Tell them what you're doing. Tell them you can't wait to get home. It'll mean the world to them to get a letter from you."

Nelson spoke barely above a whisper, his eyes fixed on the blank pages in front of him. "Chaplain, I can't write. I don't know how. I can sign my name, but that's it."

Poling looked at him, kind and stern at the same time. "Son, there's nothing to be ashamed of in that."

Nelson looked up.

"Everybody has different gifts. You got some; you didn't get others. How many people in this room do you think could shoe a horse? Or grow a sack of potatoes?"

Nelson sat a little straighter.

"You know what?" Poling went on, "I'll bet you're not the only man in this room right now who can't write. But you're the only one who cares enough about your family to worry about it.

"I'll help you write your letter. And depending how long we're here on this little adventure together, I'll teach you what I can so you can write yourself."

"No foolin'?"

"No foolin'."

Chaplain Poling picked the pencil up from a crease in a sheet of paper where Nelson had placed it to keep it from rolling off the table in the swells.

"OK," the chaplain said, tapping the edges of the paper on the tabletop to even the stack. "Let 'er rip."

"Dear Mom, Pop, Amos, Cassie, Maggie, and Mark,

"I know you're surprised to get a letter from me. A nice chaplain is helping me write. I'm on a big ship in the middle of the ocean. We're on our way to an island near Canada, but I don't know where we're going after that. It's cold and rocky out here in the water, but I'm fine. I miss Mom's biscuits and cornbread, but otherwise the food is real good. Have you heard from Willie? I hope he's giving those Germans what for. I miss you so much. This is another world out here, and home seems awful far away. May God keep you safe and bring me home safe is my earnest prayer.

"How does that sound?" he asked.

"Private Nelson—Sam—it sounds wonderful. I know your family will be proud of you for doing this."

"Here, let me sign it." Chaplain Poling turned the last page so it faced him, and handed him the pencil. "How do you write 'love'?"

Poling wrote the word very lightly in pencil at the bottom of the letter. Nelson traced it carefully, then signed his name.

"Would you keep this and mail it for me?" Nelson asked.

"Be glad to. It'll be safe in here." The chaplain unbuttoned a shirt pocket on his uniform, slipped the letter inside, and buttoned the flap. "Say, I almost forgot. I'll need a mailing address. I'll do the envelope for you later."

"Oh—right. Just mail it to the Nelson General Store, Bluefield, West Virginia. They'll get it."

"I'll see to it," Poling replied. He rose to leave.

"Thank you, chaplain," Nelson said. "God bless you."

"Hey, I'm supposed to tell you that," the chaplain answered jovially.

Chaplain John Washington had been on deck for less than ten minutes. Even so, his face was red and windburned, his glasses covered with salt spray, and every inch chilled to the bone in spite of his thick new army greatcoat. The rain had been gone for some time now, but the wind and cold were as intense as before. The unrelieved wall of steel-like sky had transformed into a mottled swirl of various gradations, bringing the promise, however slight, of sunshine some time in the future.

At some point, the priest thought, *the cold air is better than the air inside. A guy's gotta get a breath of air somebody else hasn't already breathed first. Then at some other point—like now—the air inside is better because at least it's warm.*

Returning to his cabin, Washington took off his heavy outer clothing, shucked his rain boots, and sat down on one of the two lower bunks. He was a man of action; sitting around was always hard on him. But there were nine hundred souls aboard, and no doubt an interesting story lay behind every one. No doubt a need for spiritual strengthening and guidance. He was there to seek out those needs and meet them. They sure weren't going to come looking for him.

Washington heard a knock on the frame of the open door and looked. It was a young officer in the engineering corps, about the same age as Washington, with close-cropped red hair and freckles.

"Chaplain?"

"Chaplain Washington here. Come in, Lieutenant. Please. If I had a chair, I'd offer it to you. Pull up a bunk and sit down." He gestured toward the bunk across from him.

146

"Chaplain, you're Catholic, right?"

"Right. Every chaplain is here for every soldier, but I'm a Catholic priest, yes."

"I was wondering, that is, several of us aboard ship were wondering—by the way my name's Shanahan, Lieutenant Michael Shanahan—were wondering if you would hear confession."

"Of course. In fact I was making plans to do that but hadn't worked out all the details with Captain Danielsen yet. It was good of you to seek me out and make the request. I should have everything in order by tonight. I'll be sure to let you know."

"Chaplain—Father—could you hear my confession now? You don't know me. I don't know you. It doesn't matter whether you see me or not."

Washington considered for a split second. "Yes. Let me just do this." He took a piece of notepaper from his drawer in the dresser and scrawled a few words on it. Holding it by the edge with one hand, he pulled the stateroom door almost shut with the other, positioned the paper on the outside, then latched the door, securing the note between the door edge and its frame so anyone approaching the closed door would see it.

"Bless me Father, for I have sinned . . ."

A minute later, Rabbi Goode, heading to his quarters, was surprised to find the door closed. He had his hand on the lever before he saw the note: "In conference—thanks, Ch. Washington." Silently releasing his grip, Chaplain Goode continued on down the passageway.

★ ★ ★ ★

Entering the mess for a cup of ever-present coffee, Goode saw a cook's helper wiping down tables in the room. It was one of those rare times during the day that there was little activity going on. In one corner, enjoying a cigarette and a moment of leisure, Morris Jones loomed over his domain. He waved nonchalantly to Goode as he entered. Goode served himself from the coffee urn, then walked to the table where Jones sat.

"Have a seat, Chaplain. Take a load off," Jones offered.

"Thanks. Don't mind if I do. Busy day?"

A low chuckle rumbled out from deep within his massive frame. "Every day's a busy day. Three meals, three shifts each. Twenty-five hundred to three thousand meals every twenty-four hours, depending on who feels like a snack and who's off somewhere feeding the fish."

"I know just what you mean. I've been on the verge of feeding them a time or two myself these last couple of days."

"Say, you Greek? Italian?"

"Born in Brooklyn, New York."

"No kiddin'. You got that kinda foreign look, you know?"

"I know. I heard about it plenty growing up. I'm a Jew. A rabbi like my father."

"You and me both been picked on, then."

"I guess we have. When we moved to Washington, the kids there called me Jew Boy."

"On good days they called me Jigaboo. Other times they weren't so nice."

They sat in silence for a moment. Wanting to keep the conversation going, Goode spoke up.

"I'd hate to think of making this trip without you. You do an incredible job. I can't believe so much food comes out of a kitchen that size."

"What saves us is the coolers. Just got two great big ones that hold a powerful lot of chow. Come on, I'll show you."

With obvious pride Jones led the chaplain back through the kitchen where a small army of blacks toiled away at various jobs: chopping meat, making salad, loading potatoes in the automatic peeler. "I want all you to meet a friend of mine." There was a pause in the commotion. "This is Chaplain Alex Goode from Brooklyn, New York. Chaplain, meet . . ." here he paused for dramatic effect, "the galley slaves!" Jones let out a roar of laughter that filled the low-ceilinged room. Goode and the other men joined in.

Chaplain and chef continued their tour. They walked by a baker's helper kneading bread dough. "We make 120 loaves a day," Jones said as they passed by the big table in the low room. "Bread on the shelf spoils at sea in two days, but the ingredients last forever: flour, water, lard, and salt. So we keep on makin' it, and people keep on eatin' it."

Jones opened a big latch and clicked on a light. There was space there half the size of the kitchen, piled to the ceiling with boxes of provisions, fruits, and vegetables. "Whaddya think about that, chaplain?"

"Impressive. No wonder we eat so well."

The two returned to the corner table where Jones had left his cigarette. He crushed it out and lit a fresh one.

"Smoke?" He offered the pack.

"No thanks." He watched the smoke curl up to the low ceiling where it dissipated in a thin layer. "Seeing as many people as you do, I guess you get to know everybody on board."

"I see the same faces every day," Jones answered, "but I'm too busy to chit-chat much, you know. Most everybody's just one of the mob, you might say. Some seem a little nicer than average, some a little meaner than average. It all works out, I guess you might say."

"Who'd you think you'd put in the mean category?"

"Oh, I guess two or three troublemakers come to mind. Adams, maybe."

"Who's Adams?"

"Sergeant Wesley Adams. Got something eatin' at his craw for sure. I don't know what it is, and I don't much care. I'd just leave him plenty of room if I was you."

"Would he be kind of stocky? Brown-headed? Rough complexion?"

"He would at that. And speak of the devil . . ."

Through the doorway into the mess came the surly-faced seaman the chaplains had seen the night they came aboard. He filled a coffee cup and started out of the room.

"What say, Adams?" Jones called out across the empty tables to the disappearing figure.

"What say yourself," Adams mumbled without looking around.

Jones and Goode watched him as he left. The two were a dramatic study in contrast sitting across from each other at the small corner table: the huge, black man whose life was marked by hard physical labor, and the slight, bright-eyed scholar who had dedicated himself to a life of faith, teaching, and preservation of ancient customs and truths. Each in his own way had been marked as an outcast, and each in his own way had made his peace with the world.

Later in the afternoon, walking down a companion-way, Goode happened to see Adams up ahead. Adams looked straight ahead over Goode's shoulder as they drew near, his mouth a thin line, never making eye contact. Goode moved slightly away from the wall toward the middle of the passage.

"Adams? Chaplain Goode. We met in the mess earlier this afternoon."

"Good Chaplain Goode. What can I do you for?"

Goode deftly ignored the snide comment. "I was thinking it'd be nice to sit down together soon and share a cup of Jones' all-night coffee. Get acquainted."

"I'm not the get-acquainted type," Adams declared flatly. "You're a lieutenant. I'm enlisted. You say do something, I do it."

Goode turned around in the narrow companionway to walk with Adams. The two walked down the passage together to a staircase, descended, and continued along a hall on the deck below. "Chaplains aren't here to give orders. Being officers lets us get things done that maybe we couldn't do otherwise. There's no rank in the chapel."

"Maybe there's something rank in here," Adams said sniffing the air loudly, an unmistakable edge to his voice.

"A friend of yours warned me something was eating at you," Goode admitted. "I can see now what he meant."

Adams stopped at a bulkhead door leading to the sailors' quarters. "Look, Chaplain. Thank you for your kind expression of concern." His words dripped sarcasm. "If you have an order for me, I will obey it. If you want to be my buddy, you can forget it. If you want to save my soul, you've given yourself a helluva job. Good night, Lieutenant Goode."

"Good night, Adams," the chaplain said at the door that closed behind his prickly companion. Aloud to himself he continued. "There are four of us and one of you. Challenge accepted. Shalom."

CHAPTER 11

TORPEDO JUNCTION

The convoy turned northwest, continuing a long, slow arc that would bring them to safe harbor at St. John's on the eastern shore of Newfoundland. It was the beginning of their third day at sea—a day that, if all went according to plan, would see them securely into friendly territory.

This morning the convoy's plotted course would take it at last through the notorious sector of the western Atlantic familiar to soldiers and sailors everywhere as Torpedo Junction. Because of the prestige that came with sinking the most American tonnage, commanding a U-boat at Torpedo Junction was a plum assignment for the brave, intensely patriotic men who captained the vessels of the German submarine fleet. Competition was keen for the opportunity to prowl there, patrolling at periscope depth by day, riding on the surface by night, lying in wait to pounce on the big, slow transports and cargo ships that passed within torpedo range. The term "wolf packs," coined to describe these eager, aggressive, and deadly hunters, was accurate in more ways than one. In their small, cramped, dimly lit room, the ASDIC operators aboard the *Dorchester* maintained their intense and quiet vigil. Their listening station was next to the radio room, which had been rendered eerily quiet by orders of radio silence. An operator stayed on duty to monitor radio traffic, but he hadn't pressed the microphone button since the *Dorchester* sailed past Sandy Hook more than fifty hours earlier.

The ASDIC cubbyhole, though equally quiet, resonated with a much greater feeling of tension and expectation. Continuing to alternate their watches at the console, operators listened hour after hour for any indication of underwater activity—staring into space, eyes fixed at random on a single point in the room. It was as if, having concentrated all their sensory energy and receptiveness in their auditory nerves, facility in the other senses had been drained away: smell, touch, taste, sight shriveled temporarily to redirect all receptive power to the soft hiss and static pop of the big speaker that so dominated the room.

This was the first voyage the *Dorchester* had made since the new high-sensitivity ASDIC was secretly installed. So far the operators had heard nothing but the steady machine-generated "boop" that drifted off into the dark waters and disappeared, once every five seconds, 17,280 times a day. Apprehensive at the thought they might have to distinguish between a hull of Krupp steel and a school of fish, the ASDIC technicians had not even had that to test their mettle. The only sound, beyond a constant low hiss of atmospheric static, was edgy silence.

Huddled over the receiver, the two ASDIC technicians wondered aloud what the unbroken stream of static meant.

"No change. Nothing."

"Do you think it's busted?"

"It's still sending the signal out."

"Yeah, but what if it's hard of hearing? What if a vacuum tube is shot? How would we know?"

"Your guess is as good as mine. But hey, we're the experts, right?"

"Right."

★ ★ ★ ★

Chaplain Alex Goode sat at a table in the dayroom holding a better-than-average bridge hand. He hadn't been too sure he could scare up a foursome for such a highbrow game on board, but in fact it was easy. The more Rabbi Goode got to know his fellow passengers, the more interested he was in the range and variety of their experiences. There were schoolteachers, storekeepers, night watchmen, farmers, salesmen.

His partner across the table was a former car dealer from Indianapolis named Fred Baxter. "There weren't any more cars to sell," Fred had told Goode when they introduced themselves to each other the day before, "so I thought I might as well do something for the good of the cause. Instead of making Dodges and DeSotos, the factory switched over to trucks and half-tracks. Even if it puts me out of a job, I'm all for it if it gets us to those Japs and Germans faster. We can't pummel 'em fast enough for me."

Lieutenant Baxter and Chaplain Goode were playing against two lieutenants from Maryland, Cal Foster and Monroe Williams. Childhood friends, they had enlisted as soon as they got out of college and had spent their entire eighteen-month military career together. Their long-standing friendship gave them a big leg up when it came to bridge; they were beating Baxter and Goode handily, though Goode felt at the moment that the cards in his hand might well put him on the comeback trail.

"So you lived in Washington, Chaplain?" Lieutenant Williams was saying. "Cal and I took the train in several times a year to see the Senators play when the Orioles were out of town."

"I went to school in Baltimore," Goode responded. "I got caught up in the Orioles–Senators battles myself. Say, have you met Chaplain Washington? He's a big baseball fan. I think under other circumstances he might have gone pro—although I have to admit I think the team he chose is the best of all—God's team." A murmur of lighthearted approval worked its way around the table.

"Yes," Goode continued, answering the question. "I moved from Brooklyn to D.C. and enjoyed my time there."

"Was your father in government service?" Lieutenant Foster asked, looking at his hand as he prepared to bid.

"He was a rabbi."

"So, you're carrying on the family tradition."

"In a way, though that wasn't why I did it. In fact, my father wanted me to be an engineer. I wanted to honor his wishes, but it wasn't for me."

When he talked to new friends about Washington, he never mentioned the feeling he had there of being an outsider. The unkindness of the neighborhood boys had only strengthened his resolve. With help from money raised by area synagogues, his faith and love of learning took him out of that neighborhood to Hebrew Union College in Cincinnati. And it was later, while he worked toward his doctorate at Johns Hopkins in Baltimore, that he became an Orioles fan.

Goode's stalwart patriotism was part of the bedrock that shaped his life and character even then. Before Pearl Harbor plenty of Americans said the war in Europe was a "phony war." No less a luminary than Colonel Charles Lindbergh had taken a strong antiwar—some said pro-Nazi—stance. He'd even reported favorably on the German military to the U.S. government in 1939 and accepted a medal from Reichsmarschall Hermann Göring. To Goode and tens of thousands of other American Jews, however, the tragedy that unfolded in

Germany and neighboring countries beginning with the Nazi rise to power in 1933 was never a phony war. Many Jews had been relieved when Lindbergh, his loyalty questioned by President Roosevelt, resigned from the Army Air Force in 1941.

Though the *Dorchester* had been at sea scarcely three days, everyone cast together on this adventure felt they had been together forever. Passengers and crew had gotten accustomed to the endless pitch and roll of the ship on the water, the crowded, dim quarters, the constant throbbing of the engines, and, underscoring and permeating everything, the fear that out there somewhere probably was an enemy submarine— or two, or ten—watching the convoy, looking for an opening, patiently biding its time in the timeless tradition of the hunter stalking the hunted.

After lunch the four chaplains convened in their stateroom to assess the situation. They took their accustomed spots, two sitting on each of the two lower bunks. "Shall I start us out with a prayer?" Chaplain Fox asked.

The others nodded their assent and bowed their heads.

"Our Father and our God," Fox began, "we come before you grateful for the opportunities you've given us to bear your light to these hundreds of soldiers. Some of them are scared; others are angry, lonesome, bored, and mixed up in all sorts of ways. Help us to know how to reach out to them—how to comfort them in your name.

"We pray for this voyage and this mission. Lord, we don't know where we're going or what we'll face when we get there. But help us never to forget that you're always with us, your arms always encircled around us. Help us as chaplains to be a worthy example to others, supporting one another in a true spirit of brotherly love. We're from different branches of your faith, but we know that a lot more in our beliefs draws us together than divides us.

"Give us wisdom as we talk here now and consider what we can do to lift the spirits of the men on board. Some of them, we know, are not walking with you. They don't know you, don't want to know you. Even these, we pray, will be touched in some way by our work in your name.

"These men are strangers, but they're our brothers under God. Thank you for this great opportunity to meet them at their point of need and turn them toward your incomparable and perfect light.

"In the Lord's name, Amen."

Chaplain Poling raised his head. "I think we all sense that we need to do something to lighten the atmosphere."

"All it would take to light this atmosphere is a match!" Washington rejoined as the other chaplains chuckled their approval.

"We need to come up with some sort of event that will bring out a sense of community. We're sharing a real adventure here, and we ought to celebrate it," Goode observed. "What we need is a party!"

A chorus of approval greeted his suggestion.

The four chaplains soon formed a plan of action. After dinner that night, the dining hall and dayroom would be transformed into party headquarters. They'd spread the word for everybody to gather for refreshments and whatever entertainment they could scare up.

"I'll check with the captain and make sure everything's cherry," Fox offered.

An hour later Captain Danielsen welcomed Chaplain Fox to the bridge. In reality it was a modest little wheelhouse, seemingly undersized like everything else aboard the *Dorchester,* but the captain presided over his modest domain with an aura of military precision and efficiency.

The two walked back to the captain's private day cabin, seated themselves, and Fox explained the chaplains' plan for a party.

"A fine idea, chaplain," Captain Danielsen responded. "Even though we'll be in the harbor at St. John's by tomorrow morning, it would be a wonderful way to end the voyage—at least this part of it—and get everybody started off on a positive note for the next. Remember, we still don't know what in the blue blazes we've got facing us after we get to Newfoundland.

Washington may send us over the Pole to attack the Krauts in Norway."

Expecting the captain's approval, the chaplains had already bounded into action, consulting with Morris Jones on whipping up some extra desserts, rounding up participants for a talent show, and planning decorations. "Making a joyful noise unto the Lord has never sounded like a better idea than it does tonight," Chaplain Goode said as the four chaplains gathered again later in the day to exchange information about their progress.

"And wait'll you see what I found," Washington teased. "Something you'd never expect to see on this tub in a million years, but something you can't have a real party without."

"Frank Sinatra?" asked Chaplain Poling.

"Closer than you think," Washington answered with a conspiratorial grin.

Word spread quickly that the chaplains on board had cooked something up, and anticipation was keen. Just the thought of something to break the routine took everybody's mind off their physical discomfort and the edginess that came from a sense that hostile eyes were always following them, never resting, looking for the moment to strike.

Someone had made paper streamers to hang from the low ceiling. Many of them were cut from the blue pads of message sheets that normally streamed out of the radio room any time the *Dorchester* was underway. "Since we can't use the radio this trip, might as well get some use out of these things," the signal officer had said, maintaining his position in the radio room strictly to monitor any stray enemy communication or coastal broadcasts from New England or Nova Scotia.

The dishes from the evening meal were hardly cleared away when Morris Jones emerged from the kitchen with two huge layer cakes balanced on each arm. Acknowledging the applause of his admiring audience, he returned to the kitchen and came back with four more. Stacks of plates and forks appeared; the ever-present coffee urn was filled with a fresh supply.

One of the men brought out a guitar and strummed, obviously self-conscious. But with a little prompting he was soon charging ahead, enthusiastically taking requests as a group gathered around to sing along.

Another group formed around one of the dining tables to watch an arm-wrestling match organized by some of the enlisted men, with prizes for the winners—and a healthy amount of wagering on the side.

In less than an hour the festivities were in full swing. No tuxedo-clad swells aboard the *Queen Mary* ever enjoyed entertainment on the high seas any more than the officers and men of the *Dorchester* that night. Added to the knots of people singing around the guitar and watching the arm-wrestling matches, another group formed to play charades. Others sat down to play hearts, gin rummy, poker, or bridge. Since the rain outside had stopped, the portholes were even opened in the two rooms for brief intervals, allowing bracing, spray-laden sea air into the spaces, though somehow the jovial mood seemed to do as much for the atmosphere as fresh air did.

Even Helga and Kristen ventured in to join in the festivities. It was the first time since the voyage began that they had felt comfortable in a crowd. Because there were so many diversions and so much to enjoy, they could feel for once like they were not the center of attention everywhere they went.

In the midst of all the activity was a commotion as the swinging doors to the pantry opened and out came Father Washington and five other men pushing a grand piano. Those around them who could see what was going on applauded as they rolled the piano into the room and secured it to the floor with special clamps.

"Where in the world did you get that thing, chaplain?" a spectator called out.

"Ask and ye shall receive," Washington answered, prompting a ripple of laughter and applause. The fact was, the piano was original equipment on the *Dorchester*, and Washington had literally stumbled upon it in storage when he was looking around in the hold for party ideas earlier in the day. It had once graced the music room of the vessel, entertaining passengers during afternoon recitals, evening cocktails, and Sunday morning chapel services.

The party had a piano, but what wasn't clear, at least at first, was exactly who would play it. After a little shuffling around, Chaplain Washington slid onto the bench to the collective oohs and aahs of the crowd.

He hammed it up, flexing his fingers and cracking his knuckles in grandiose style. The noise in the room died down a little as he turned to face the keys and struck a dramatic pose. Hunched over the keyboard, he looked to the right, then to the left, then slowly began playing "Chopsticks" with two fingers. A rumble of laughter and scattered applause nearly drowned out the end of his simple solo, but he stuck with it to the end.

He paused a moment, relishing the thought of what was to come. Half closing his eyes, he launched into a scorching boogie-woogie. The crowd noise rose, and those nearby surged to the piano to see who was playing.

"It's the chaplain!"

"Imagine that!"

"Look at that cat go!"

The card players and arm wrestlers left what they were doing and joined the growing crowd around the piano, clapping their hands, snapping their fingers, bobbing their heads in time with the music, and shouting encouragement.

Washington segued from one tune to another, running up and down the hit parade, playing a range of style with seemingly no effort at all.

With a final flourish he ended his set to a roar of applause. The cramped quarters were completely forgotten, along with the war, the Germans, seasickness, and even the always present fear of the unknown. Every apprehension was lifted up and swept away by the strains of Jelly Roll Morton, Count Basie, and Hoagy Carmichael.

As the applause peaked at last and began to diminish, a voice from the crowd called out, "Chaplain, where'd you learn to tickle the ivories like that?"

"Well, that's my sermon topic for next week," Washington replied.

The sound of exaggerated groans was combined with heartfelt laughter and a smattering of applause.

"Really," Washington went on. "If I'm lyin' I'm dyin'."

"How can playing the piano have anything to do with a sermon?" came the voice again.

"Glad you asked that question," Washington fired back, to another swell of good-natured groans mixed liberally with laughter.

As the crowd settled down, an astute observer would have noticed a change in the room. The crowd had relieved its tension, spent its pent-up nervous energy, and had wound down to a quieter, more introspective state. In the same way they had been so eager, without

165

consciously realizing it, to hear Washington play, they were eager now to hear him speak—not because they wanted a sermon or felt they needed one but because the shared experience of the music was so fulfilling to soldiers and sailors embarked on a dangerous mission on dangerous seas. The music was over, yet the audience as a body somehow desperately wanted the shared experience to continue.

Father Washington pivoted around on the piano bench to face his eager audience. Looking out from his low vantage point, and with the low ceiling in the room, lowered still further by the festoons of shredded blue radiogram forms, his entire field of vision was filled with eager eyes looking back at him. Looking for peace, comfort, forgiveness, the blessing of forgetfulness, and so much more. The corners of Washington's mouth turned up in a smile. Wasn't it incredible, he thought, how God always seemed to have a reason for everything? Think of the opportunity he had here before him, thanks to a mysterious piano in the cargo hold and piano lessons he had taken, under duress, half a lifetime ago.

"How can playing the piano have anything to do with a sermon?" Washington repeated. "Here's the story.

"I took piano lessons, at least in the beginning, because my mother made me."

"Same here," someone interrupted, "but I quit after 'Chopsticks.'"

The merrymakers reacted, and Washington's smile broadened.

"My mother wasn't satisfied with 'Chopsticks.' I'd be sitting there in the living room practicing, and I could hear all my friends outside playing baseball. I hated not being there. They'd call to me through the window as they walked by on the way to the park: 'Hey, Four-Eyes! You play Beethoven, we'll play ball!'

"That was what kids in my neighborhood did—played baseball. I loved baseball. Still do. But what I figured out before too long was that I could really play this thing." He gestured toward the piano behind him. "Not only could I play; I thoroughly enjoyed it. I had a gift, and I truly enjoyed using it.

"That was my first lesson that what other people think you should do—your friends, even your mother—isn't as important as what you know in your heart is best for yourself.

"Everybody on this ship—everybody in this world—is unique, a unique creation of God. We come together to fulfill God's purpose for our lives, even when we don't have any idea what it is. But he's our shepherd, and if we follow him faithfully, he'll eventually lead us to safety.

"And that's how playing the piano gets turned into a sermon topic."

The last self-deprecating sentence brought his impromptu homily to an end as it flooded the room with warm feelings of camaraderie and good cheer.

It was late now, and though a few of the chaplain's listeners went back to their card games or conversations, many began drifting toward the companionways leading back to their quarters.

One of the men still grouped at the piano said, "Hey, Chaplain, can you play any hymns on that thing?"

"Good question. I was hoping nobody would ask." He smiled. "The hymn writing has ended up mostly in the hands of the Protestants." He stood up and opened the top of the bench. Reaching in with one hand, he pulled out a well-thumbed green book. "Look at this. Here's the army and navy service book. Hmmm, let's have a look."

"I know one." It was Rabbi Goode, standing at the edge of the circle of men who remained around the piano. "How about 'The Navy Hymn' to commemorate our being here together by the grace of God on the high seas?"

"You know that one, Rabbi?" Washington said, amused.

"Hey, good music is good music, even if it isn't in Hebrew," Goode answered.

The dog-eared book lay flat on the music rack. Washington smoothed the page with his hand and started to play. The singing was robust and from the heart:

> Eternal Father, strong to save,
> Whose arm doth bind the restless
>   wave,

168

Who bidd'st the mighty ocean deep
Its own appointed limits keep;
O hear us when we cry to Thee
For those in peril on the sea.

One hymn followed another until Washington raised his hands in resignation. "No more tonight. I'm beat. I think God gets the picture. Good night, everybody."

Moving quietly down the companionway so as not to disturb those who had gone to bed earlier, Poling and Washington were startled to hear a whimpering noise down a short aisle that led off the main hall. Exchanging glances, they turned down the aisle, which led to a small storeroom. Stopping at the door and listening intently, they heard the unmistakable sound of a man crying.

Chaplain Poling rapped softly on the small, heavy wooden door with the knuckle of his forefinger.

The sobbing stopped abruptly. "Go away!" ordered a muffled voice on the other side.

"Chaplain Poling and Chaplain Washington here. Can we be of some assistance?"

"I said beat it!"

Poling turned the knob and slowly opened the door inward.

The small room, lit by a single lightbulb in the ceiling, was a linen closet lined with shelves, the floor covered with heavy canvas laundry bags full of sheets and towels. Perched on top of a pile of bags, chin resting on his knees and hands clasped across his shins, sat

Sergeant Wesley Adams with tears streaming down his face.

First annoyed, then startled, then with an unmistakable sigh of relief, Adams said evenly, "Oh, it's you."

"Didn't you hear me say who it was?" Poling inquired.

"Maybe I did," Adams sniffed.

"In any case, looks like you could use a cup of coffee," Poling went on.

"Don't think I'm up for it right now," Adams answered. "Maybe later."

"Anything you want to talk about at all?" Poling continued.

"Like what?"

"Like whatever's on your mind. There's a lot about this mission to make a man unhappy. It's nothing to be ashamed of."

"Who says I'm ashamed?"

"Nobody. Nobody says you are."

Adams thought for a moment. "Well, pull up a chair."

The two chaplains squeezed in and sat down on the pile of linen. Washington pulled the door partly shut but propped it open with a laundry bag. They waited for Adams to speak.

"This idea of me knowing what's best for me—what Chaplain Washington was talking about in there a little while ago . . ."

"Yes," Poling prompted.

"I know what's best for me. No doubt whatever about it. But somehow things never seem to work out. I don't know . . . the way he talked about it just got to me."

"Why don't you and Chaplain Washington and I talk it over with a piece of leftover cake and a cup of all-night coffee?" Adams hesitated, motionless and silent as the other two men rose to their feet.

The sergeant seemed about to reply. But in the split second before the words could form, an ear-piercing sound split the dark night, shattering the calm and jolting everyone already asleep from his slumber.

The general quarters klaxon!

The shrill bleat of the alarm shot through every soul like a lightning bolt. Within seconds the gangway was filled with soldiers and sailors scrambling to their assigned battle stations, pulling on boots, heavy coats, and dragging life jackets along behind them.

The trio shot from the linen room to take their assigned places. Naval personnel on board were in charge of the six guns; other officers and men traveling as passengers had battle station assignments as gunners' mates, lookouts, or other jobs.

Chaplain Poling moved quickly to his assigned station as a lookout. On the way up through the superstructure to the boat deck on the starboard side where his post was, he heard two senior officers exchange a few brief words. Stepping inside the wheelhouse, his eyes met those of Captain Danielsen only briefly, but long enough to know what he had heard was true.

"The ASDIC operator reports a suspicious signal, consistent with the profile of a U-boat at attack depth."

CHAPTER 12

LONE WOLF

Aboard the U-223, Captain Karl-Jürgen Wächter peered calmly through his attack periscope at the slow-moving convoy rolling through the North Atlantic. These were moderate-to small-sized ships—and only six of them—when convoys at this stage of the war often numbered sixty vessels or more. In a way, going after such a small prize was scarcely worth the risk to his command. But some of the ships were certainly transports filled with enemy soldiers. And besides, Captain Wächter was, as those enemy soldiers would have said, on a roll.

He had been at sea for only three weeks, sailing from the U-boat base at Kiel, Germany, two weeks after Christmas. It was his second trip to Torpedo Junction, and he was determined to make this voyage even more successful than the first. Over one four-day period the previous November, his crew had sunk sixty thousand tons of Allied shipping. That was good enough for serious bragging rights back home, good enough for Wächter to get a medal of commendation and a personal, handwritten letter from Admiral Karl Dönitz himself, mastermind of the wolf pack offensive that had so successfully hindered the flow of American troops and supplies across the Atlantic.

As every U-boat commander had drilled into him, every ton of shipping sunk meant one more ton of weapons, ammunition, food, fuel, and manpower that Churchill would never have. Just as important, it kept the fear of U-boats alive in the hearts of the British, stranded and isolated on their island home, and frustrated the Americans, who saw their soldiers and resources sacrificed in vain and sent in defeat to the bottom of the sea.

Wächter at twenty-six looked like the Hollywood stereotype of a German officer: tall, fair, blonde, blue-eyed, square-jawed, ruthlessly efficient. Over the course of the war, the average life expectancy of a U-boat officer would come to be fourteen months. Out of every hundred who left port, sixty would die at sea. If Wächter knew any of that, he didn't care. In an ironic way his skill as an officer had robbed him of some of the glory he thought was his due. He had served as an instructor for almost a year after the war began; shore duty had denied him his share of Allied spoils. Now he was making up for lost time.

He had tracked this little convoy for almost two days, since they had hived off from the larger group. He thought at first they were heading for Greenland or England and was surprised to see them change course toward Newfoundland, a desolate and sparsely settled outpost of the British Dominion of Canada. There was a fine, well-protected harbor at St. John's on the eastern shore. But why go there? Nothing but ice and rocks and codfish.

It seemed clear that one ship in the group was setting the pace, eleven knots more or less. Looking at it through his periscope, he could see it was a coastal vessel, hardly ideal for a crossing in wartime. *If this is what the Americans are using to send men to England,* he thought, *they must truly be desperate.*

In the eyes of the German command, the United States had been desperate from the beginning. Every Kriegsmarine officer knew the story or some version of it: In 1941, almost thirteen hundred Allied vessels had been sunk by Axis warships, more than four hundred of those by U-boat. In 1942 more than sixteen hundred Allied ships were sunk, with U-boats responsible for more than eleven hundred.

Newly transferred from the North Sea or Arctic patrols, German sub commanders arriving off Cape Hatteras early in 1942 could take their pick of torpedo targets virtually untouched, with only the single Coast Guard cutter *Dione* to oppose them. By the time she got word of an attack and chuffed to the scene, the damage was done, the Allied craft were sunk or sinking, and the enemy was nowhere to be found. On February 26, 1942, a U-boat torpedoed an American tanker loaded with over seventy-eight thousand barrels of fuel oil within sight of the New Jersey shore with the loss of thirty-nine of her forty-one officers and men. Two days later the same sub torpedoed and sank the American destroyer *Jacob Jones*; out of a complement of nearly two hundred, eleven men survived. That week set the stage for a year of loss and apprehension on the eastern seaboard.

By the beginning of 1943, the Germans were having a harder time of it, in spite of developing a bigger, more capable U-boat design. Americans had finally begun to rise to the challenge, flushing the Germans out of the Gulf of Mexico and driving them eastward away from Cape Hatteras and the Grand Banks. Reconnaissance aircraft and torpedo planes pushed them as far as the range of those airborne defenders would allow. But out of that range, competition among Kriegsmarine captains was keen. The recognition brought by sinking record tonnage was an incredible enticement. So though their area of operation became more and more restricted, the concentration of attacks was greater than ever.

Another defense the Americans had tried with varying results was the new supersensitive sonar system, which the British called ASDIC. Wächter knew about sonar but felt no threat from it. It was unreliable, inaccurate, and had a range of only a mile or so. Let them send their primitive boops his way. By the time they knew he was there, he could already have a torpedo dispatched in reply.

U-223 carried a dozen torpedoes that could be fired out of any of four forward torpedo tubes or one aft. Wächter's "Unterseeboot" was a Type VIIC, the backbone of the German submarine fleet, displacing 750 tons and manned by a crew of forty-eight. The Type VII, of which nearly seven hundred were built, was the first design capable of crossing the Atlantic with enough fuel and supplies to wage war on the American shore and still return safely to Europe.

Virtually all her time was spent on the surface where, cruising at twelve knots, she had a range of sixty-five hundred miles. Top speed on the surface, powered by her efficient, low-maintenance diesel engines, was seventeen knots; while submerged, running on batteries, top speed was only seven to eight knots with a range of twelve miles. Slow underwater cruising lengthened her maximum range on battery power to about eighty miles. Design depth was 250 feet, though U-boats had survived dives of six hundred feet and more to escape Allied depth charges.

Wächter knew that the Type IX, the Reich's latest engineering triumph, would bring an even more powerful weapon into the Atlantic. At twelve hundred tons it was a third larger than the VIIC, which was one design newer than U-223 and the current top of the line, with a faster cruising speed, longer range, and room for more ordnance. He had also heard rumors of a supersecret design that replaced diesels with another kind of propulsion. Even the Allies used diesels in their submarines, after years of unsuccessful experiments with gasoline engines and oil-fired steam turbines. The new design would be turbine driven, but the heat would come from a chemical reaction instead of combustion; the ship would run on hydrogen peroxide, meaning the only limitation to its underwater range was how much breathable air could be stored on board.

By that time, he knew, the Allies would be on their knees begging for peace.

Wächter called for the officer of the watch, Lieutenant Joachim Fels, and asked for the latest report on the convoy.

"We have confirmed two freighters, one troop transport, and three escort cutters, sir," Fels reported. "At least one vessel is equipped with an ASDIC listening device. There have been reports depth charges are also aboard some of the ships, but we have not been able to confirm that."

"Good. Thank you, Fels. That will be all for now."

Should he give chase or not? This would take some careful thought. He lowered the periscope and walked down the crowded, dimly lit corridor to his quarters.

Had it been possible to travel back and forth between U-223 and the *Dorchester,* an observer would have seen some curious similarities. Both were dark and crowded; both had a significant complement of seasick men; and both were filled with stale air and the stench of fuel oil. The U-223 had the additional distinction of requiring the entire crew to share a single toilet, which didn't always work and could not be flushed when the vessel was more than eighty feet below the surface.

Closing the door to his cabin, Captain Wächter sat on his chair, drew it up to his tiny desk, put his elbows on its empty and immaculate surface, and bent forward to cradle his forehead between his thumbs and index fingers. What should he do?

He looked around the cabin, momentarily lost in thought. His was the only private room aboard ship. Though at eight by four feet, it was hardly larger than a closet, it was beautifully detailed in Bavarian walnut and a model of German efficiency. He had a desk and chair, a small wall safe with a door no larger than a book cover, a chart case, locker, bunk with storage drawers below, a tiny porcelain sink in the corner with a mirror above, and a table with an intercom handset on it and bookcase below.

He pulled a chart from the case and, with practiced precision, unrolled it like a scroll to the part he wanted and positioned it on the desk. It was such a small convoy. Six ships—and relatively small ones at that—weren't much of a prize. By chasing them he might lose the opportunity to go after much bigger game a day or two later. He'd be out of position and maybe low on torpedoes as well. What would happen then if a truly prize convoy came through and one of the other U-boat commanders got it instead of him? What would happen to his stock back in Berlin? What would Dönitz think of him if he went chasing the little fish and let the big ones slip out from under his very nose?

On the other hand, this convoy was slow, lightly armed if at all, and there were no other U-boats in the area. The Allies were sitting ducks. He remembered stories other captains told him earlier in the war when he was on training duty in Kiel, straining at the bit to have his turn at the fat American prizes. Along the coast, they'd said, American cities blazed with lights. They could read lighted highway billboards through their periscopes. Silhouettes of ships passing in front of the bright lights of Charleston or New York stood out like shapes in a fairground shooting gallery. Thinking they were safe in shallow water near the shore, ships lumbered up and down the coastline, outlined by streetlights and illuminated by channel markers. All the Germans had to do was surface at night and wait for a target, then submerge, ease forward, and fire.

The situation was a lot less simple now. Like other U-boats, the U-223 awaited its prey on the high seas, where weather this time of the year was often cold and visibility limited. Every officer in the Kriegsmarine was looking for the kind of high-profile victory that had proclaimed unequivocally the preeminence of wolf packs on the North Atlantic just short of a year ago, the victory that would prove the U-boats were as all-powerful as ever.

If he got two or three ships of the convoy, which he considered possible, that would certainly raise his status both in Kiel and Berlin. One or two, depending on which they were, would not be as likely to get him the attention he deserved, he thought. The English had a saying, "A bird in the hand is worth two in the bush." Here he had his choice of six birds but hesitated to give up torpedoes, time, and the advantage of surprise if something more impressive were to come along.

Captain Wächter rerolled his chart, replaced it in the case, and returned to the bridge. The convoy was still heading toward the harbor at St. John's at eleven knots. Moving closer to pick up what visual information they could in the dark of night, the sub had come within a thousand yards of the vessel nearest them, the low-slung civilian coastal cruiser. Noting the close distance, the captain ordered his helmsman to drop back to twenty-five hundred yards and shadow the enemy from there.

As the helmsman snapped his acknowledgment, Captain Wächter spoke a few words to the duty officer, then returned to his cabin. It was time for bed, and he had some more thinking to do. Closing the door once again, he took off his duty uniform, smoothed it out carefully with his hands on the sheet covering his bunk, then hung it in his locker.

Holding his web uniform belt, he thoughtfully fingered the engraved words on the back of it: "God with Us." He coiled the belt, then lay down on top of the sheet in his shorts and undershirt. "God with us," he mouthed. It was on the back of every Nazi uniform buckle. Not that he thought much about it, but he figured it was reasonable to believe God was on their side. He thought of his family, his wife and four young children at home at their apartment in Cologne. Surely God was protecting them.

As he dozed off, calmed by the familiar hum and roll of the vessel, he wondered, poised for an instant on the line between consciousness and sleep, whether Americans thought God was on their side too.

CHAPTER 13

RACING

WITH THE MOON

Lieutenant George Fox was sound asleep in the chaplains' cabin. It had been a long day, and he'd been ready for some sack time. The first night or two aboard the *Dorchester* had been a little restless for him, with the constant noise and movement of the ship, the vibration of the engine, and the fetid air. People passed up and down the corridor outside all night, and he could hear every word and footstep through the louvered panel in the door.

Though he had only been in bed a few minutes, Chaplain Fox was already dreaming the vivid dreams of a man far from home. Stories and settings flashed from one to the next without warning, all connected some-how with his family and people in his life.

He wondered about his son in the marines. He and his wife had heard from him regularly up until the chaplain left North Carolina for his new duty assignment. He wondered what Wyatt was doing. His wife seemed to take it well, two of her men being in the military service at the same time. And he was a strong, capable young man. Fox was proud of his son. Still, he was only eighteen.

Eighteen. It seemed awfully young to a father. But hadn't he himself enlisted to fight in France a quarter century ago at an even younger age?

The army had represented a new beginning for the strong-willed youngster from Pennsylvania. His mother loved him but was powerless in the face of his father, stern to the point of abuse. To Papa everything was black or white, and in young George's eyes things seemed mostly black. Joining the army had been a relief.

The voyage to France had been the most exciting experience of his life up till that time—a week across the ocean to Cherbourg, then by train to the front. He was an ambulance driver. The same mechanical advancements that produced tanks and other horrible instruments of war could also produce machines and equipment that saved lives.

Fox's ambulance was painted white—it reminded him of a milk wagon—and had a large red cross on each side. But that didn't always help at night. Or when visibility was poor because of smoke or fog. Or when the enemy, frustrated, enraged, or bored, decided it just didn't matter.

Chaplain Fox dreamed about all these things and, still dreaming, braced himself for what he knew would follow. What always followed.

A soldier standing outside the rubble of an old brick building waved him down. He left the engine idling and followed the soldier inside to a temporary shelter where several wounded soldiers huddled for warmth against the chilly dampness of the overcast autumn day.

Concentrating on the wounded, young Fox never saw or heard the explosion. All he saw was a bright light and the feel of a concussion in the air, followed by a searing pain as though his back were being sliced in two by a flaming knife.

Everything went black. But in the blackness there began a sound, faint at first then growing to fill his consciousness. Somehow the report of German mortar fire transformed into a new sensation of noise: a shrill, repeated clanging and buzzing that pushed every other image and feeling aside.

Aaaank! Aaaank! Aaaank! Aaaank!

Chaplain Fox's eyes flew open. The klaxon. General quarters. The lieutenant sat bolt upright, paused for an instant to collect his thoughts, then scrambled out of bed still in his undershirt and shorts, grabbing his heavy wool overcoat in one hand and his life jacket in the other as he headed for the door. Walking quickly down the corridor toward the mess kitchen, he slipped his arms through the armholes of the jacket and pulled the coat over his shoulders like a cape.

Fox's battle station assignment was in the kitchen, designated as the field hospital under combat conditions, to help treat the wounded. As he arrived, a naval officer entered the room, quickly and efficiently organizing the team into work groups, laying out first-aid supplies and checking the availability of hot water.

Fox saw Chaplain Washington, also assigned to the field hospital, come out of the pantry with a steam table tray full of medical supplies and bottles of alcohol, disinfectant, Mercurochrome, and boric acid.

Forbidden to communicate with other ships in the convoy, the *Dorchester* could not request evasive action for the whole contingent. She could, however, move around in her designated area within the convoy like a finger waving on a hand. She could zigzag and move forward or back relative to the other ships inside a predetermined area.

The vibration increased as the engineers worked to coax more power from the faithful old engine deep inside the belly of the ship. Since the convoy speed was set by the *Dorchester*'s cruising speed, the reserve power produced only two or three extra knots, enough to close a prescribed amount of the distance separating her from the vessel ahead. Then she could back off a little, but not too much for fear she would get too far behind to catch up.

As they worked in the kitchen, Washington and Fox felt the ship turning. A container of medical instruments slid off a counter and rattled to the floor, scattering them across the room. The two chaplains hustled to gather them up, scooping scissors, probes, hypodermics, and more back into a container to be sterilized later.

"Make a note," Fox deadpanned as he and Washington crouched on the floor, stating the obvious in an attempt to relieve the tension. "We've got to keep everything in here tied down, including the wounded."

★ ★ ★ ★

In the radio room Captain Danielsen and Chaplain Goode, reporting to his battle station there, huddled with the ASDIC operator around the table holding the system's large cloth-covered speaker, now silent. The captain peppered his man with questions, short, direct inquiries shaped to get important answers fast.

"How far away was it?"

"About a mile or a little less, sir. It seemed to be closing on us, but now it's dropped back out of range."

"What heading?"

"Starboard side aft, sir, heading one-one-zero."

"And how can you tell it was a U-boat and not an oversize tuna?"

"A tuna's softer than a sub, sir. The signal would be a lot weaker because most of it would be absorbed."

"Wrecks? Floating debris?"

"They'd be almost stationary. This target was moving faster than we were."

"Size of target? Depth?"

"Don't know, sir. No way to determine that with this gear."

Chaplain Goode listened intently, learning, taking it all in. "Where is it now?" he asked.

Donning headphones plugged into the control bank in front of him, the operator raised his hands for silence. All eyes in the room watched the eyes of the operator, who stared straight ahead, straining to hear anything through the extrasensitive headset.

After a long moment he stood up with a start. "There it is!" he exclaimed in a hoarse whisper.

Reaching out to the control panel, he flipped a switch. The big speaker came to life with a soft hiss of static.

Then: Boop . . . biiing. Boop . . . biiing. Somehow its softness made it all the more frightening.

The listeners exchanged looks all around as the sound grew steadily louder, then stopped abruptly. The operator fiddled with his dials, and they all listened some more—but in vain. For breathless minutes the only sound was the ticking of the clock on the wall above them.

"Where is it?" Captain Danielsen demanded.

"Gone, sir." The technician listened intently for another minute, turning dials with great deliberation. Another minute went by. "Gone."

188

The captain looked at the men around him, looked at the speaker, then stood up straight from where he had been hunched over the table. "Stand down."

"Aye, aye, sir," replied a junior officer who had been standing beside the door and rushed out to give the order. Throughout the ship a whistle signal was sounded, and the men with duty stations began to pack up and secure whatever equipment they had taken out. Shaken, men returned to their cabins. Evasive maneuvers were discontinued, and the *Dorchester* forged ahead toward St. John's, now less than eight hours away.

Goode left the radio room and went out on deck. There was a half-moon in the clear night sky. The wind was bitter cold but dry, and the rabbi found the feel of it on his face both bracing and refreshing after the tense moments inside. He looked out at the sea. Somewhere out there was a German submarine tracking him. Watching him. Waiting for the chance to do him evil. Even American Jews weren't safe from Hitler's Nazi wrath. He had thanked God for his deliverance from the persecutions the Jewish diaspora had endured in Poland, Czechoslovakia, and Germany; by God's grace he and Theresa were safely on the other side of a vast ocean from the butchery. Yet this same ocean that protected her now concealed a deadly German war machine.

A movement caught his eye. Ambling forward was Chaplain Poling, also in search of a little quiet and calm after his frantic few minutes at his lookout post. The two nodded to each other, then stared out at the sea.

Poling broke the silence. "It's beautiful, just like my father always described it."

"Has Dr. Poling traveled a great deal?"

"He's been around quite a bit. Loves the sea."

"It is wonderful. Powerful but peaceful at the same time."

"And yet sinister. The unseen killer lurks. He can see us, but we can't see him."

"Almost a metaphor for the world, don't you think?" Goode mused.

"How so?"

"The world hides an awful lot of evil beneath the surface."

"True enough," Poling rejoined. "But it's God's sea and God's world in which to work his divine will."

"Praise ye the Lord," Goode rejoined. There was another silence.

Poling pointed at the reflection of the moon on the ocean surface. "Look. It looks like we're racing."

"Racing with the moon," agreed Goode. "Wonder if we'll beat it to St. John's?"

Poling smiled. "Who's to say?"

"Who indeed?" Goode echoed.

They stood there a long time, braced against the wind, the shoulders of their heavy overcoats almost touching, looking out at the stars, the moon, the water, and the sparkling lunar reflection on its surface; each man lost in his own thoughts of home, the mysterious task before them, and tonight's unexpected reminders of God's awesome majesty, beauty, and power.

CHAPTER 14

HARDBALL

When the sun first began to rise dead astern, the *Dorchester* and her convoy were wrapped in wisps of fog. As it rose higher in the sky, the fog drifted and shifted away, swirling from the paths of the ships. By the time the last traces of mist lifted, the coast of Newfoundland appeared on the horizon ahead. The six ships in the convoy moved into a tighter formation in preparation for forming a single line to enter the harbor.

There wasn't a better protected harbor anywhere in this part of the world. The entrance was formed by a narrow inlet with five-hundred-foot hills on either side, ideal for gun emplacements and observer stations. Framing the mouth of the harbor, they looked like open arms, welcoming the threatened ships to safety. Underwater, the extra precaution of submarine nets added another level of security. One by one the ships sailed between the hills, men lining the railings to watch as the buoys marking the submarine net went by. By mid-morning the *Dorchester*, bringing up the rear, entered the harbor and tied up at the dock. She was safe.

This was as far as anyone knew the story. They'd been ordered to St. John's to await further instruction. There was no indication what that word would be or how long it would take to get it. Even Captain Danielsen didn't know.

Everyone was assigned quarters onshore at a barracks that had been built literally in a matter of weeks. Created at the beginning of the war, its sole purpose was to house military personnel in transit. It was nothing much—a plain, boxy, prefab affair, but to the convoy passengers it looked like a palace: fresh hot water, stacks of fresh towels, pure clean air, reasonable privacy, and a floor that wasn't moving.

Over the course of the day, the ships emptied, and the barracks filled. Men relished the simple pleasure of a long, steaming hot shower and some extra elbow room at every turn—and no cursed life jackets! The enjoyment of their first day was tempered somewhat by orders that they would be confined to a secure area alongside the harbor. There would be no shore leave to explore the quaint, historic town of St. John's.

When he got the word of their quarantine, Chaplain Fox went directly to Captain Danielsen for clarification.

"Come in," Danielsen said at the sound of the chaplain rapping lightly on the door frame. "What's on your mind?"

"Thanks for seeing me, Captain. I'm wondering about this order restricting the men to the barracks and the immediate area. They've been under a lot of strain, and nobody knows what's up next. This might be the only time during this mission—whatever it is—that they can relax and cut loose a little. Isn't there any way they can have some more freedom?"

"You raise a good point. I realize some of the men are wound tight as a banjo string. Exercise will help. I can authorize the men of my command to go to the park and the soccer field at the end of Wharf Street. Maybe you and the other chaplains can organize some activities for them. I'll also have the men do calisthenics and drill." He was warming to the subject. "Yeah, I think some drill and a little cal will make a big difference in attitude."

"Captain, I appreciate it, and I know the men will too. I'll talk with the other chaplains, and we'll be ready with our ideas as soon as you want them."

"Thank you, Chaplain Fox." The chaplain turned to leave, then turned back as he heard the captain's voice once more. "And Chaplain, thank you for your concern. I know it means a lot to the men."

"Thank you, Captain. I was once a scared young soldier myself."

Orders were issued giving everyone in the convoy permission to venture as far as the public park Captain Danielsen had mentioned. Beginning the next day, military personnel were allowed more freedom of movement. However, they were only to go to Wharf Park escorted in small groups of twenty, and their visits were marked by calisthenics, marching and drill, makeshift obstacle courses, and footraces.

While these activities were a clear improvement over earlier restrictions, it seemed to Fox and the others that there ought to be a much more enjoyable way for nine hundred men to shake out the wrinkles. Their second day ashore Father Washington and Rabbi Goode sat together in the canteen right next door to the barracks.

As they savored their hot coffee, complete with real Danish rolls, Washington suddenly clapped his hands together and said, "Rabbi, I'll tell you what this place needs right now. Some serious baseball."

"Baseball!" Goode exclaimed in reply. "What are you talking? It's freezing out there. You going to run the bases in your overcoat, or get frostbite sliding home?"

"Hold it," said the priest. "It's the all-American sport. I think the guys would love it. Football is played in weather like this all the time, and it doesn't seem to bother the teams. Anyway, I can't stand to see these poor guys marching up and down the street. Time's a-wasting. We need some hardball."

Goode sipped his coffee. Washington's enthusiasm was contagious. "Hardball, eh? You may have something there after all. I wouldn't mind a little game or two myself."

"You a fan?" Washington asked.

"Love to watch it, love to play it."

"So you play, too? I thought about turning pro once, but God had other plans. Not to mention the bum eye."

"I've noticed one looks a little different from the other."

"You know how your mother always told you, 'Stop that! You could put your eye out'? Well, mine was right. When I was twelve, a friend back in Newark accidentally shot me with a BB gun. The doctor did his best, but the eye was pretty much a total loss. I can see light and shapes out of it, but I can't even read a billboard at six feet with that eye alone. Hard to imagine the Dodgers offering me a contract."

"Baseball was great, but track was my favorite sport. Even got a scholarship, but ended up in Cincinnati at Hebrew University instead."

Washington was genuinely surprised. "What are you talking?" he said, in his best Chaplain Goode imitation.

With a shock of recognition, Goode paused, his hand halfway to his coffee cup, then let out a roar of laughter. Washington joined in, and the two men doubled over laughing, rocking back and forth, fighting for breath.

A young canteen volunteer ambled over to see what all the commotion was about. "You guys put something in the coffee?" she asked, giggling a little at the two laughing lieutenants.

"We've got something better than hooch in the java," Goode said, gradually regaining his composure. "Friendship. Baseball. A plan of action."

Once the two got their breath back, the conversation continued. Before the day was out, sign-up sheets appeared throughout the barracks for the First Annual St. John's Deep Freeze Baseball Tournament. By the end of the next day, enough players had signed up to field eight teams.

The chaplains would each coach a team, though Chaplain Poling disclaimed any expertise in baseball, and Fox insisted he was too old. Washington and Goode, on the other hand, vowed not only to coach their teams to victory but to be star players themselves. They decided to have three days of practice and then get the tournament under way, assuming they weren't under way to their mysterious new duty station by then.

Washington scanned the sign-up sheets looking for familiar names. Morris Jones was there and Sam Nelson, whose letter to Bluefield, West Virginia, Chaplain Poling still carried dutifully in his pocket. No sign, though, of Wesley Adams. *What a mixed-up and unhappy guy that soldier seems to be,* Washington thought to himself. He realized he never had given Adams the chance to finish the story he'd started the night of the U-boat sighting. In fact, Adams must have been avoiding him, because he couldn't remember even seeing him since then.

The first day of the Deep Freeze Tournament, the eight teams gathered at Wharf Park, elated already that they hadn't had to march there for a change. It would be a double-elimination tournament, so a team had to lose twice to be out of the running. Two games could be played at once, one in an open field at the park, and a second on the soccer field. It was a crystal-clear morning, the cloudless sky a rich royal blue. The temperature hovered around twenty-five degrees, forcing the players to choose between warmth and agility in assembling their game clothes.

More than a hundred men had signed up to play, and at least twice that many more came to watch, sitting on picnic tables and benches, playground equipment, in trees, and on the frozen ground. Spectators soon picked their favorites, cheering and booing as the action demanded, and making a steady stream of wagers on the outcome. Rumor had it that the smart money was on the rabbi's team, but word of Washington's legendary exploits on the diamond kept the odds respectable.

After two days of play, four teams were still standing, including Goode's and Washington's. The other two were captained by Sergeant Oscar Blackmun from Omaha, Nebraska, and naval Lieutenant Roger McCallum, from Phoenix. As teams were eliminated, the defeated players good-naturedly joined the crowds on the sidelines to cheer the remaining contenders.

Late that afternoon, as the chaplains returned to the barracks to wash up for evening chow, they had just gotten through the door when a corporal entered with an envelope. Taking it with a word of thanks, Chaplain Poling opened it and read aloud.

"Confidential. Eyes only. You are hereby ordered to report to the dining hall aboard the *U.S.A.T. Dorchester* at 2100 hrs tonight. Carry this order with you." The chaplains' names were listed at the top. The orders were signed by Lieutenant General Marshall R. Blackstone, USAAF.

"Army Air Force. And three stars," Fox observed. "This may be what we've been waiting for."

They said little during dinner and ate even less. Not that they were afraid, but the excitement and apprehension seemed to squeeze out every other sensation, even hunger. As they prepared to leave the barracks for the dock, Chaplain Goode said, "Gentlemen, any objection if we begin this little outing with a word of prayer?"

The others quickly welcomed the idea. "Why don't you lead us, Chaplain Poling?" Goode continued.

Unconsciously, almost instinctively, the four gathered in a tight circle. Chaplain Poling prayed aloud, softly but confidently. "God of our fathers, we humble ourselves before you and ask your blessing on us as we go about your work. Calm our fears. Strengthen our resolve. Give us brave and confident hearts. You are our rock in every storm. Thank you for loving us. Amen."

It wasn't until the men began to step toward the door that they realized they had locked elbows during the prayer. It may have been a gesture of brotherhood inspired by the emotion of the moment. Or a symbol of friendship. None of them stopped consciously to think about it at the moment, or, with one exception, made any reference to it whatever. But they all thought about it, each in his own way—four men of different ages, with different religious beliefs, from different parts of the country, all brought here in God's good time and for a purpose only he could see. A spiritual intimacy, a bond of faith, was finding its own expression.

"We'll never get through that door like this," Father Washington said, straight-faced. Sharing a hearty laugh of brotherly understanding, the four men broke up their circle and went outside to the *Dorchester*, waiting at the dock.

At the foot of the gangway was an armed sentry. "Your orders, please, sirs." Chaplain Fox handed them to him. He glanced at them briefly but with an expert eye, returned them to Fox and saluted. The four chaplains returned his salute, walked up the gangway, and made their way along the familiar decks and passageways to the dining hall.

The group was a small one. The chaplains were the only junior officers in attendance. They saw the six ship captains at one table and a scattering of executive officers from the base—navy commodores and army colonels—at a few others. There were maybe forty-five or fifty men in all, moving in and taking their seats without delay.

After a minute or two a deep voice suddenly barked out, "Attention!" The room rose as one, as General Blackstone and his staff walked briskly in and stood in a line at the front of the room. One of them, a crusty lieutenant colonel, spoke first.

"Be seated, gentlemen.

"You may be wondering what in the world you're doing meeting on the *Dorchester* when there are much more hospitable quarters ashore. The reason is that this is a secure area. Everyone in this room received orders directly from General Blackstone. We're here to begin telling you more about a mission only a handful of people even know exists. We can't take any risks that unauthorized personnel might get wind of it.

"General Blackstone is in command of U.S. Army Air Force North American operations. This mission is his baby. General?"

General Blackstone took two steps forward, planted his feet, and squared his shoulders. He wore a fatigue uniform and a field jacket. The only insignia was a row of three stars on each collar point. Long before another soldier saw them, though, he knew this was a man whose life was the army. Marshall Blackstone had been flying airplanes since he was a teenager and had spent thirty-one years in military service. He wasn't a tall man but seemed taller than he was, ramrod straight, his piercing gray eyes darting like an eagle's.

"Gentlemen, good evening. Within a very few days you will receive orders that will send you on one of the most important missions of the war. Its success will save untold thousands of lives and probably shorten the conflict by a year or more. These orders from the president will come to you through me. I expect them at any moment.

"What I can tell you now is that you will be serving overseas. You will remain together as a unit throughout the mission. Your activities will carry the highest top secret security clearance. Only the people now in this room will know the big picture. Everyone else will know only what is essential to perform his individual function."

The general switched gears a little. "I understand there's a baseball tournament going on. Excellent. A great way to keep the men occupied. You'll be playing hardball with the Germans soon enough. Better enjoy yourselves while you can. Colonel?"

The lieutenant colonel took a step forward. "Attention!" The officers around the tables stood as General Blackstone and his staff filed quickly out. At the sound of "Dismissed!" the room broke into a dozen animated conversations at once.

"What do you make of that?" Chaplain Poling said to his three companions as they gathered up their hats and coats. "This whole operation gets more and more mysterious."

Bundled against the cold, the four chaplains walked onto the deck of the *Dorchester* and down the gangway. The others noticed Chaplain Fox lost in thought.

"What's on your mind, Fox?" Chaplain Goode inquired after a moment.

Fox smiled and nodded. "Off in my own little world, wasn't I?" The four were back on shore now, walking toward the canteen, which was still open for a few more minutes. "I was just thinking of how chapped I was at being stationed in North Carolina, combing the skies for German bombers no one ever expected to be there. I was so excited about being reassigned. Then, honestly, I was a little disappointed about not going into combat. Now I'm excited again. There's something important going on here, and I feel there's going to be a special part in it for us."

"When you know how a situation's going to turn out," commented Chaplain Poling, "you can really enjoy the journey. And we all know how this one's going to turn out: God wins!"

★ ★ ★ ★

The next morning Chaplain Poling remembered the letter he had started to Betty what seemed like ages ago, though in fact only a little more than a week had passed since he folded it away unfinished in a notebook. This letter, as with every letter mailed by a serviceman from an army post office during wartime, would be censored to remove any mention of where he was or what he was doing. He scanned back over what he had already written, then poised his pen below the last completed line.

"I imagine you and Corky (and Thumper!) playing in the snow and having a wonderful time, then coming in to warm up by the big fireplace. I think about you constantly and about our church and the work God is doing there. We're so blessed, Betty, and I'm thankful every moment for the gifts God has given us. Is Mrs. Sorensen still in the hospital? If she is, send her my regards and prayers for a speedy recovery. I know Dr. Lawrence is doing a fine job in the pulpit. Tell him hello for me, and thank him for his willingness to stand in the gap until I return.

"Since I don't know when I'll have time to write again, please give Father my love and tell him I'm praying for his church and his ministry. I miss you all, but at the same time I have a true peace that my place is here. I've met three other chaplains—Catholic, Jewish, and Methodist—and we're spending a lot of time together. Of course there are important theological differences between us (though we haven't talked that much about them), but we definitely have more in common than in conflict. Now we're going to team up to play some hardball with the Germans, and we'll make quite a team."

Poling wondered momentarily whether the censors would take out the part about the Germans. He went ahead, leaving the words as they were.

"Read this letter to Corky, my love. I'll enjoy knowing you spoke these words I write and that he heard them from you. God hold you in the palm of his hand until we meet again. All my love, Clark."

Poling tapped his shirt pocket where he'd put the letter he helped Private Nelson write. After sealing and addressing his letter to Betty, he took out Nelson's letter, holding it in one hand and his own in the other.

How interesting it was, he mused, that though their lives could hardly have been more different, their love for their families was so much the same. The two of them had, as it were, the same index of feelings: devotion, concern, loneliness, apprehension. What a remarkable reminder that God's creative power was endless and that as different as people in his world were, they were also brothers.

Because so few men knew that an explanation of their mission was on the horizon at last, and because those officers in attendance aboard the *Dorchester* for such news as there was did their duty and kept mum about what they learned, the atmosphere inside the secure compound was no different than it had been. The baseball tournament concluded with Chaplain Washington's St. Isidore Icebergs the exultant winners. "We won this one for the Dodgers," he exclaimed joyfully. National League Pennant winners in 1941, the Brooklyn Dodgers had gone down in defeat to their crosstown rivals in the World Series that year.

In '42 the Yankees had their comeuppance at the hands of the St. Louis Cardinals. Seeing the Yankees humbled made Washington feel good, but no better than this decisive victory as coach and star of the Icebergs.

After dinner following the game, the four chaplains gathered at the canteen. As they sat there around the metal table with their cups of coffee, there was an unspoken awareness that they were developing a bond different from any they had formed with anyone before, drawn together by a common calling to stand against a common enemy. The canteen was nearly empty, which gave them the sense they could relax and speak freely in confidence. And there was no shortage of material for conversation.

"What have you heard lately about our two mysterious ladies?" Chaplain Poling ventured. "I haven't seen them since the day we sailed."

"With the odds at about 450-to-one, I can't say I blame them," Fox replied. "They're engineers. I wonder if they're some kind of specialists. Otherwise why would the brass want to bring women on a mission like this?"

"Beats me," said John Washington. "But I've heard all kinds of speculation. You know how it is, when there aren't any facts to explain what's going on, rumors rush in to fill the vacuum. I've heard they're spies, members of the Danish royal family, hookers, and officers in the OSS."

"I don't guess they could be all four, could they?" Alex Goode interjected. The men chuckled. "I've heard something else that sounds a lot closer to the truth."

"And what would that be?" Poling said, encouraging him on.

"Two of the world's foremost authorities in cryogenic metallurgy. In laymen's terms, experts in building stuff out of metal in very cold environments."

"Maybe they're going to build a baseball stadium down the street in honor of Washington's victory!" Fox suggested good-naturedly. Washington blushed and remained silent during the murmur of approvals. After the ribbing had run its course, there was a short pause in the conversation until Poling picked up a thread.

"Come to think of it, who's to say the rumors of a spy on board aren't true? There must be three thousand people in this convoy. If it's as important as the general says it is, don't you think the Germans have some idea of what's going on?" He didn't say it out of fear, but more as an intriguing intellectual exercise.

"Certainly they could," Fox answered thoughtfully. "I guess the whole point of being a good spy is that you don't look like a spy."

"No trench coat!?" Goode exclaimed in mock horror. "No sunglasses? I'm crushed. Life is such a disappointment sometimes. No wonder the men have the problems they do."

Though he said it half in jest, Chaplain Goode's remark about the men refocused the conversation in that direction. The chaplains agreed that the men they knew aboard the *Dorchester* were holding up remarkably well under the circumstances.

"My biggest concern," Chaplain Fox said, "is what's going to happen when it's time to leave here for wherever we're going next. When we left New York there was a sense of excitement—taking on the unknown. Now the men know what it's like out there: cold, rough, smelly, cramped, and never knowing when you might be in the crosshairs of a German periscope. My guess is that our real challenge as chaplains is still in front of us."

"Speaking of real challenges, has anyone seen Sergeant Adams?" asked Washington.

"Just seen him here and there since we landed," Clark Poling replied. "Can't seem to corner him long enough to ask any questions."

"He and I have some unfinished business to attend to," Washington continued. "If anybody here gets a chance to talk to him in private, do what you can to draw him out, and send him to me if you have the chance."

"Will do," Poling said, answering for the group. "It's sad to see what the thought of war and combat does to people."

"Interesting, too," said Goode, "how differently one person takes it compared to another. Just walking

209

around, I can tell who has a spiritual center to hang onto. It gives the ones who do a little pool of calm, quiet confidence deep inside them. And that assurance affects everything they do."

"I think that's one of the great discoveries I've made in my life," George Fox responded. "If you've got that assurance in your heart, you're on the right track."

CHAPTER 15

THE SECOND
ENVELOPE

Twenty-four hours later the four chaplains were back aboard the *Dorchester*, waiting in the dining hall as before for General Blackstone to arrive. Just after breakfast they had been approached by a thin-lipped army captain with piercing eyes that seemed never to blink ("I don't know what OSS looks like, but I bet that's it," Chaplain Washington had ventured) and had been ordered to report at 2100 hours that night.

The room stood on command at 2100 hours precisely as the general and his small entourage filed in and stood in a line. This time the general stepped forward at once, without introduction or formality. He had a manila envelope in his hand.

"Be seated, gentlemen." He began opening the envelope.

"There's only one copy of these orders. They're too sensitive to have them duplicated, so I'll read them aloud. Actually I already know what's in here, because I wrote it. But the president decided that it would be better for me to present them to you in person." He handed the empty envelope to the staff member closest to him, glanced at the sheaf of papers it had contained, then looked up at the assembled officers.

"This mission actually began almost two weeks ago at the Staten Island docks. That was when a carefully selected force was assembled for what will be one of the most important defensive operations of this war. You were brought there in secret, then opened orders at sea that told you only to come here for further instruction. This procedure was followed to reduce the chance of leaks, whether accidental or otherwise. If a man doesn't know where he's going, he can't tell anybody.

"This morning I received orders from the president that this program is to move forward at the earliest possible moment. That moment is now. No notes will be taken at this briefing. You are not to discuss anything you hear this morning or answer any questions from anybody for twenty-four hours from now. After that point you can talk all you want because it won't make any difference."

General Blackstone held the papers up and began to read.

"Orders to special forces mission team at St. John's, Newfoundland by order of the Commander in Chief, Washington, D.C., January 27, 1943: Proceed with Operation Thunderbolt."

The general slipped the paper he was reading to the back of the stack and handed the stack to one of his men.

"The rest of this is all background and specifics. I'll give you the highlights now. Operational details will be passed on to the navigation officers and unit commanders.

"Protection of Atlantic shipping is crucial to defeating the Nazis. We have to be able to safeguard ships sailing from North America with men, fuel, equipment, spare parts, and other supplies.

"The great danger continues to be German submarines. Current models have a range of sixty-five hundred miles, and more advanced designs are in sea trials. This range allows them to wait in the western Atlantic just out of coastal air surveillance and bomber range, to target vessels and convoys as soon as they sail into unprotected waters. From that point until they come under the protection of bombers based in England, our ships are like ducks in the shooting gallery.

"Operation Thunderbolt will turn the tables and turn them fast. Your mission, gentlemen, will be to build and maintain a network of remote airfields to supply a fleet of aircraft carrying top secret microwave radar equipment. Using radio waves, conventional radar can locate enemy subs on the surface—or aircraft in flight, for that matter—at night. The Germans cruise topside at night because it saves their batteries and doubles their speed. But the U-boats can detect radar signals aimed at them while they're still too far away to give us a shot. As soon as they know we've located them, they submerge.

"Microwave radar is different. Because of the frequency of the signals, the Jerries can't pick them up. To the wolf packs, we're invisible. They don't know we have a bead on them until a torpedo comes knocking on their hatch."

A controlled yet intense wave of excitement rippled through the room. The potential for this mission was almost unimaginable.

"The first Operation Thunderbolt installation will be Blue West One, northwest of Cape Farewell near the tip of Greenland. Greenland, as some of you may know, became a U.S. protectorate after the Germans invaded Denmark in '41. It's safe, isolated, and geographically ideal for our mission.

"Your orders are to build, operate, and—if necessary—defend, a major airfield installation there, complete with support housing, maintenance, and repair hangars, a major fuel depot, roads, and harbor facilities. Some of you will be involved only in the construction phase. Others will remain after the facility is complete as operational or support staff.

"We want to keep Operation Thunderbolt and the Blue West One facility a secret from the Germans as long as we can. The less they know about it, the less they'll modify their plans to counter it.

"From the field at Blue West One, Allied planes can be dispatched to find and destroy U-boats in mid-ocean for the first time. Within a matter of months from now, a new long-range aircraft, the B-24 Liberator, will be available to extend the coverage area even more.

"Using airborne systems and more powerful, land-based radar, Operation Thunderbolt will give Allied shipping the most effective defense ever against U-boat attack. As Blue West Two and Three come on line, we will ultimately have a virtually airtight defensive perimeter.

"There are other reasons for Operation Thunderbolt that go beyond protection of convoys. The first is that the Germans have cracked our communications code. We have unmistakable evidence that troop movements, convoy sail dates, and other highly classified information is now regularly available to the enemy. On the other hand, we have had absolutely no luck with their Enigma code. There's a new derivation sequence for every letter in every word of every message—no pattern whatever. The Brits have got a whole house full of people working on it twenty-four hours a day: not only code experts but musicians, chess players, mathematicians, psychologists, and anybody else they think might be able to come up with the key. Germany knows our secrets, but we don't know theirs. Operation Thunderbolt will help us level the playing field.

"Another reason Thunderbolt is crucial is that the time is coming when the Allies will launch their counteroffensive from the British Isles. Once that happens, a steady supply of convoy goods will be essential for maintaining the drive. We can't afford to have offensive units stranded in the middle of a campaign by a lack of equipment.

"Third and most unlikely, though also the most potentially dangerous, is a secret project for harassing the U.S. mainland. The Germans are working on supersecret, ultralong-range bombers that could fly from Norway or the Azores to America and attack East Coast cities, particularly New York and Washington. Imagine what the propaganda value would be of a German bomber flying over the Capitol? They're also working on unmanned missiles they could launch from Europe and hit those same East Coast targets. With Operation Thunderbolt in place, the Third Reich won't last long enough to put these plans into action. And the longer it takes them to find out about Thunderbolt, the longer they'll waste their time on an expensive project that's doomed to failure.

"We've spent a fair amount of time assembling this convoy. It is self-contained and completely self-sufficient. Other than the highest level of command, no one outside this room knows anything about it.

You're carrying all the equipment, tools, building materials, fuel, and labor needed to complete the installation at Blue West One. Those two ladies some of you have seen aboard the *Dorchester* are two of the foremost experts in the world on cold-climate construction techniques. You have doctors with you, cooks, carpenters, concrete finishers, even four chaplains on board." He gestured subtly toward them.

"You men"—he was looking at the chaplains—"will have your work cut out for you. It's going to be cold, dark, lonely, scary, boring, and who knows what else on a godforsaken rock pile not far from the Arctic Circle." The general's gaze shifted back to take in the whole room again. "But nothing is more important to the success of our forces in this conflict than the completion of this radar base and its effective use to deter hostile action. We think we can cut tonnage sunk in half with this operation. If we do, we'll have you and your commands to thank.

"Keeping our own spirits up will be the biggest challenge over the next few days. Once you arrive at Blue West One and get to work, you'll be too busy to be scared. Anyway, Greenland is U.S. territory for the time being, and I expect the Germans will think long and hard before they rattle your cage there. But between here and there you've got to run the U-boat gauntlet one more time. By now members of your command have had a taste of the high seas that they don't much like. In a lot of ways, going out this second

217

time will be harder than the first because you all know what to expect. Help them. Be an example.

"Good luck, and God bless you." Then he and his staff were gone.

The excitement and anticipation that had been building as the general spoke burst out into a deafening roar of shouts, cheers, whistles, and applause. The *Dorchester*'s dining room pulsated with the eager, emotion-charged reaction of the men to the news revealing at last what their ultimate mission was to be.

Still flushed with the intensity and drama of the moment, the chaplains walked ashore, paused at the entrance to the canteen, then went on to their quarters, anxious to discuss what they had heard and realizing their room was the only place safe enough.

"Man," said Father Washington as soon as the door was shut, "I never expected this!"

"'The Lord works in mysterious ways his wonders to perform,'" quoted Chaplain Poling.

"What can we do that will help the men most?" Chaplain Goode wondered aloud.

"It's going to be a challenge, that's for sure," agreed Chaplain Fox. "You know they're bound to ask us what's going on. We can't lie and say we don't know, but we can't exactly tell them everything we do know."

"Think of the opportunities this could bring us, though," Chaplain Poling said. "Times like this are when men look the most desperately for what's missing in their lives. Maybe we can't give them pat answers about where we're heading. But we can give them spiritual truth and assurance that will change their lives from here on out."

"Here, here!" Chaplain Washington rejoined. "Suddenly we have a chance to answer our calling in a way we'll probably never have again."

Next morning it was announced that the convoy would sail with the tide in only a few hours. The news was a blow to the troops who, as predicted, dreaded the prospect of leaving the quiet comfort and safety of the harbor at St. John's—the two hills at the harbor entrance standing guard and the submarine net blocking out any brash hidden would-be invader—for the stale, cramped quarters, seasickness, homesickness, and the age-old fear of the unknown.

Mission commanders were wise to leave the convoy so little time between the announcement and departure: it gave malcontentment little time to take root in the rocky provincial soil. Tension and discontent could easily manifest themselves at sea, as the chaplains well knew. They would have their hands full keeping a lid on things for the next few days until the convoy reached Cape Farewell. After that, once the men realized how safe they were and how important their mission was, it ought to be smooth sailing for a while. Then the boredom and darkness would set in, and the chaplains would be there to counter them at every

219

turn, keeping Operation Thunderbolt encouraged, enthusiastic, and confident.

As troops headed for the ship, the chaplains saw some of them moving with slow, unwilling steps; in many faces there was a look of concern, of foreboding, of fear.

"Corporal Simmons," Chaplain Washington called out to one of the young troops who had toured Manhattan with him a few days before.

"Hey, Chaplain," he said, his face downcast.

"You don't look so chipper. You miss that deli cooking already?"

Simmons did his best to smile. "Chaplain, I'll shoot straight with you. I don't feel good about this. About those wolf packs and all."

"Nobody does," Washington replied matter-of-factly. "But the sooner we get where we're going, the sooner we'll get home." He gripped the corporal's shoulder through his heavy topcoat. "Cheer up. It's contagious."

"Come on, men," Chaplain Fox shouted to another knot of soldiers making their way slowly to the dock, gesturing to others within earshot, "let's show these grandmas how to march. Hut! Hut! Hut, two, three, four . . ."

The men fell into step. Their scowls disappeared. They waved and jeered proudly at the men around them as they marched smartly by. Other men hustled up to join ranks.

Watching them, Chaplain Poling thought, *If only it were as easy to revive them spiritually!*

In their quarters just minutes before departure, each chaplain reflected silently on what had happened and what was to come. Alex Goode took a photo of Theresa out of his pocket and stared at it for a long moment. He loved her so much. She was so understanding about his desire to serve both his country and his God in this time of crisis. Her famous Uncle Al—Al Jolson—was hard at work, too, entertaining the troops overseas and raising money from war bond sales.

Clark Poling started another letter to Betty, though he had no idea where he'd mail it from—was there a post office in Greenland? Since Denmark was under Nazi control, would he need German postage stamps? He smiled at the thought.

As he did so often, George Fox found himself thinking about his son, wondering where he was. Was he safe? Did he have enough to eat? Was he afraid? Would he be brave when the time came? Certainly their relationship could hardly have been more different than his with his own father. Fox was so thankful for that. His son was also his friend, growing in the nurture and admonition of the Lord.

John Washington moved his lips silently as he prayed. There was no way to number how many thousands of times he had said those comforting words, yet each time they brought him peace and assurance afresh.

In a small, felted box, John Washington kept a pocket watch his father had given him. Whenever he looked at the watch, he imagined the shop of the watchmaker in Dublin, the teeming streets, the emerald green of the forests outside the city. He had never seen any of it, but he felt he knew it as well as he knew his old Twelfth Street neighborhood. He imagined the brave but frightened man who carried it across the Atlantic to a new life and away from the great Irish potato famine almost exactly a hundred years before. It was a reminder of family and heritage and the faith that ties people together across oceans and generations. *And now,* Washington thought to himself, *after all these years, it's headed back toward home, even if only part way.*

In a scene repeated throughout the *Dorchester* and other ships in the convoy, each of the chaplains was lost for a few moments in his own thoughts as the six vessels passed beyond the welcoming arms of the harbor entrance. Dead ahead, beyond the safety and protection of the submarine net beneath them, far from the spaciousness and clean air and baseball behind them, concealing the ruthless enemy all around them, the ominous Atlantic waited.

CHAPTER 16

THE BLINDFOLD
OF FEAR

Sailing single file out of the harbor, the ships in the convoy established their positions once again as soon as they reached open sea. The *Tampa* led the way, forming the apex of a triangle. Behind her were the ships she was there to protect, sailing abreast of one another: the *Lutz* to port, the *Dorchester* in the center, and the *Biscaya* to starboard. Behind and outside them were the other two cutters forming the second and third points of the triangle, the *Comanche* on the port side and the *Escanaba* to starboard.

The chaplains sat together in stateroom B-14 and considered their options. The invigorating days at St. John's had been a godsend to the whole convoy. The only downside was the way life aboard ship suffered now by comparison.

"It's tough," Chaplain Poling observed. "We've seen already how leaving this has been a lot harder on the men than New York was." The others nodded in mute agreement. "You heard them. You talked to them same as I did. You saw how hesitant they were. They definitely don't want to be here. When we left from Staten Island, none of us had any real sense of what we were doing. It was an adventure into the great unknown. Now everybody knows what to expect: seasick bunk mates and the threat of a German torpedo in our belly any time of the day or night."

"Here's the irony, though," Chaplain Goode replied. "This ship and these conditions we hear so much complaining about—and complain about ourselves if we're honest—is taking us to one of the most important top secret duty assignments of the war. We'll be giving spiritual guidance and confidence and assurance to people whose work will save thousands of lives—maybe tens of thousands."

Father Washington spoke up cheerfully. "Some of us are happy with any ship."

"That would be the nonswimmers, I suppose," Poling answered.

"What are you talking?" Goode said with surprise. "You can't swim?"

"Not a stroke," Washington said with a smile.

"And so what are you doing here?" the rabbi went on with mock seriousness.

"God only knows!" the priest shot back. "Glub, glub!"

The stateroom rocked with laughter, not because Washington was all that funny, but because they desperately needed something to laugh about.

The laughter faded, leaving each man with his own thoughts for a moment. Chaplain Fox broke the silence. "Chaplain Washington, Chaplain Goode, you guys are living proof that God has a sense of humor." A ripple of chuckles affirmed his statement. "But you know, it's a good question. What are we doing here? A priest who can't swim. An old man with back trouble like me. Cooks from Mississippi and illiterate privates from West Virginia. All brought here by God for some great purpose only he can see. What are U-boats doing taking a bead on us like kids shooting for Kewpie dolls at the county fair? What are the Nazis doing rolling over Poland and France and Scandinavia?

"The Bible tells us we see 'through a glass darkly.' God's clear vision is dim to us and will be till we meet him in heaven. The way I figure it, we're here to help everybody else pick their way through the dim light the best they can. And 'here'—for the time being—is a ship in the Atlantic Ocean."

"We've established a lot of good relationships already," Poling observed. "I pray they'll help us be what these men need us to be for them."

"How about a little buddy system prayer," Goode suggested. The other chaplains eagerly agreed. And so in the prearranged manner, Goode prayed for Washington, then Washington for Poling, then Poling for Fox, then Fox for Goode, completing the circle.

★ ★ ★ ★

Later that day the rest of the convoy was informed where they were going and what their mission was to be. Information about microwave radar and the new B-24 Liberator was kept sketchy; each man would be given details on a need-to-know basis. The Allied command was taking no chances on any leaks. Though there was absolutely no hard evidence of spy activity on this special component of Convoy SG-19, rumors persisted, being stamped out one place only to surface in another.

Initially there was a renewed sense of excitement aboard the *Dorchester* at being reminded they were insiders involved in a secret mission. The enthusiasm soon faded, however, and a sense of tension began to tighten around the passengers and crew like a vice. The chaplains had seen the seeds of it as the soldiers reboarded the vessel at St. John's.

"Four chaplains can't do much to brighten up a whole shipload of scared, suspicious people," Poling commented later on, when the four of them were together again. "But the chaplains know who can."

"I think you're on to something there," Fox quickly rejoined. "What we need is a chapel service to remind everybody in this sardine can that God put them here for a reason and that they can always turn to him for help, for assurance, for peace of mind. Even out here in the middle of nowhere, nobody is alone."

They spread the word and organized a simple service from the army and navy service book they all carried. At the appointed time two hundred or more men gathered in the dining hall, each taking a service manual from a stack as they entered. The room was full but not crowded. Leaning over to Washington, Chaplain Goode said, "Maybe if this works, we'll have even more next time." Washington winked in reply.

Chaplain Poling began the service. "I'm glad to see you all here, men. The other chaplains and I have had a chance to speak with some of you since we left St. John's. I know a lot of you are unhappy to be back out here, especially now that you have some idea of what to expect for the next couple of days.

"I'm not going to lie to you. We've got a dangerous voyage ahead of us. But we've got a Savior watching out for us every minute. I'd like to start by reading something to you. It's a prayer President George Washington prayed to remind the country of the power of God and the importance of his blessing on our country. It's every bit as true now as it was then:

> "Almighty God, we make our earnest
> prayer that thou wilt keep the United
> States in thy holy protection, that
> thou wilt incline the hearts of the

citizens to cultivate a spirit of subordination and obedience to government, and entertain a brotherly affection and love for one another and for their fellow citizens of the United States at large. And finally that thou wilt most graciously be pleased to dispose us all to do justice, to love mercy, and to demean ourselves with that charity, humility, and pacific temper of mind which were the characteristics of the Divine Author of our blessed religion, and without an humble imitation of whose example in these things, we can never hope to be a happy nation. Grant our supplications, we beseech thee, through Jesus Christ our Lord. Amen."

When he finished, the room was completely silent except for the constant rumble from the engine room. After a few quiet seconds Chaplain Washington played an introduction on the piano. Everyone in the room recognized the popular tune and joined in with feeling on the chorus:

God bless America, land that I love;
Stand beside her and guide her
Through the night with a light from
above . . .

Chaplain Goode stood up to lead a responsive reading.

"Happy are they that dwell in thy house," he said in a robust, confident voice. "They will ever be praising thee."

The room responded with conviction: "Happy is the people that is in such a case; yea, happy is the people whose God is the Lord." Even as they read, the men felt their spirits lifted.

A hymn followed, then a heartfelt prayer from Chaplain Fox for the safety of the convoy.

When the crowd began to disperse after the benediction, the chaplains split up to greet and talk with as many men as they could. It scarcely seemed possible that these same men—busy in animated conversations and obviously at ease—could be the same withdrawn, haunted men who had entered the dining hall less than an hour before. Comparing notes later, everybody agreed with Poling's succinct assessment: "I think it helped. Let's do it again."

★ ★ ★ ★

The next morning after breakfast, Lieutenant Aubrey Burch approached Chaplain Fox as he sat in the dayroom reading one of the Canadian magazines that had recently been brought aboard.

"Hi, Chaplain. Lieutenant Burch. Remember me?"

Fox looked up from his magazine. "Sure. You're in charge of all that mysterious sub-finding gear."

"That's right."

"Pull up a chair."

Burch was young, eager, and very serious about his work. He sat on the couch next to Fox's chair. The chaplain put down his magazine. His first thought was that this young officer was hardly older than his son Wyatt. He couldn't help thinking for a split second about what he might be doing at that instant. He hoped he was safe and comfortable and that if he had questions about his life or faith that there would be somebody there to listen and talk to.

"Chaplain, I know you've heard some of the rumors going around on the ship."

"Here and there."

"This is the kind of scuttlebutt that gets the men worked up. It gets me worked up."

"I know what you mean. I've heard some doozies. What specifically do you think we ought to run down?"

"Maybe it's because I spend so much time in the radio room, but sometimes I feel like I'm in the path of every wild rumor on the Atlantic." The more he talked, the more animated the young lieutenant became. "Orders are we're on a secret mission to Greenland. But do you think that's really where we're going? I've heard men say we're actually a decoy. That all the secret gear— all the microwave radar stuff—is on another ship in the convoy and we'll be sacrificed to the Germans because they think the gear is aboard the *Dorchester*. The convoy flagship leaked radio transmissions saying we had it."

"You're in the radio room all the time, Lieutenant Burch," Chaplain Fox commented. "Have you heard any transmissions from the flagship? Anything reported to you? Written in the logbook?"

"No, Chaplain, I haven't. But that doesn't mean they weren't sent."

"I see your point. Go on."

"The next one is even stranger: that we're going to Greenland, then march overland to the North Pole and down the other side of the world for a surprise attack on the Germans at the Russian front."

"I've got to say that's a great idea," Fox responded, trying to defuse the situation. The young officer was clearly concerned. "I wish we could do it. But if you think about it a minute, you'll realize nobody has ever walked over the North Pole from Greenland to Siberia. And my guess is, the first to do it won't be a convoy load of soldiers and sailors without the training. You've heard what our mission is. A radar base in Greenland will do a lot more for the Allied war effort than a bunch of greenhorn soldiers marching over the ice cap."

The lieutenant grinned sheepishly. "Of course you're right." Then as suddenly as the smile had appeared, it evaporated. "There's something else floating around that worries me even more."

"What's that?"

"The rumor there's a spy on board."

"A spy?" Fox replied. "I've heard it mentioned."

"In the radio room. With access to the ASDIC. In other words, me."

"You?" answered the chaplain, still calm. "What makes them think that?"

"I don't know. And nobody's actually said anything to me face-to-face. I've only heard it around. But the way some of the guys look at me, I know something's up."

"Well, Lieutenant, you don't look like a spy to me. Of course, I guess if you did, you wouldn't be a very good spy. I think you care deeply about your position as an officer and your participation in this mission. As an officer, you know rumors have got to stop with you. Don't encourage them; don't pass them on. They only hurt morale and make the troops skittish."

"Yes, sir, Chaplain."

"Something else to remember is that you can't control how other people feel about you or anything else. You can only control how you feel. I'd like to pray for you, Lieutenant, that you'll remain confident, remain in control of your feelings, and serve as an example to the other men until we get through this mission."

The young lieutenant's chest swelled with pride. "Yes, sir, Chaplain."

As the two lieutenants—one a graying veteran of an earlier war, the other a sincere but apprehensive man half his age—bowed their heads together, Chaplain Poling and Private Sam Nelson were engrossed in an animated conversation of their own in B-14.

There too, Lieutenant Burch was a central character.

"I tell you, sure as you're born, that Lieutenant Burch is a spy. Just look at him! And if Burch isn't a German

232

name, I don't know what is." Private Nelson was convinced he and everyone aboard the *Dorchester* were doomed.

"Nelson, I'm sure you've thought a lot about this," Poling answered calmly. "But remember, the lieutenant is young and a little jumpy. He's under a lot of pressure. I don't think there's any reason in the world to think he's a spy."

"Spies don't always look like spies, do they?" Nelson asked rhetorically. "And that name, that's the kicker."

"I don't know if Burch is German or not."

"It sounds German to me, all right!"

"It does sound German. Know what sounds even more German?"

"What?"

"Eisenhower."

Nelson was dumbstruck for an instant, then found his voice. "Good Heavens, Chaplain, you're right."

★ ★ ★ ★

At the same time, at a dining hall table near the never-empty coffeepot, Chaplain Goode spoke with a new acquaintance, Sergeant First Class Arnold Greene. Each of them had met few other Jews in the military, though Sergeant Greene had been in the army five years. Their conversation revolved around the question that was on the lips of the whole Jewish world as the reality of Hitler's "final solution" became clear: Why?

"This was my war long before Pearl Harbor," Greene was saying. "From the time Hitler came to power in

'33, I have felt every blow against the Jews in Europe is a blow against me." He punctuated his speech by pounding the table with the side of his fist. "I have relatives in Poland I haven't heard from in two years. Are they dead? Probably. But not knowing is worse than knowing they were dead. A Jew understands. Other people can read the newspaper and listen to the radio and say, 'Oh my goodness, how awful!' but they'll never feel what we feel."

"Don't sell your Gentile brother short," Chaplain Goode advised. "There are millions of people dedicated to freeing Jews from the Nazis. Not all of them are sensitive. Not all of them are particularly nice, even. But this is a war being fought by every American, for every American. Leave it to God to give Hitler his due. He's up to the job whether you or I are or not. You pray. You put everything you have into this mission. God will honor that."

The fourth chaplain found himself in the most unexpected and remarkable situation of all. Walking down a companionway, Chaplain Washington heard his name and stopped. There, outside the linen storage room where their earlier meeting had been interrupted by the U-boat sighting, stood Sergeant Wesley Adams.

"Chaplain!" a voice hissed again. Washington saw who it was and held out his hand in greeting.

"Adams, I've been hoping I'd run into you. Don't think I saw you the whole time we were in St. John's. We've got some unfinished business."

"I was tied up," the sergeant said with no further explanation. "But that was then. This is now. I got a question for you." Adams made no move to go into the storeroom or anywhere else, so the two men stood talking in the narrow aisle leading from the companionway.

"Anything," Washington responded, seeing Adams's willingness to talk as an answer to prayer.

Adams leaned forward conspiratorially. "I've heard this ship is carrying huge underwater tanks of aviation gas. We're a floating bomb!"

"Adams, you're a real veteran, and I'm not. You know a lot more about fighting and surviving and espionage than I'll ever know. But even I know the *Dorchester* could never make eleven knots with gasoline tanks welded to its bottom."

"But Chaplain, gas is lighter than seawater."

"But the gas has to have big steel tanks with all kinds of drag to hold it. Even if they were empty, they'd slow us down. You're a sharp guy. You can keep rumors like that from spreading."

"What makes you think I'm so smart?"

"You came to check out your facts. That's good."

"I used to be Catholic, you know."

He said it out of the blue. Chaplain Washington suddenly felt he had a live one on the line. "No, I didn't know."

235

"Yeah."

"I'd like to know more. Maybe we could go somewhere a little more comfortable and talk about it?"

Without saying a word, Adams nodded and stepped into the companionway. As the two walked toward the chaplains' stateroom, the door opened and an army private came out followed closely by Chaplain Poling. Deep in conversation the two headed down the hall in the opposite direction without noticing the newcomers' approach.

Washington sat on one of the lower bunks, and Sergeant Adams turned the desk chair around to face him. The chaplain waited for his guest to speak first.

"Sailing in this convoy is like running blindfolded through a roomful of knives. Those U-boats are all over the place. We know they're there but we can't see them, and there's nothing we can do about it." The words came out in a torrent. They had been bottled up tight, and now the dam was bursting.

"You said you used to be Catholic," Washington observed. Adams nodded. "When you were Catholic, did you believe the Lord would protect you?"

"Maybe. I guess."

"That God's Spirit protected sailors and travelers at sea?"

"I guess."

"Wouldn't it feel good to have the Holy Spirit in your heart right now?"

Adams's eyes welled with tears. "I guess."

"Isn't it more than a guess?"

Adams nodded slowly.

"If you're here to talk," the chaplain said, "I'm here to listen."

Adams's shoulders slumped. He buried his face in his hands and sobbed with abandon like a little boy. Washington waited until Adams raised his face, wiped his eyes on his sleeve, took a deep breath, and began.

"I grew up in the church. My parents and kid sisters and I went to mass every day. Went to confession every week. I always liked the parties we had at church in the summers. That's where I met Madeline. She was the prettiest girl I had ever seen, and I fell in love the minute I saw her across the room. We were just kids— both sixteen. But you know how it is; when you're that age, you think you're bulletproof and invisible. Nothing can hurt you, and you're never going to make a mistake you have to pay for.

"We went to different high schools, but we saw each other every afternoon. We spent every Saturday together, went to church together, introduced our families to each other. We never really talked about it, but after a while we just assumed we'd be getting married. By the time we were seniors, we had it all figured out. We'd get married the summer after graduation. I had a good job waiting for me at a machine shop where I was working part-time, and she was going to work in her uncle's department store. We even had a little house picked out, white clapboard with red shutters and a picket fence in front. I had the world by the tail.

"But we didn't live happily ever after."

"I had a feeling," Chaplain Washington replied.

Adams swallowed hard and went on. "When we met, neither one of us had, you know, 'done it.' But we decided that since we really loved each other and knew we were getting married, it would be OK. Deep down I guess we knew it was wrong, but it seemed so right. After a few times it caught up with us. She got pregnant, and it absolutely scared her to death. She thought her parents would throw her out of the house.

"Sure enough, her parents went ape and so did mine. Hers wanted to have me arrested and mine did too. Lucky she was eighteen, so there was nothing the law could do. But our families said we couldn't see each other again. Even the church turned against us. So we ran away. One night we just took off together. Didn't know where we'd end up but knew we'd go together. As soon as we got settled somewhere, we'd get in touch with our folks, make up sooner or later, and everything would be good again.

"We drove from Springfield—that's where I'm from, Springfield, Illinois—as far as Lincoln, Nebraska. Figured out west would be a place we could make a fresh start and all. We stopped for the night at a tourist court on the edge of town. Two or three in the morning Maddie started to hurt. The pain got worse and worse, and she said something was wrong with the baby. Said we had to get to a doctor quick. We ended up having to go all the way into Lincoln to the hospital. By then Maddie was practically screaming her head off.

"We got inside, and a nurse rolled her away down the hall. I sat and waited for hours. It was broad daylight by the time a doctor came out to tell me my baby was dead. 'Mr. Adams, I'm sorry to tell you that your daughter didn't make it.' That hadn't sunk in before I heard, 'And you'd better come on back to Mrs. Adams right away.' They assumed we were married, and I didn't tell them any different.

"I followed the doctor back to where Maddie was. She was so white. And her eyes glowed like they were on fire. I sat on the bed and cradled her head in my lap.

"'Little Margaret's gone to be with Jesus,' she said. We hadn't talked about what to name the baby, but I thought Margaret was a wonderful name.

"'Margaret,' she said. Then softly, 'I'm so sorry. I love you.' Then she closed her eyes and died in my arms. It would have been our wedding day.

"After that I wanted to die myself." His voice grew louder. "How could a God who cares about anything let people like that die? A beautiful young mother? A perfect, innocent baby girl? Where was God then?" He hurled the last question at Washington inches from his face.

"If that's the way God runs the world, I don't want any part of it. I want to be left alone, thank you very much. I'll just make it on my own."

239

Both men were drained. They sat facing each other in silence, feeling the motion and vibration of the ship.

At last Washington spoke. "Thank you, Wesley, for sharing that with me. It took a lot of guts. And my guess is that if you still wanted to be left alone you wouldn't have flagged me down back there by the laundry room."

Adams smiled an unaccustomed smile of sincere joy.

The chaplain went on. "Terrible things happen in this world. Maddie and Margaret are examples of that. Hitler's another. The wolf packs out there waiting on us are another. I can't explain God's plan to you or anybody else because I don't know what it is, and he doesn't owe me an explanation. He sees a big picture we can't, a future we can't, our place in the lives of others we can't. If it were obvious, it wouldn't take faith to believe. But God calls us to be faithful. Jesus said that God has prepared a place for every one of us. You believed that once. I pray that one day you'll believe it again."

There was nothing left to say. The two men rose, and Washington put an arm around Adams. Then Sergeant Adams left the room.

While it was fresh in his mind, Father Washington pulled a notebook from his drawer in the chest the chaplains shared and began writing down his reaction to Adams's heartfelt story. After five minutes or so he finished and opened the drawer to replace the book. Out of habit he glanced at the corner where the felt bag containing his father's and grandfather's gold pocket watch always rested.

The bag was open, and the watch was gone.

CHAPTER 17

HARD CONTACT

Between St. John's and Cape Farewell the convoy observed the same communications blackout as before: absolute radio silence, no semaphore lights, no flares. If one of the ships was disabled or hit, orders were to leave it behind for search-and-rescue operations as soon as they could be organized.

Heading north-northeast, the convoy began passing through fields of icebergs. The weather, which had held clear and beautiful the whole time they were in harbor, turned foul again. Heavy winds drove the sleet sideways so that it struck any exposed skin like tiny needles. A layer of rock-hard sheet ice again coated the rigging, railing, and deck of the *Dorchester,* making a turn aboveboard for some fresh air a treacherous proposition.

Though plenty of passengers still ventured forth, none of them stayed topside more than a few minutes.

With poor visibility and the ice field adding to the burden of heavily bundled lookouts keeping watch for a telltale periscope wake, Captain Danielsen ordered the watch doubled and the time on watch cut in half. The captain knew it was unlikely a sub would be sighted during the day. Spotting periscopes, the smaller of the two periscopes most U-boats had, were designed to have as narrow a profile as possible, making them extremely hard to pick out. It wasn't until a torpedo run was contemplated that the Germans typically switched to the better—but larger—attack periscopes that left a more visible wake.

The captain reminded himself that daytime attacks were relatively rare. U-boats usually spent their days submerged. Most of the traveling—and stalking—came at night when, under cover of darkness, U-boats surfaced and switched to diesel power, easily outpacing the convoys they shadowed.

Torpedo Junction was in their wake now, Captain Danielsen thought with some relief. The good news was that the most concentrated danger was behind them. The bad news was that out here in the North Atlantic, U-boats could still appear anywhere, any time. This was the danger zone their mission would soon eliminate with the construction of Blue West One.

The first night out all passengers and crew aboard the *Dorchester* were ordered to wear life jackets twenty-four hours a day for the duration of the voyage. Crowded conditions below decks were bad enough; cinched up with buckles and straps, bumping into each other's bulky kapok life jackets day and night, and sweating and chafing beneath their stifling mass only added to the discomfort.

Whatever men did to occupy their time, no one's thoughts were far from the radio room where Lieutenant Burch and his command kept vigil over the panel of knobs and wires connecting them to the electronic ears that could save their lives. Burch spent virtually every waking moment in front of the ASDIC now, along with pairs of operators rotating in six-hour shifts, each of the pair taking an hour on and an hour off.

Both at the captain's request and by their own preference, Helge Thomasen and Kristen Sorensen had kept a low profile during the entire voyage thus far. They spent most days in their stateroom, with occasional visits to the captain's dayroom, which they had been invited to use whenever he was busy elsewhere. As the only women in the entire convoy, they were the center of attention wherever they went. It wasn't something either of them enjoyed. They had a mission to carry and felt honor bound to fulfill it. It was important to the Allies; moreover, it was important to the future of their native country.

They were friends as well as colleagues and had lived near each other since their university days in Leipzig.

Helge, with white-blonde Scandinavian hair and fair skin, was of medium height; Kristen was an inch or two taller, her hair a light strawberry. Both were natives of Frederiksberg on the outskirts of Copenhagen. Denmark had been the first country to sign a non-aggression pact with the Nazis. Even so, it had been overrun with German soldiers in the first months of the war; the Reich insisted its troops were there to protect them from Allied attack. Even now, Denmark still claimed itself a neutral country, but no one knew what would happen next.

The ladies' common origin made them fast friends as soon as they met at engineering school, sharing a longing for familiar places and a homesickness for the brisk weather, the bustle of the port, and the families they left behind.

Helge's husband was Norwegian; he had left the haven of his adopted country to fight for his homeland. The two of them agreed they could do more for the war effort separately than together and had parted more than two years ago, not knowing when or whether they would see each other again. The first one to make it back home to Frederiksberg would wait for the other.

Kristen was single. From her first days inside the ancient walls of the university, her engineering career had been her life. She was far more interested in the mysteries of fluid dynamics, tensile strength, and plasticity than in the unfathomable confusion of human relationships.

Both women graduated with honors, both specializing in extreme cold weather construction techniques. After Helge's husband left for Norway, Kristen moved into the apartment to keep her company. They were both working for the civil government designing bridges and port facilities when a man approached them one day and said he was from the OSS. The Office of Strategic Services was America's eyes and ears behind enemy lines. His question was simple: Did they want to help the Allies go on the offensive against Hitler?

They were elated at the chance to take a direct part in bringing the war to an end. The two of them spent four months in America learning about microwave radar installation and working on preliminary designs, and now they were heading back to within a few hundred miles of home, to a top-secret job that would sweep the hated U-boats from the Atlantic. And, they hoped, sweep the Nazis from Danish soil.

The women were lonely, though certainly not for the attentions of men. That sort of diversion was far from their thoughts; besides, Captain Danielsen had made it his personal responsibility to see that the women were protected from any unwanted advances. They longed for conversation and relationships to divert their attention from where they were and what they were doing. Their only outlet aboard the *Dorchester* was to spend time with the chaplains.

Since their first meeting with Chaplain Fox in Captain Danielsen's office at the beginning of the voyage, the two looked forward to afternoon sessions almost every day with one or two of the chaplains. Neither Helge nor Kristen had been taught much about religion, or thought much about it, yet there was a calmness and confidence about the chaplains that attracted and encouraged them.

The second day out of St. John's, the heavy weather continued. Rain and sleet lashed the *Dorchester* without, and heavy seas roiled her passengers within. The captain would be in the pilothouse in the afternoon, and so Chaplain Fox and the two women agreed to meet in his office at three o'clock. The trio arrived at the same moment. The captain's orderly was expecting them and ushered them into the room, immaculate as always and free from any hint of clutter.

Taking their seats, the three couldn't help pointing and chuckling at one another, cinched into life jackets on top of their clothes.

"Looks like a snowmen's convention," Chaplain Fox decided, moving awkwardly to serve the ladies from the coffeepot the steward had left.

"I feel like *l'homme Michelin*," Helge complained good-naturedly.

"You've got to quit eating all those potatoes," Kristen shot back with a giggle.

As he passed the cream and sugar, Fox said, "Well, we ought to be nearing the halfway point between St. John's and Blue West One. I wonder if you're as anxious as I am to get off this thing and onto dry, solid, vibration-free land for good."

"You bet," Kristen answered, trying out a little of her new American slang. She and her friend spoke excellent English, accented with a curiously appealing combination of German and Danish overtones. "This place really bugs me."

"Bugs?" Helge interjected. "What are you talking about?"

Kristen leaned over to Chaplain Fox in a mock serious tone. "I watched a lot more movies in New York than she did."

"Who's kidding who?" asked Helge, catching the spirit of the exchange.

"You mean *whom*!"

"I mean youm, that's whom! I mean I can't wait until I can speak Danish on the street again!" Helge continued playfully.

"You and me both, sister," Kristen concluded.

These exchanges marked the only times the women could truly relax and enjoy themselves. Any of their fellow passengers who saw them in these visits with the chaplains would scarcely have recognized the quiet engineers they knew as the witty friends who tossed American slang back and forth with such pleasure.

After a short while the talk turned, as it usually did, to the disheartening isolation the women felt. "It gets so lonely being an outsider," Kristen admitted. Her friend nodded in agreement. "We're egghead engineers. We're women. We're foreigners. That's three strikes, you know. We're different in absolutely every way. If not for these wonderful conversations with you and your colleagues, I doubt we would be able to talk to anybody at all. We'd explode with frustration."

"Even our country's not our own any more," Helge said. "Germans all over the place telling us how we need their protection from the warmongering Allies. Greenland, even England, seem so far away, so helpless to rescue us."

"I don't know how the two of you feel about religion," Fox began.

Helge interrupted. "I was baptized, confirmed, and married in the church. I go there every holy day . . ."

"Whoa, there. I'm not challenging your Christian pedigree. Nobody has a right to do that, and besides, it doesn't affect what I have to say. What I will do, though, since you brought it up, is to repeat what an English writer I admire said about going to church: it doesn't make you a Christian any more than going to the garage makes you a mechanic."

The comparison delighted the Danes. "That's a good one," Kristen admitted.

"Anyway, what I started to say was that God tells us in the Bible that he has a plan for each of our lives. You may feel out of place here, but you never have to feel out of place with God. You're here for a purpose, even if you don't know what it is right now."

"I'd like to think that's true," Helge answered deliberately.

"Would you like me to pray for you," the chaplain suggested, "that you'll feel God's direction in your heart?"

"I think . . . yes," Helge said.

"It couldn't hurt," Kristen added.

As the three bowed their heads, there was an urgent knock at the door, and the steward entered quickly, wide-eyed. "Sorry to disturb you chaplain, ladies, but Chaplain Poling needs you in the dining hall immediately. You better come right on."

With a few brief words of comfort and apology to the engineers, Fox rose and walked rapidly out the door, careening from one side of the narrow jamb to the other as he hit his life jacket in passing by.

He heard the commotion even before he saw it, the buzz and shout of excited voices cascading along the hallway to meet him. Bursting through the door he saw a room crammed full of men (all but a few in their life jackets as ordered) surrounding an open area in the center where two men faced each other, fists raised.

On one side of the space loomed Morris Jones, his cook's apron torn, his face hardened in an angry scowl. On the other side stood Wesley Adams with a bloody nose, a split lip, and a waver in his stance. However the confrontation began, Adams was clearly getting the worst of it.

"I'm going to give you one more chance to take it back," Morris was saying evenly. The tightness in his voice made his words a stifled growl.

Adams seethed with anger all but out of control. "I'm not taking anything back. You're a low-down dish darkie as sure as you're born, and there's nothing on earth you can do about it."

Judging from his condition, Fox figured Adams wouldn't be repeating his accusation more than another time or two before he was pounded unconscious by the beefy chef.

As he rapidly considered how best to defuse the situation, John Washington ran into the room, summoned to the scene as Fox had been.

"Adams!" the chaplain barked with a military demeanor that surprised many of the men who had talked with him in private over the past two weeks.

The sergeant froze in position, fists up, jaw set. A big drop of dark red blood hung from the tip of his nose, moving back and forth in a short arc as his body moved with the rolling of the ship. The room fell silent.

"This isn't your fight, Chaplain," Adams declared weakly.

"It isn't yours either." Washington stood at the edge of the circle of men, an arm's length or a little more from the young sergeant.

"Adams—Wesley—what does being mad at the world get you? It gets you a bad reputation and a bloody nose. Look at you. It's eating you alive."

"You don't know. You'll never know." Adams stumbled. "It isn't fair."

"Life isn't fair. It's life. You've had a raw deal, no question. But you can't control what's happened. You can only control how you feel about it. That's tough to do all by yourself. Less tough when you realize God's on your side.

"What's it going to take to convince you of that? How many explosions? How many insults? How many years?"

Adams dropped his fists but otherwise remained motionless.

"You'll never know," he repeated. He turned his back to Jones. The onlookers parted, making a path for him from the center of the room to the door as he walked out in silence, eyes glazed and looking straight ahead.

As he left the room, the animated murmur of conversation filled the room. Jones, unhurt and seemingly unruffled, ambled back to his kitchen with half a dozen men streaming along behind him all talking at once. Goode had arrived breathless from elsewhere on the ship and listened as the other three chaplains explained what happened.

"You've spent the most time with that guy," Chaplain Goode said to Washington. "What gives?"

"He's a work in progress. Just like the rest of us."

"Well, maybe more work than progress."

★ ★ ★ ★

As the chaplains continued their conversation in the dining saloon, Lieutenant Burch leaned forward intently in his windowless listening post two decks above. There was an operator on duty with him, and the officer of the watch had just come in on his rounds. Burch suddenly clapped his palms tightly over his headphones, pressing them into his ears until the lobes grew red around the edges. His eyes flitted back and forth. He closed them.

"Could be company," Burch said softly. The only sound in the room was the footsteps of the watch officer going to inform the captain. Danielsen entered the room almost immediately.

"What do you hear, Lieutenant?"

In reply Burch flipped a switch activating the speaker in front of him. As soon as it hissed to life, the captain heard the ominous sound everyone in the room strained to hear every minute of every day. Boop . . . biing. Boop . . . biing. The sound got louder and more clear, the two tones almost on top of each other. Boop-biing. Boop-biing. The men exchanged glances.

Suddenly the sound stopped. It had grown steadily louder and now stopped without a trace.

"Lost him," Burch said tersely. "But there's a U-boat in the neighborhood."

"No alarm," Captain Danielsen said with a confidence born of years of making decisions under stress.

"This time we'll wait a little. No use letting the Jerries spook us. We all need our beauty rest. Wait for hard contact."

"Aye, aye, sir," Lieutenant Burch answered.

George Fox stood at the railing on the lee side of the *Dorchester*. The buttons on his overcoat were stretched tight over his life jacket. Staring out at the whitecaps, seeing other ships of the convoy off in the distance in the dreary afternoon, he pondered the strange feeling he had inside. He hadn't felt it since he was a soldier in France—like something was going to happen. It wasn't one definable feeling but tiny fragments of an infinite number of them jumping around inside him.

One feeling he could define was the pain in his back. Cold, wet weather always made it worse, and this was the coldest and wettest he had been since he could remember. But it hurt whether he was topside or below, so he figured he might as well have a little constitutional before he hit the sack.

In two days the convoy would heave into port at Blue West One, and a whole new chapter in the adventure would begin, with him and the other three chaplains doing everything possible, he thought, to keep a small city full of strangers from snapping under the strain like Adams had earlier in the day.

As he always did when he was alone, he thought about Wyatt and the marines. Boot camp was over now, and he wondered where his son was tonight. Wondered whether he was thinking about his old dad. Was the young Fox peering out into the mist at that moment thinking about him?

He wouldn't stay out much longer. Getting too cold. His thoughts drifted back to Adams. It was an absolute miracle everyone on the ship wasn't just like him. The good news was that the voyage would be over in a day or so. Meanwhile here they were: a huge Negro from Mississippi, a car dealer from Indianapolis, a troubled misfit from Illinois, two lady engineers from Denmark, chaplains from the four corners of the Judeo-Christian tradition. Either God had an amazing plan or one incredible sense of humor. But here they all were, because they believed in freedom, "one nation, indivisible, with liberty and justice for all." Guess that's worth getting seasick for.

Fox went below to the chaplains' stateroom to get ready for lights out. The other three were already there, going through their individual routines of reading, writing, praying, and winding down. With a grateful tug Fox unfastened his life jacket and took it off in order to undress, sat on the bed and pulled off his boots. Rabbi Goode was reading in bed; Chaplain Poling was writing a letter with a flashlight beside him, in case he wasn't finished by the time the others were ready to turn in.

Chaplain Washington had his back to the others and had just opened his drawer in the chest to replace his notebook when he let out an involuntary gasp of surprise.

The other three men looked at him, concerned. They saw him turn around slowly, grasping something in his fist, a puzzled look on his face. He lifted his hand, and held up a beautiful gold pocket watch dangling from a chain.

CHAPTER 18

PURSUING AND

PURSUED

Captain Karl-Jürgen Wächter looked up from his paperwork at the sound of a knock on his door. "Come in."

"We have reached the coordinates, Captain," a young officer reported.

"Very well. Thank you."

Wächter closed the folder he was reading from and followed his informer to the bridge on the U-223. He glanced around him, seeing much in a single sweep of the room. The crewmen around him moved quietly and efficiently about their tasks.

"Periscope depth," the captain ordered.

"Yes, sir."

When the sub had cruised up to the prescribed level, Captain Wächter ordered the periscope raised. In line with standard procedure, the snorkel was also deployed, rinsing out the fetid atmosphere the men had been breathing and rebreathing all day with a sudden refreshing burst of bracing sea air. Reflexively the men took in great sighs of it, quickening their moves and savoring the simple pleasure of feeling the sweat evaporate from their grease-smeared faces and clothes. The moment marked the end of another day of sitting in a hot, dark, cramped underwater metal tube laboring slowly through the depths, and the transformation of U-223 into a sleek, fast predator under cover of darkness.

"At least the Americans have fresh air all day," Wächter said aloud to no one in particular, unaware of the facts to the contrary. Through the periscope he watched each ship in the convoy in turn, their silhouettes just visible against the dull night sky. The ship in the center of the formation caught his attention as it had the day before.

"Any idea what they're carrying?" he asked a bridge officer beside him.

"Probably the same thing most of them do this time of year. Furnace oil and coal to keep those pasty-faced limeys from freezing. There's also a transport."

"I'm looking at it now. The one we shadowed last night. Not a deep-water ship, I would guess, though she rides fair from the look of her."

He continued watching the *Dorchester* through the spotting periscope. She wasn't too different from the steamers Wächter saw sailing up and down the Elbe and the Rhine and calling at continental or Scandinavian ports in the North Sea. She rode low in the water—fully loaded, perhaps, with soldiers.

The curious question about this convoy was where it was going. Leaving the Grand Banks, the ships' heading took them first more or less directly toward England, destination of virtually every eastbound vessel either alone or escorted. As they gradually turned more to port during the first day, they were on course for occupied Denmark or Norway. Now their course was even more northerly, toward Iceland or Greenland. The former, Wächter knew, was under British control and the latter under American, though both islands were legally Danish territory. Their names to the contrary, Iceland was surprisingly warm due to the Gulf Stream and dotted with fisheries and livestock farms, while Greenland was all but covered by a gigantic ice cap.

What lure could Greenland or Iceland have for these Allies? What was their mission? Kriegsmarine intelligence had nothing on them. Wächter took pride in the fact that neither the Americans nor the British had had any luck cracking the German Enigma code, even though the Nazis had deciphered American coded messages almost since the first months of the war. If something important was happening, the High Command would know about it and so would U-223.

The great question that remained in the balance was whether to use one of his precious torpedoes on the target before him. This coastal steamer was easy game. Sinking it would be a feather in his cap and a few hundred less reinforcements for Churchill. But so small a ship! The same torpedo would sink a twenty-thousand-ton tanker to far greater effect—and, since score was kept in tonnage, far greater accolades to the U-boat captain responsible.

"Increase speed to fourteen knots. Let's go in again for a closer look."

"Yes, sir."

Most passengers aboard the *Dorchester* were asleep when Lieutenant Burch stiffened again at the sound coming through his headphones.

Boop-biing. Boop-biing.

Captain Danielsen was informed, and within a minute he was in the room with Burch. The lieutenant switched the speaker on. The sound was unmistakable and stronger than ever.

"General quarters!" barked the captain.

Seconds later the klaxon screamed to life, jolting hundreds of sleeping soldiers and sailors from their bunks, propelling them up ladders and staircases as they yanked on overcoats and ran toward their battle stations.

With beads of sweat standing in two neat, glistening rows on his forehead, Lieutenant Burch listened to the speaker as a small audience of officers gathered around.

"Can you tell how far away it is? How big?" Captain Danielsen asked.

"No, sir. Just that it's out there."

The sound had a mesmerizing, hypnotic effect. Listeners in the room blocked out every other sensory message to focus every ounce of their attention on the sound projecting from the constant background hiss of the speaker.

Boop-biing. Boop-biing.

"Heading three-two-zero, sir. Straight at us."

Then the sound stopped as before, suddenly and without warning. Fifteen seconds passed. Thirty.

Then it was back, so loud it made the listeners flinch.

Boop-biing. Boop-biing. Two signals and then silence again. Thirty seconds passed. A minute. Two.

Lieutenant Burch looked up at the captain. "Gone, sir."

Two more minutes passed.

"Stand down!" Captain Danielsen ordered. "Double the lookout again. If there's anything out there I want to know about it."

"Aye, aye, sir."

Throughout the ship the order to stand down was met with a combination of relief and irritation. The companionways reverberated with comments from tired, tense, sleepy men roused to a fever pitch and scared half to death twice now in two days:

"This is making me nuts."

"Man, I gotta get out of here."

"Who's driving this bus anyway?"

"That's it for these pajamas."

Everyone was under orders to wear a life jacket day and night. A significant number had been caught by the klaxon without them. Out of sight in their own bunks, they thought they could disobey this most disagreeable order without anyone ever knowing. Yet when forced to race to their battle stations, 20 percent of the men either carried life jackets in their hands or had none at all. This second false alarm won even more soldiers over to the view that wearing a life jacket to bed on a rolling ship in eighty degree air below decks was ridiculous.

The four chaplains returned one by one to stateroom B–14. "We need to take some preemptive action," Chaplain Goode insisted. "Some of these men are near the end of their rope. The false alarms are almost worse than the real thing. All that pent-up energy has nowhere to go."

"Knowing there's something evil out there and we can't do a thing about it is a tough thing to deal with," Chaplain Poling declared. "This time tomorrow we'll be in Greenland. What time is it? Just past zero hundred hours? So it's already the third. Make that this afternoon. This afternoon the ride will be over, and we'll be part of a mission to keep this from happening to people who come after us."

"What do you say we have another little prayer service?" Goode suggested.

"Now, in the middle of the night?" Poling asked.

"Now's when we need it."

"I'm for it," Fox said. Washington quickly agreed. "Bet our attendance improves too."

Fifteen minutes later the dining hall was packed to overflowing with soldiers and sailors. As the chaplains began to speak, their audience listened so intently they didn't even notice Helge and Kristen enter quietly and take seats just inside the doorway.

Since the meeting was Goode's idea, the other chaplains insisted he start things off.

"Some of you I've met. Many more I haven't," the rabbi began. "Maybe I'm the first Jew some of you have ever seen. I see some things differently from you, believe some different things. But what matters right now is that we all stand together against the enemy. He's out there now, making our lives miserable—or trying to. We can't control whether he breaks our body; only God can do that. But we can control whether he breaks our spirit. And he can't do it if you won't let him.

"My relatives, and maybe even some of yours, have been enslaved by the Nazis. The mission we're on will bring the day their slavery will end closer. It's worth losing a little sleep when others have lost so much."

He glanced at Chaplain Poling, who took his cue. "I've got a little one at home and another on the way," Poling said. "There's not a minute I don't wonder what they're doing and how my wife is getting along on her own. God didn't mean for man to be alone. In fact, he himself made woman to keep us company. But here we are, alone and worried about loved ones—maybe a wife, or a mother, or a kid sister—making it on their own back in the States. My prayer is that you can trust the people you love to the only one who loves them more than you do: the God who created them. Whatever happens to us on this mission, whatever happens to your families, you can bet your last cent that God loves them. And loves you."

Fox spoke next. "This is my second war, and I don't like it any better than the first one. In spite of the stories I told around the dinner table about fighting in France, in spite of a back that hurts like the dickens on days like this, I've got a son about the same age as some of you who enlisted the same day I did. He heard all the bad stuff and went anyway. Because he—like every one of you in this room—feels there's something more important in all this than any one life. We can fight for freedom in the world only if we realize that to win, somebody—maybe the guy you're standing next to right now—will make the ultimate sacrifice. If you didn't believe that deep down, I don't think you'd be here on this mission. God bless you."

As Chaplain Fox finished his remarks, the piano was wheeled out of the storeroom and secured in place in the dining hall. Father Washington sat down on the piano bench.

"Some of you were surprised," he said, "to hear a Catholic chaplain playing hymns out of the Army and Navy *Song and Service Book* the other day. You may know that Catholic congregations don't sing much in church. We make the clergy do it by themselves. But music is one of the traditions that all our religions have in common. In this book"—here he held up the small black book—"there is music about *El–Shaddai,* God Almighty, from the Jewish tradition; words written by Saint Francis of Assisi, founder of a great Catholic order; and timeless lyrics by Charles Wesley, the "sweet singer" of Methodism.

"It's all here." He gestured with the book.

"And here." He made a sweeping gesture taking in the whole room.

"And here," Chaplain Poling added, pointing to the four chaplains in turn.

"And most of all, here," concluded Chaplain Goode, touching his hand to his life jacket over his heart.

Washington started playing an introduction. When he began the verse, the whole room joined in, their voices filled with strength and power. Those who didn't know the words hummed; those who couldn't sing mouthed the words. As their voices joined, so did their hearts. Captain Danielsen, the engineers, Morris Jones,

Hardaway, Shanahan, Nelson—even, all but unnoticed in a corner, Sergeant Adams.

The hymn served too as their closing prayer. As the last notes died away, the crowd dispersed quietly, reflectively, to bed, each of them with his own thoughts.

★ ★ ★ ★

Aboard U-223, Captain Wächter was two miles from the only troop transport in the convoy and closing slowly. To use a torpedo or not? He wondered how other U-boat captains had fared since he had been on patrol. Were they ahead of him this time out? He made a mental note to plot an average of tonnage sunk per torpedo used to improve his odds at a time like this.

Then he remembered something that had not up to now played a part in the decision. Admiral Dönitz, the commander of the U-boat force who had himself awarded Wächter a medal after his last Atlantic tour of duty, had just succeeded Admiral Räder as Grand Admiral—commander in chief of the entire German navy. Perhaps this war prize that beckoned would be a worthy honor to bestow on so great a leader to mark the occasion of his promotion. He could dedicate the kill to Dönitz, play up the timing, and catch the admiral's admiring eye even if the little ship ahead of him was a garbage scow.

Wächter ordered five torpedoes loaded and armed in five tubes.

He had surfaced enough to clear the conning tower shortly after sighting the convoy and had been on the surface for a while now. The submarine rolled easily in the swells. The rain and sleet stopped, and stars began to appear overhead. Wächter stood at the top of the conning tower ladder peering through binoculars, forearms resting on the hatch opening, catching sight of the ship in front of him as it bobbed in and out of his field of vision. The enemy evidently had detected nothing.

He climbed down the ladder. A crewman closed the hatch.

"Flood the active torpedo tubes," he ordered. Though he spoke calmly, there was a tinge of excitement in his voice that those who knew him recognized.

"Congratulations, Admiral," he said aloud softly, rehearsing his speech. "Allow me to pay my respects in honor of this glorious day for the Kriegsmarine, and for the Reich." Coolly he turned to his ordnance officer.

"Schiessen!"

CHAPTER 19

HELL ON ICE

S hortly after midnight the wind died down, and the stars shone through parting clouds. For lookouts aboard the *Dorchester,* the clearing weather was doubly welcome, first because it made the water surface easier to see, and second because it brought relief from the rain and sleet. The cold was still with them as always; now it would be intensified by the loss of insulating cloud cover. Every exterior surface—deck, railing, rigging, anchor chains, lifeboats, windows, bulkheads, everything except the funnel—was coated with a clear film of ice built up in thin layers first by the precipitation and then by the ocean spray. Not the white rime ice that could be knocked off with a boot heel; this was remarkably transparent and rock hard.

Normally the night lookouts had floodlights to help them, but mission orders prevented it now. They strained into the darkness with only binoculars, a sense of responsibility to the mission and their own fear of the unknown to serve them.

Captain Danielsen had posted four times the standard complement of lookouts for this last night of the voyage, so that there were four times the number of spotters at any given time, and each man still stood only half a watch in order to remain fresh. In less than eight hours the late-appearing midwinter sun would rise, and in four more after that the convoy would be secured dockside at Blue West One. Danielsen was not the kind of master of a vessel to take frivolous or unnecessary gambles—hence the order to wear life jackets around the clock—and since he had made it this far, he planned to do everything he could think of to make it the rest of the way.

An hour or so after midnight, two young seamen stood at the starboard rail on the bridge deck, within sight of two other lookouts, scanning the water and the horizon for any sign of icebergs or enemies. The icebergs, they decided, would be easy to spot, stark white as they were and the size of office buildings. The superstructure of a U-boat, black and about the size of a delivery truck, would be vastly harder; a periscope, smaller than a human silhouette, would be practically impossible, though both would leave telltale wakes an attentive and experienced lookout would recognize.

The two fought the cold and the lateness of the hour. They wrestled with boredom too, in spite of the importance of their assignment. In the cold, five minutes stretched on interminably; thirty minutes seemed like a lifetime. There was little room to move around, and the two men paced back and forth. Dressing as warmly as possible, they had donned insulated union suits under their uniforms and heavy overcoats on top, with life jackets buckled into place on the outside, which kept them warmer than putting the coat over the life preserver and not being able to button it up completely.

The lookouts kept a conversation going, though they spoke little because their faces were numb with the cold. It was more a mental exercise to help them stay awake and alert. Also it was a sharing of two men, strangers half a month ago, who were now embarked on a crucial top secret mission as brother warriors.

"This is plenty cold, all right," one of them was saying. "If we were on dry land, it wouldn't be too different from the farm back home."

"Where do you live," asked his companion, "the North Pole?"

"Minnesota. My family's got a dairy farm in Bimidiji. What about you?"

"We've got a farm, too, outside Tallahassee. Man! This is like living in the freezer at the icehouse."

"Not too cold there, I guess."

"Sometimes it gets down in the forties."

"Forties? That's swimming-hole weather."

"You're welcome to it. I'll take that good old Gulf breeze any day of the week."

"A little whiff of it right now wouldn't hurt, I guess."

There was silence as the two looked intently out toward the northeast. This was the way it was: bursts of short conversation, silence, then more talk, often about something completely different: Frank Sinatra rejected for military service with a perforated eardrum, the owner of the Cubs starting a women's baseball league, favorite foods, cars, girlfriends, what's going to happen after the war—anything except the army and the present moment.

The whitecaps on the wave crests made a regular pattern extending as far as the men could see, the foam tracing a ghostly undulating presence that reflected what starlight and moonlight there was. Eyes well accustomed to the dark, the men saw the sea clearly, the white foam peaks standing out in bold relief.

As one of the men looked, holding the binoculars to his eyes with thickly gloved hands, he saw the pattern of white on dark interrupted suddenly by an alien shape, very nearby—twin parallel white lines moving rapidly towards him. Once the lines caught his attention he tracked them for a second or two more, intuitively trying to place them relative to anything he had seen before.

It wasn't ice; it wasn't any sort of marine life he could recognize.

"Look!" He nudged his companion and pointed. "Straight out there, low in the water." The other lookout swung his binoculars around. "No, lower," he said, more urgently. The second man looked over his field glasses at the spot then held them back up to his face.

He saw the movement then and started to respond, but by the time words could form in his mouth, it didn't make any difference.

★ ★ ★ ★

Except for the lookouts and the crew members on duty, everyone else aboard the *Dorchester* was in his bunk. Captain Danielsen slept comfortably, having twice reinforced his lookout, and left his vessel under the command of a seasoned and trusted officer of the watch. There would be much to do later in the morning as the ship prepared for landfall and disembarkation, thus as many officers as possible were getting as much rest as they could.

Below decks about 870 men and two women slept—everybody who was not on the night watch—anticipating their arrival in Greenland and all the busyness that would fill the coming hours. Temporary quarters had been built onshore, as well as fabrication sheds and other basic facilities that would serve as headquarters while permanent structures were being designed and built, and while the airstrip was being reconfigured into a state-of-the-art military base with runways wide enough for formation takeoffs.

As they slept, the passengers aboard the *Dorchester* early that winter morning dreamed many different dreams. True, some were not dreaming, some who never dreamed. But many more traveled through their nocturnal subconscious to happy memories or the anticipation of things to come. From longing for long-absent wives to remembrances of favorite childhood toys, high school antics, practical jokes, spring flowers, spiritual fulfillment, a new house, a job after the war—such were the dreams of these souls making for Cape Farewell, now less than a hundred miles ahead of them through the Atlantic night.

BaarROOOM!

An ear-splitting sound ended the dreams abruptly as a rattling, concussive shudder ran through the ship from forepeak to fantail. In the hot, damp darkness of the cabins, men were thrown by the dozens from bunks and sent sprawling to the floor. In the confused state between wakefulness and sleep, some thought somehow the noise itself had catapulted them across the room. Night-lights in the corridors flickered and went out, adding the confusion of darkness to the disorientation of the moment.

Men called out in the black void, forming a sonic jumble of shouts, cries of pain, and the names of missing buddies. In no more than a minute, the rooms were permeated with the smell of smoke and fuel oil.

In the engine room amidships, six men were already dead, blown apart by a German torpedo that pierced the hull and exploded with horrible precision. Through the ragged opening the dark, frigid Atlantic came streaming.

Jolted awake, the four chaplains wrestled into their coats and boots and headed topside. They were some of the first on deck and took a few seconds to rearrange their clothes, unfastening their life jackets—which they slept in as ordered—rebuckling them over their top-coats, then putting on lined uniform gloves that were toasty warm but useless for doing any high-dexterity work.

The doorways and hatches began disgorging con-fused and disoriented soldiers. No one knew yet what had happened or what kind of danger the *Dorchester* was in. There was no sense of fear or panic, though people shouted apprehensively into the night, "What's happening?" "What's goin' on?" "What the . . . ?"

Seeing the chaplains grouped on deck, men instinctively came up to them. They were an island of steadiness and leadership in that first moment when something unexpected happens and the response sys-tem, though swift to act, is still taking shape.

"Chaplain, what's the story?"

"Hey Chaplain, you got the skinny on this?"

"Chaplain, what gives?"

"Don't know. We're trying to find out. We'll tell you as soon as we get the word."

The four chaplains worked their way up to the pilot-house against the tide of men heading for open deck.

Captain Danielsen was already there, working by flashlight, standing next to the helmsman. The *Dorchester* was still making slow headway, though the outlines of other ships on the horizon had disappeared. Forbidden to call for help on the radio or to send a distress flare, the *Dorchester* was going to have to make it the last few hours until landfall on her own.

"Well, see what you can find out," Captain Danielsen said into the intercom as the chaplains entered. He saw the four lieutenants and nodded, then spoke to the helmsman, though loudly enough for the chaplains to hear. "I can't raise anybody in the engine room. The chief engineer is in the gangway in front of the door. It's jammed, and there's no answer from the other side.

"He hears water."

It was clear to the chaplains there was no way they could help the captain for now, so they headed back toward the main deck. As they descended the dark stairs along with a throng of others, they noticed that only about half the men were wearing life jackets. A few more carried them in their hands, but many had none.

Chaplain Poling felt a pang of foreboding flash through him. He turned to the young corporal coming down the stairs beside him. "Where's your life jacket, soldier?"

The man patted his chest as though he thought he had it on; his eyes registered astonishment, then a memory, then mild panic. "I forgot I took it off, sir. It's inside. It was so hot inside when I hit the sack, I took it off.

Kept it in the bed right beside me, but I couldn't find it in the dark. I know we're supposed to be wearing . . ."

"Put one on. Now," Poling ordered.

"Yes, sir." The corporal obediently peeled off from the surge of men moving toward the main deck and went back inside by the nearest doorway.

On the main deck the ship's crew was organizing the men into groups in case they had to board the lifeboats. Other crewmen had opened big wooden storage lockers on the promenade deck and were handing out spare life jackets to some of the many men emerging without one.

There were many lifeboats and plenty of jackets. The *Dorchester* originally carried ten lifeboats; four more had been added when she started transporting troops, along with a variety of rafts and emergency floats—enough to carry more than twelve hundred passengers in all. There were also fourteen hundred life jackets on board—one for every passenger with almost five hundred to spare.

Chaplain Fox tapped the three soldiers closest to him. "Men, let's go back inside and bring out more life jackets. Everybody who needs one can't get downstairs at the same time. Let's save them the trouble."

Fox and his three volunteers clambered down the stairs, pressing themselves against the wall as a steady line of men still continued out. The chaplain had only one flashlight. He shined it around the staircase and gangway, then into staterooms and cabins. That there was a full supply of jackets was both good news and bad: there would be jackets for everybody, but an alarming number had left theirs behind. If the ship was not badly damaged, there would be time to hand them all out, but no one knew what shape the *Dorchester* was in.

The first thing most men thought when they were jolted awake was that they had been hit by a torpedo. They had heard nothing but rumors about U-boats and wolf packs and Torpedo Junction since they left Staten Island. Word that a torpedo was indeed the culprit made its way across the deck, now filled with people milling around, beginning to organize themselves around the lifeboats because they saw the crew members working on them. Other news circulated among the men: Aubrey Burch had been executed as a spy; the convoy flagship had seen the explosion and was coming back for everyone aboard the *Dorchester;* this was the diversionary tactic planned as part of the mission, and the ship would be sacrificed so that the others would make it safely.

The chaplains spread out along the starboard deck within sight of one another but far enough apart to allow a teeming huddle of men around them to ask questions and hear the facts. No, Lieutenant Burch wasn't dead and wasn't a spy; no, this was not part of the plan. Yes, the ship had been hit by a torpedo, but the extent of the damage was still not known.

Nearby, two crewmen faced an unexpected obstacle in preparing their lifeboat for launch. The rigging and pulley that held the boat in its davit were encased in a solid ball of ice. The men were winded, and their hands were numb from their vain effort to break the pulley free and lower the boat to the edge of the main deck for safe loading. They had tried knives, mallets, hammers, even a fire ax. The ax was best but still slow, painful, frustrating going.

An officer appeared below them and shouted their names. The two stopped their work and leaned over the boat gunwale. "Man the lifeboats and prepare to lower."

"Aye, aye, sir," they answered in tandem. "That is," one added to the other, "if we can get this bloody pulley working."

The *Dorchester* was now dead in the water. She had also begun to list noticeably to starboard. Word spread quickly that the lifeboats would be loaded. That put the number eight lifeboat crew in the spotlight, and suddenly all eyes were on them as they took turns, one holding a flashlight and the other pounding the ice-encrusted pulley.

"Hey," said one of the two, "we're never going to get through this thing. Cut the rope!"

"We can't do that!" the other replied. "We'll lose the whole boat. Even if we didn't, we couldn't hold it over the side while people got in. No way."

"I tell you we haven't got a snowball's chance. It won't do us any good stuck up here!"

As their frantic exchange continued, a lifeboat on the other side of the *Dorchester*, somewhat more protected in the lee of the weather, began creaking in its davits, swinging out and down toward loading position. A cheer went up from the men at the sight. Its crew positioned it expertly at deck level, and the men around it, some still without life jackets, climbed over the railing of the ship and into the boat.

Once it was fairly well loaded, it began creaking down toward the dark ocean. Its passengers looked back and forth from the others on deck to the water below. The closer they got to its surface, the more agitated it appeared. The seas were not extraordinarily high. Whether it was the cold, or the dark, or carelessness, or the motion of a wave that no one could have foreseen, the boat had no more than hit the water when a wave crashed across it, slamming it into the side of the *Dorchester*. The crew struggled to loose the ropes, while those at the oars tried to push off and row. One rope dropped, but the second got tangled, producing a pivot point for the boat as the waves whipped it around.

The boat shipped some water, then shipped some more. Two men stood on the gunwale to get at the twisted line. Both of them lost their footing as the boat jerked, falling in between the boat and the side of the vessel where, at the next wave, both were crushed. The lifeboat capsized, spilling men into the icy water. Two of those without life jackets struggled to strip the two dead men of theirs. Wet straps, wave action, and cold water made it impossible. As the two struggled, men on deck threw life rings to those in the water.

Some swam toward the ship and climbed up lines thrown to them.

The *Dorchester* rocked with a second explosion. This one sent billows of acrid fumes up the funnel and out several of the ventilation shafts. An engineer's mate standing by Chaplain Goode had an explanation. "There's still fire down there somewhere, and it's touched off the ammonia in the galley refrigeration system. Chemical reaction."

The fumes sent another wave of men out onto the deck. Chaplain Fox, busy passing out life jackets, called to one of the volunteers who had gone below with him to bring back abandoned jackets.

"Take this flashlight and get some guys to go below with you. Bring back another load of life jackets."

"Will do, Chaplain." The soldier took the flashlight and disappeared.

In the pilot house Captain Danielsen dismissed the helmsman, the navigation officers, ship's engineers, and Lieutenant Burch's signal officers. There was no reason for them to remain.

CHAPTER 20

NO GREATER LOVE

The *Dorchester*, listing heavily to starboard, began settling at the bow. Each time the forepart of the ship bobbed in the Atlantic swells, it rose a little less. The motion itself was imperceptible to the men on board, busy as they were with buckling on life jackets, pounding on frozen rigging, and making their way around the rolling deck in the dark.

Men from the foundered lifeboat who had been pulled from the water sat on the deck or leaned against the superstructure, wrapped in heavy wool blankets and shivering with shock and cold. The water was thirty-six degrees; anyone left behind would have about twenty minutes to live.

Watching the failure of the first lifeboat made the crew of the second more cautious. Having less ice to contend with, they had an easier time of it to begin with and drew incentive from the tragedy they had just seen.

The davits swung outward, and the knot of men who had been waiting beside them climbed aboard. When the boat was filled, the crew lowered it toward the water. Unable to judge their height above the surface, the sailors slipped the ropes and let the boat fall to the water with a jolting slap. The boat heeled hard over, shipped a little water, but then righted itself.

Men at the oars strained to take the boat safely away from the hull of the *Dorchester*. As soon as it was clear the boat was away, a cheer burst from the crowd watching at the rail. They waved at the lifeboat passengers, who excitedly returned the gesture. To any who stopped to considered it, it would seem ironic that passengers aboard a small wooden open boat would be relieved to be there instead of aboard a sturdy steel ship a nine-hour voyage from Greenland.

Watching the drama of the lifeboats as he worked, Chaplain Fox continued handing out life jackets from the storage locker to men who had gone to bed without them in violation of the captain's orders.

He shouted to one of the men who had gone below with him before. "Round up some men and go below for another load of jackets!"

The soldier nodded, collected a squad of men to accompany him, and disappeared through a doorway. Moving through the empty interior of the ship by flashlight, the group descended past the point where Fox and the others had scoured the area for jackets earlier. They made a turn on the landing and saw that the bottom of the staircase was under water. The water surface radiated cold like an open freezer. The men met the chill as they descended the stairs as far as they could. Looking at the water level on the doorway below them, they could see that it was already shoulder deep. Watching the level rise slowly up the step below them, they discussed what they should do.

"How about we wade down there and keep looking?" wondered one of them aloud.

"We don't know how far we are from any more jackets," said a second. "By the time we get back here, the water could be too high to get through the hallway."

"We'll get soaked for nothing," warned a third.

Six jackets came floating out from the doorway. The men scooped them up and returned topside.

Chaplain Fox saw the men emerge. "How'd you do?" he shouted, noticing they carried only half a dozen jackets in all.

"Water's coming up inside, Chaplain," one of them answered. "This was the best we could do."

"Hand them out, then. That's six more men with jackets."

In the lifeboat with frozen pulleys, the two men at work on the davit mechanism exchanged heated words. At last they swung the boat over the rail, but the ropes and tackle holding it in the davits were frozen, unmovable as the steel plating of the *Dorchester*'s hull. One of the men pounded his fist in disgust and climbed out of the boat. The remaining man pulled a sheath knife from the survival kit on the lifeboat and started sawing at the ropes. His plan, dismissed as insane by the departing sailor, was to cut nearly through the ropes at each end of the boat, then fill it with passengers until the ropes broke simultaneously, dropping the boat to the sea.

He cut the ropes to the point he had in mind, then motioned the men standing around the boat—men who had watched the whole argument play out—to get aboard. The group hesitated, and in that moment there was a popping sound as one of the cut ropes broke and the stern of the boat dropped, dumping the sailor into the water. The boat hung briefly suspended in the air like a giant minnow, then the bow rope gave way, sending the lifeboat vertically into the water. The sailor disappeared beneath the shape of the boat; then the boat bobbed vertically like a cork before pitching over, hull up, and rolling over slowly, filling with water as it went.

Inside a doorway a first aid station was set up for the men who had been fished from the water and for others who had been injured below by the blast, or by their scramble to get topside in the dark. Father Washington was one of the officers organizing the treatment, arranging supply soldiers brought up from other parts of the ship, talking to the injured.

One young soldier lay wrapped in a blanket on a cot, his hair matted with seawater. He was in the first lifeboat to be launched and had pulled himself up a line onto the deck even though both his legs were a dangling, broken mass.

"You're doing well, soldier, doing all right," Washington said briskly. "We're going to get you warmed up here in a minute."

"Chaplain," the soldier asked weakly, "are we going to get out of this?"

"We'll get out of it one way or another, guaranteed," Washington answered with a smile that brought a smile in return.

"You know what I mean, Chaplain," the soldier said with more animation.

"And you know what I mean. We pray to God, and God does what he will."

"Chaplain, could you say a prayer for us here?"

"That's my specialty," Washington replied. Other injured men within earshot turned to listen as he began praying aloud in a firm, confident voice.

"Holy Father, we come before you in crisis. We are driven down by our enemies and look to you as David looked when his enemies threatened to destroy him. We are powerless to save ourselves and pray that you will bless and preserve us. In the name of the Father, the Son, and the Holy Ghost, Amen."

As Chaplain Washington prayed, Chaplain Goode stood in a lifeboat hung between its davits on the other side of the ship. As a man exhausted himself in pounding at the ice-laden pulleys, another came up to take his place. Goode was heaving a wooden mallet at the frozen mass—not the most efficient tool but the best they could find. Pouring all his athletic conditioning into the task, he succeeded in blasting apart the ball of ice that trapped the mechanism in front of him. A cheer rose up from those watching, and Goode stepped aside to let sailors continue the task of lowering the boat.

The boat was swung out and lowered to deck level. As men began to board, one of the sailors shouted, "Hop aboard, Chaplain."

"Thanks, but I'll wait a little," Rabbi Goode answered. "Got a lot to do. Lots of ice to pound." The soldier had no gloves, and the chaplain noticed his hands, red and raw from his exertions against the pulleys. He was trying to protect them under the armpits of his overcoat; its pockets were blocked by his life jacket.

Goode stripped off his gloves and held them out. "Here. You look like you need these."

The man looked at the gloves. His eyes widened. "For me? Thanks, Chaplain, you're a lifesaver!" He grabbed them eagerly and put them on.

"I wouldn't go quite that far yet, Soldier, but I think you can use them. I'll find another pair."

The soldier waved to Chaplain Goode as the boat filled with men and then inched toward the ocean. The keel met the surface, and the boat settled gently on the water. Once again cheers rang out in the dark Atlantic night as another few men rowed away to safety.

The bow of the *Dorchester* was riding low in the water now, sinking imperceptibly with every wave, and the hundreds of men on deck began a gradual, almost unconscious migration toward the stern of the ship. Chaplain Poling stood on the listing rear deck, leaning to keep his balance. He answered questions as fast as he could and soothed nerves here and there that were beginning to fray. Scanning the faces peering out from heavy coats, he recognized the two Danish engineers almost frozen and holding on to the rail, and walked quickly over to greet them.

"Hello, ladies," he touched the brim of his cap with a gloved hand. "Glad to see you made it up safely."

"Thank you, Chaplain," Helge answered, her teeth chattering. "It doesn't look good, does it?"

"I haven't seen the captain. Obviously we're not going anywhere in this ship, but the crew is launching lifeboats as fast as they can."

"You forget we're engineers," Helge said with an inclusive gesture at Kristen. "It doesn't take a marine architect to know we'll all be underwater in a very few minutes. The mass of the ship, the rate we're sinking—it won't take long."

It was the first time the chaplain had heard anybody say the word *sinking,* and the sound of it startled him. Recovering quickly, he said, "I have no idea whether you're right or wrong about that, but it looks like we have room in the lifeboats—and plenty of life jackets if we can just collect them. I see you two are all fitted out." The two had life jackets buckled on outside their overcoats. "If you'll stay close by, I'll get you in one of these lifeboats when they're ready to launch." He pointed at the two boats they could see—in rearmost positions on both starboard and port sides—where crewmen struggled to complete their work.

Three lifeboats had been destroyed by the torpedo explosion, and two more were lost so far in an effort to launch them. That left nine, plus the rafts and floats.

Toward the bow, out of Chaplain Poling's view, another lifeboat was freed and its davits rotated into position. But as the boat began its descent to deck level, the ropes became tangled, suspending it three feet above the deck at a crazy angle.

Crewmen attacked the ropes again, but the weight of the boat made it impossible to get any slack in order to work the knots loose. The lifeboat moved back and forth with the motion of the waves, tantalizing and useless.

Chaplain Fox handed out the last life jacket in the storage locker. He looked up at the next man in the line that had formed and held up two empty hands. It was Sergeant Wesley Adams.

"No more?" he asked, eyes wide.

"We'll have to go around to the locker on the other side," Fox answered. Word passed among the others who waited that the supply of jackets was gone. The buzz of the men grew suddenly louder and more agitated. Some of them shouted in anger. Some swore. Others began to cry.

Fox saw their reaction, closed the empty locker, and stood on top of it. "Men, this is not the time to lash out in anger or to give up. This is the time to stay strong, hold on to your faith, and help one another. There are more jacket lockers. There are more lifeboats. The Lord has given us tools. Let us make the most of them."

The words were simple, but they had a pronounced effect in calming the men. Fox then led them around the stern of the ship toward the other side. On the rear deck the chaplain noticed Chaplain Poling standing near the Danish women. He approached him but was intercepted by an army lieutenant who had come from the other side of the ship.

"Chaplain, we've handed out all the life jackets in the portside lockers. Are there any more starboard?"

"We've handed out all ours too," Fox answered. "We were just coming around to see if there were some left on your side."

"All gone, I'm afraid. We've salvaged a few from the water, and retrieved some that floated up. Those idiots who left theirs below!"

Fox replied, "Idiots or not, those men need help, and it's up to you and me to figure out how to help them."

Adams, overhearing the chaplain say the life jackets were gone, burst into a wild fit of anger. At that moment Rabbi Goode and Father Washington rounded the superstructure on their way astern. Both had done their best—Goode against the ice and Washington for the injured men—and had come to where the greatest concentration of people was to see how they could help.

Noticing Adams, Washington rushed up to him immediately. "Adams—get a grip! You're not helping yourself or anybody else acting like that, and you know it!"

"The life jackets are gone!" Adams exclaimed. "I'm going to die!"

"You'll die when God says so and not a minute before," Washington admonished. "It's out of your hands."

"I'm going to die!"

"Nothing, Wesley, is beyond the power of God. Not even saving you from yourself—again."

"What do you mean?"

"All your life you've run from yourself, from your decisions, from your responsibilities. Stop running, Wesley. There's nowhere else to go. There never has been."

Adams fell silent and watched as Chaplain Washington turned to speak to another man.

The *Dorchester* continued to settle so that the fore-peak was now completely underwater. The stern became more crowded as men moved away from the surface of the water that crept slowly from the front of the vessel. Some were starting to jump into the water, hoping to catch a raft later; some waited, straddling the deck rail in an effort to maintain their balance. Others hurled themselves overboard out of panic or the feeling that all was lost. The lower she rode in the water, the more the *Dorchester* rolled with the action of the waves. No more lifeboats were launchable because their rigging was hopelessly frozen or they were rendered useless by snarled lines and disabled machinery or they had been smashed when the *Dorchester* listed heavily. The rest of the men—and the two engineers—were on their own.

Standing at the rail, Morris Jones surveyed the scene before him. Men were packed shoulder to shoulder on the afterdeck, continuing to inch toward the back of the ship away from the rising water. In his overcoat and life jacket, Morris appeared even more huge than usual, the extra bulk somehow making him proportionally larger than others dressed in the same protective gear. As Jones watched, men grabbed some of the dozen or so wooden life rafts stowed throughout the upper decks and tossed them to the desperate swimmers who were jumping overboard.

The black cook felt another life jacket bump against his. Turning, he found himself facing Private Sam Nelson, his face ashen between the upturned collars of his coat.

"We're going to die, Jones. You know that," he rasped.

"I don't know any such thing," Jones replied calmly. "And you don't either. Only one man knows that time for us all, and he ain't telling. We got our life jackets; we still got hope. You have hope as long as you want it. Nobody can take it away from you; you can only give it up. I'm not giving mine up. Don't you give up yours."

Open-mouthed, Nelson looked at the huge black figure then gestured toward the scene in front of them. "You think anybody's going to live through this? You're out of your mind!"

"I can't argue with you there," Jones said.

On the other side of the deck, Sergeant Adams was one of two hundred or more men still without life jackets. As word of the situation spread, those passengers took the news in as many different ways as there were people to hear it. Some resigned themselves to it in silence, eyes downcast. There were those who renewed their search for jackets, cursing their careless disobedience as they scoured toolboxes, medical kits, chain lockers, and other unlikely places in a desperate quest. More men jumped into the water and swam toward two wooden life rafts that bobbed barely visible in the dark nearby, though none of them made it: from the deck the rafts appeared deceptively close, the waves deceptively calm.

In the ever-tightening mass of men on deck, Adams caught a glimpse of Chaplain Washington praying with a knot of soldiers. They were circled together hands over shoulders like a football huddle. Within a few feet of him, the other three chaplains stood surrounded by groups of their own, praying, consoling, reassuring.

Adams stood beside Washington until he raised his head at the end of the prayer. When their eyes met, Washington moved through the crowd to him.

"I was wondering where you were."

"This is it, Chaplain!" Adams replied, almost frantic. "We're dead as doornails. What a pointless life it's all been."

"You're the last person on this ship I'd expect to say that."

For a moment Adams was so surprised he forgot to be angry and afraid. "What do you mean?"

"I've seen the Wesley Adams behind the tough-guy act." The two stood on the crowded, rolling deck of a sinking ship in the dead of a North Atlantic winter night. Yet for the way the chaplain spoke, they could have been sitting in a coffee shop back in Adams's Springfield neighborhood.

"You've got a direction in your life because you want to change. You want to put your anger and disappointment in the past and follow God into the future. I feel that. I know you feel it."

"Right now I feel like a failure. This is what I deserve, I guess. God gets the last laugh."

"You stole my pocket watch."

"I don't know what you're talking about."

"You stole it and then gave it back. Why?"

Adams was stunned with surprise, then spoke. "Because I hated you at first. You made me hate myself—thinking about the long-gone past, dredging up all the bitterness. Then I realized you were right. Boom! In a few minutes it won't matter anyway."

"Everything in this world matters, Wesley. You and I can't always see it, but right now in the middle of all this, everything we do matters. Not a sparrow falls apart from God's awareness and purpose."

Chaplains Poling, Goode, and Fox had worked their way through the crush to Washington, and the four stood together on the fantail. As it settled further in the water, the dry area astern got progressively smaller, forcing men into an ever-shrinking island of listing decking. An urgent swarm stream of men, some with jackets and others without, now dived and jumped into the water to make for the lifeboats or climb onto any of the floating debris that radiated out from where the *Dorchester* lay—tables, civilian suitcases, lockers, and other items that floated up the staircases from below decks and out onto the sea.

It was the first time since being jolted awake in stateroom B-14 that the chaplains could talk together. Emerging on deck—only fifteen minutes earlier, though it hardly seemed it could have been that recently—they had immediately fanned out to serve in separate capacities; only now were they finally reunited, the group of four separated a little from the throng as though even in this desperate moment there was a special deference and respect toward them.

"I found the Captain," Chaplain Poling told the others. "He thinks a rescue ship will come out from Blue West One, but it won't leave for here before the rest of the convoy arrives. There are also some other ships that could come after us, if they get the word soon enough."

Chaplain Fox looked down the port side of the *Dorchester* at the lifeboats still on board. "God's will be done," he said to himself in a voice so soft the other chaplains didn't hear. "God's will be done."

"I know all of you have been praying with the men and for them," Rabbi Goode said to the other chaplains. "I expect there are a lot of people on this ship who would give anything they ever had for a little peace right now. Let's pray for them."

The four stood in a circle. As they sensed what was happening, the men immediately around them fell silent. The ones near them quieted in turn, and in that way silence radiated out from the four chaplains like a blanket of comfort, even though in the darkness and wind, against the sound of the foundering ship, hardly anyone could hear them. Chaplain Goode's first words would have surprised some of them.

"God, we give thanks and praise to you," he began. "You hold the ocean in the palm of your hand. You hold our lives, our futures, our legacies. Give us the faith to worship you always with joy in our hearts."

The breeze freshened, and as the chaplains prayed, the swells grew higher. Men near the railings held on to keep their footing. Those without anything to grab onto jostled against one another, reaching out for support and at the same time steadying the passengers next to them.

The chaplains turned their attention once more to the men, now packed tightly on the remaining afterdeck, some actually standing on the side of the ship, which was listing farther to starboard every minute. More had jumped into the water; those halfway to the bow could push off from the deck or simply wade in. Sergeant Patterson was in the water, and Ketchum, and Greene, and Shanahan, and hundreds more by now. The reaction was the same for everyone: an intense piercing pain as the freezing water penetrated their clothing, transforming warm boots and trousers into sodden ice packs. That in turn was followed by numbness and immobility. Swimming was all but impossible with the added weight of the water-soaked wool. Life jackets were buoyant enough to support the weight of a man and his clothes. Those without them quickly became exhausted from treading water and sank, drowning before they could freeze to death.

Wesley Adams looked around him in a daze. *What reason could God possibly have for all this?* he thought. *There's nothing divine about it. Insanity, pure and simple.*

God, where are you?

Chaplain Washington saw Adams leaning stonefaced against the railing. He nudged him back to awareness. "Adams."

At the sound of his name, the sergeant turned to look at the chaplain. In one selfless move Washington grabbed hold of his own life jacket, pulled it over his head, and held it out to Adams.

"Put this on. You'll need it."

A life jacket.

Adams's eyes widened in excitement mingled with disbelief.

"What in heaven's name . . . ?" he began in a stage whisper.

The sergeant eyed the jacket like a poisonous snake. Desperate and mad with fear as he had been, he could not make his arm reach for it.

"Take it." Washington thrust it at him.

"How can I?" Adams protested weakly. "Why would you do this? Are you tired of living or something?"

"Maybe it's time to move on to a more comfortable climate," Washington answered evenly. "This jacket's not mine. It's yours."

"Who says so?"

"Take it. You've got work to do."

"This is no time for riddles!"

"Amen to that."

Washington gazed directly into Adams's eyes, then turned away toward the other chaplains. He saw Chaplain Poling, life jacket in his hands, in an animated debate with a young sailor. The man was sobbing almost uncontrollably, to the point where Poling could barely make out what he was saying.

"You can't do this! You can't do this!" the soldier screamed over and over as his hands reached for the jacket and began buckling it on.

"I can't not do it," Poling said in reply.

Chaplain Fox lifted his jacket over his head and, without warning, slipped it from behind over the head of the first person he saw jacketless. The tall gangly figure turned to reveal the face of Private Sam Nelson.

In a heartbeat the private understood what had happened. "Chaplain, this means you're going to die."

"We're all going to die, son," Fox answered. "For some of us it's not such a terrible thought that it might be sooner and not later."

At the edge of the circle, Alex Goode was also without his jacket. He was placing it over the head and around the chest of one Fred Baxter, former Indianapolis car dealer, who had accepted it in silence along with the chaplain's one-word message:

"Shalom."

As the chaplains looked around the circle at one another, the same thought passed from one to the next: *We didn't plan this, didn't talk about it in advance. Yet here we are, all giving up our life jackets to others. Giving them up not grudgingly but willingly, thankful for the chance to sacrifice in the service of an all-knowing, all-loving God.*

All together in this terrible war, undivided.

Without their bulky jackets the four lieutenants found it much easier to move around. Remaining in sight of one another, they turned to helping others with newfound energy.

CHAPTER 21

THE UNBROKEN
CIRCLE

Twenty minutes after the *Dorchester* was hit, she was more than halfway submerged and slipping rapidly. Anyone who stopped to watch would see the water level rising up the deck along the sides of the ship toward the stern. The trough of each wave retreated less toward the bow; as the vessel took on more water, the weight pulled her down more rapidly, shipping water faster and hastening the descent even more.

The water surface around her teemed with men bobbing on the waves. The air rang with shouts of pain, anger, fear, frustration, and resignation. Swimmers paddling on their own generated a flurry of activity as they flailed desperately for a few minutes before sinking under the weight of their wet clothes. Some frantically peeled out of their clothing, trading direct exposure to the arctic air for the hope of staying afloat a little longer; a little longer until what, they had no idea. They were reduced to thinking about survival from one second to the next. Nothing more.

A short distance from the ship, one of the wooden rafts floated aimlessly with twenty-five barely alive frozen men piled on top of the boards.

Other passengers, buoyed by life jackets—either they had been wearing them as ordered or grabbed them on the way out—floated in relative calm. The water-activated signal lights extended above each man at the shoulder, faithfully blinking red in the dark, their beams reflected on the ocean surface. Occasionally a jacket floated by, after working its way out from inside the ship, and was snapped up by one of the weary men treading water. Bodies floated by, too, and had their jackets removed awkwardly by hands grown clumsy with cold.

Thick, greasy fuel oil floated on the surface in intermittent patches, coating men who drifted into it, caking in their hair and clothes. Small pools of it here and there were on fire, ignited by the impact of the torpedo. Their sputtering light flickered on the faces of men nearby, casting garish, jumping shadows.

Many men had seen the chaplains give up their life jackets. Partly in reply, passengers in the few lifeboats removed their own and threw them to men in the water. Some of the men wearing jackets swam to the boats and hung onto the gunwales with one or two hands. Those in the boats pulled aboard everyone strong enough to make it to them and hold on long enough to be hauled in.

Hundreds of signal lights formed undulating constellations on the waves. Some were alone, marking men who preferred to be left alone with their thoughts, or who were already frozen to death. Many more formed groups of between two or three and a dozen or so— friends who had found one another, encouragers and those needing encouragement, the injured and those willing to jeopardize their own chance for survival by helping them.

By now half the passengers who boarded the *Dorchester* on Staten Island were out of their misery, drowned, frozen, killed by the explosion, or lost in a failed lifeboat launch. Little more than half the remainder were aboard the lifeboats, scarcely able to believe their good fortune. Some, miraculously, were still alive in the water. The rest stood on the port side of the hull or the aft end of the promenade deck of the *Dorchester,* now the only parts of the ship remaining above water.

As each wave crest lapped higher up the deck, more people, soaked to the knees anyway by the wicking action of the water, walked forward off the deck and added another bobbing light to the mass that encircled them. The noise of voices grew softer as one by one they became fewer in number.

Burch had been ordered into a lifeboat to man an oar. He was wiry and strong and now returned his attention to his work at the oarlock, even as he was plotting his revenge against the Kriegsmarine. With three others who propelled the boat and one at the tiller, he maneuvered around bodies and floating debris to pick up men in the water. The oarsmen pulled alongside a man or a small group, steadied the boat—holding her position while others grabbed at outstretched hands, clothing, or whatever else they could—then hoisted half-frozen figures into the bottom of the boat, where they sat too numb and tired to move.

"I don't guess they figure I'm a spy now," Burch said to himself. A muffled laugh escaped his lips blue with the cold. Here he was blistering his hands (he bet they were blistered—he couldn't feel them) to gather up survivors and haul away from this tub before she sank and pulled them all down with the wreckage.

Some of the men Burch didn't recognize, either because he didn't know them or because he couldn't place them in the dark, their faces contorted with exhaustion and the horror of the experience. One he did know was Wesley Adams, hauled over the gunwale like a giant codfish.

"Great," Burch said under his breath. "Just what we need. A malcontent troublemaker." But as Sergeant Adams struggled into a sitting position in the bottom of the boat, Lieutenant Burch looked into his eyes.

They were not the eyes of a malcontent troublemaker.

Even in the dark, in the bottom of a lifeboat full of desperate men floating among a sea of dying ones, there was no doubt Wesley Adams of Springfield, Illinois, was different from before. Not that anybody who saw him that night consciously paid any attention. It was a change they sensed rather than observed, strong enough to invade their subconscious even as they were fighting for the next hour—the next five minutes—of life.

Adams was completely unaware of his surroundings. He didn't speak or acknowledge others speaking to him. He didn't seem to care that now he was relatively safe and dry in a lifeboat rather than condemned to certain death in an ocean four degrees warmer than ice. All he could think about was the fact that Chaplain Washington gave up his life jacket for him, sacrificing his life for Adams's. The scene replayed itself over and over in his mind.

He thought about Chaplain Poling and Chaplain Fox. Those men had families. They hadn't seen their lives ruined like his had been. And what about Chaplain Goode? The son of a rabbi. That was something to be proud of. Now there would never be a little Alex to carry his legacy forward. Adams had been proud of things in his life once; he could almost remember what it felt like.

How could a man of God be sacrificed—make a conscious decision to sacrifice himself—and a bitter, sinful man like Adams be saved? They deserved to live, and he deserved to die. But what was going on here? Adams's life seemed a disaster to him, one misery and sin and failure following another. Yet here he was alive when so many people he knew were better than he was were dead already or would be soon.

A light caught his attention. He shook his head in short rapid strokes to clear it, then looked around him. The water was on fire. With the four oarsmen pulling for all they were worth, the lifeboat knifed through the fire and away from the spilled oil. Looking back, the men inside could see the low curtain close behind them as they rowed into clear water.

In the eerie light of the flames, Sergeant Adams could recognize some of the men still on the ship. New figures arrived, climbing down from the pilothouse and joining others on the promenade deck: Morris Jones, Sam Nelson, and others, all remarkably calm. They seemed to have a sense of peace that was completely out of place as they looked back out toward him across the water.

The ship was settling faster than ever. Adams could actually see it moving. The keel of the badly listing hull was now exposed. The chaplains and the rest of the men struggled to keep their balance, eventually edging all the way around to the port side hull and standing there, which by now was more horizontal than the deck. Among the sounds of groaning and flexing steel of the ship, the fading cries of the few men still alive in the water, and the wind and waves, he heard something else. Above the din, four strong, confident voices stood out. He caught only a stray word or two at a time at first, but soon he was amazed at how clearly the voices carried across the water.

It was the four chaplains praying, lifting up their separate prayers all at the same time, interweaving their traditions and faith messages.

Goode was saying a Hebrew prayer: "En kelohenu, En kadonenu, En k'malkenu, En k'moshienu . . ."

At the same moment, Fox offered the Twenty-third Psalm: "The Lord is my shepherd, I shall not want . . ."

Washington was praying: "My God, I am sorry for my sins with all my heart . . ."

Chaplain Poling prayed the Lord's Prayer: "Our Father, who art in heaven, hallowed be thy name . . ."

As each man finished, the hearty sound they made together got gradually softer and faded away. Adams wondered what they were thinking, the four of them there, having lived upright lives—certainly a lot more upright than his, he had no doubt—and done everything right, and dedicated their lives and careers to serving God. And now there they were, bound to die as war casualties. And here he was, alive at least for the time being, with a chance of surviving.

All four of them had given up their lives for people like him. He had a life jacket but hadn't worn it. That was his choice, and in a fair world he should be paying for his own mistake. Paying with his life. But John Washington had stepped in and taken his place. Washington was dying that he, the least worthy, might live.

Why? For what?

And then a thought hit him: a memory buried deep inside, all but lost, came rocketing into the present. He couldn't remember where he'd heard it at first, but then the curtain of the past dropped away, and he recalled the simple double funeral when the two people he loved most in the world were buried. Madeline, and their beautiful daughter, Margaret.

"The Lord giveth, and the Lord taketh away."

As he sat in the floor of the lifeboat, rolling with the easy motion of the waves, with death scattered all around him, he saw life in a way he had never seen it before. Life was a gift from God. He numbers all our days. He calls us to do his will. He had called these chaplains to give up their lives for others, and they had done it sacrificially. Not because they were brave or foolhardy. But because they were obedient to God.

His thoughts were interrupted once again by an unexpected sound.

Music. The chaplains were singing.

> *Eternal Father, strong to save,*
> *Whose arm hath bound the restless*
> *wave, . . .*

They had formed a circle standing on the hull, bracing one another on the slippery surface, arms locked tightly together, singing at the top of their lungs. The music was clear and confident. The cries and noise around the lifeboat seemed to fade away until all he could hear was the music: four stouthearted voices raised in a song of triumph.

> *Who bids the mighty ocean deep*
> *Its own appointed limits keep. . . .*

The singing continued undiminished as the seawater lapped over the tops of their shoes.

> *O hear us when we cry to thee*
> *For those in peril on the sea.*

Adams watched mesmerized as the water rose up on their bodies, to their waists, and then to their shoulders. The men unlocked their arms and joined hands, Chaplain Goode's bare hands contrasting with the others in gloves. As one, the four raised their joined hands above their heads.

Soon, only the hands, still clasped in a circle, were visible in the flickering light of oil fires and flashlights. And then they were gone.

CHAPTER 22

OUT OF THE
DEPTHS

The last ripples and eddies marking the
Dorchester's position disappeared, and the sea
was quiet again. Three lifeboats bobbed
within sight of one another on the water. Designed
for forty-eight men each, one of them carried more
than sixty men, another over a hundred. The wooden
rafts supported most of the remaining survivors.
Sergeant Adams's boat was scarcely half full. It had been
swept into the water as Lieutenant Burch and the rest of
the boat crew struggled to launch it while the ship was
listing. There was no way they could have gone back for
anyone then, so now they rowed slowly through the
water looking for survivors.

Adams had been the third man they pulled alive out
of the water. A few minutes later they found a fourth.

Or rather a fourth found them. Without warning a stark white hand appeared, grasping the gunwale. Men seated the closest to it looked over the side and saw Sergeant Mike Patterson in the water, staring back at them wordlessly. Four men in the boat got up on their knees, leaned far over the rail, and hauled him aboard. He rolled onto the bottom of the boat beside Adams and lay there, his breath coming in short, quick gasps.

Thirty minutes went by, and then an hour. The dark blanket of the ocean was still studded with the blinking indicator lights on hundreds of life jackets. Some of them were empty, washed out of the inside of the ship too late to help anyone. Many more of them buoyed a lifeless body, its face frozen and white.

Anyone looking closely could have identified the bodies of Cal Foster, Michael Shanahan, Fred Baxter, Dereck Hardaway—friends, some of them husbands and fathers, all called that night to give their lives for their country and to give an accounting to their Creator. Two hours ago they were asleep in their bunks, dreaming of landfall the next day at Blue West One, ready to begin the secret project that would help sweep the Atlantic of murderous wolf packs. Now, for them, the battle was over.

Debris from the ship was scattered across the water. Sitting up in the bottom of his lifeboat, Sergeant Adams looked out at the blinking lights, the bodies, the odd table or kitchen pot floating by, and the other lifeboats in the distance. The other boats did not appear to be moving toward them, nor did Lieutenant Burch try to hail the men aboard. They were too exhausted to care about anything but surviving until daylight.

The one sight that registered with survivors above the rest was how many empty rafts and life rings there were. In the last frantic moments aboard the *Dorchester,* dozens of them had been tossed into the water by men who hoped to dive in and swim to them. Perhaps a few of those men were in one of the lifeboats now. The rest were floating lifeless on the surface or drifting slowly to the bottom of the Atlantic.

Sergeant Patterson's breath came now in short ragged bursts. Adams could feel him next to him in the bottom of the boat, shaking as he struggled to inhale once more, and another time after that. Then there were no more, and Patterson lay still.

"He's dead," one of the men said.

"What do we do now?" someone else asked after a moment.

"Wait 'til we're picked up. We can bury him at sea then."

Picked up. Adams heard the words. Maybe he would be picked up before he died of exposure and hunger and thirst. There were a first aid kit and emergency rations on board, enough hardtack and drinking water to last several days, and surely the convoy would come back for them before then. That was assuming the rest of the convoy made it to Greenland. Or maybe a ship from Cape Farewell would come out with a rescue party.

These thoughts rolled around dully in Sergeant Adams's head. He thought somewhat about the empty rafts on the water, and the prospect of rescue, and the dead man lying beside him, rocking gently with the motion of the boat. But most of all he thought about the life jacket around his chest. He thought about the look in Chaplain Washington's eyes when he gave it to him. There was nothing in it of fear or defeat or panic. It was a knowing look of contentment and success and peace. Adams had heard about sacrifice all his life. He had heard about bravery. And he thought he knew what sacrifice and bravery were. But he hadn't known until he looked into John Washington's eyes and saw them there.

Again and again his mind replayed the scene he watched from the lifeboat moments after Lieutenant Burch and the others had hauled him in.

> *Eternal Father, strong to save,*
> *Whose arm hath bound the restless*
> *wave, . . .*

The image was seared into his brain: Four chaplains standing on the aft end of the hull near the promenade deck, to the side of the dance floor where couples had once swayed to the sound of an orchestra under tropical stars. There they were in a tight circle, constantly adjusting their footing as the icy hull rolled in the swells, arms locked together, singing confidently. From somewhere deep in the recesses of his subconscious, Adams dredged up a memory of a lesson he heard—whether in the classroom or long ago in a sermon, he couldn't remember—about French Christians being burned at the stake centuries ago. They sang as the fires burned, martyr after martyr, day after day, until the authorities built a stage and had an orchestra play during the executions so the crowds couldn't hear the words to the hymns.

> *Who bids the mighty ocean deep*
> *Its own appointed limits keep. . . .*

The power of the image was almost overwhelming. It was like they had given the gift of life to him and three other passengers, and instead of losing their own lives in the bargain, they somehow gained from it. They sacrificed their lives for something better.

Corporal Tommy Simmons tapped Lieutenant Burch on the shoulder.

"What's with Adams?" he asked.

Burch glanced over and saw the sergeant looking at the seascape. Adams hadn't said a word since he entered the lifeboat and up until now appeared only dazed and shocked like so many of the rest of the men. But now there was a difference. He no longer gazed out into the night with a vacant stare. He looked carefully and attentively, his eyes bright and alert, though he remained unmoving, wrapped in sodden clothes now frozen stiff in the arctic night air.

"Sergeant Adams?" Lieutenant Burch said gingerly.

There was no response from the sergeant.

"Sergeant Adams?" Burch repeated, more forcefully. "Adams!"

315

Wesley Adams remained motionless and quiet in the bottom of the boat. If he heard the lieutenant, he made no indication of it.

A few of the men began talking about where they had been and what they had seen when the torpedo hit.

"I was in the washroom," said one of the men seated on a bench, his broken leg propped up beside him. He had caught it in the rigging as he jumped from the deck of the *Dorchester* into the lifeboat. "Standing there with a toothbrush in my mouth when the floor buckled under me and the lights went out. I don't even remember going on deck. The next thing I knew the ship was going down, and I saw a lifeboat heading for the water." His leg didn't hurt him; it was too cold to feel anything.

"I was in the dining hall playing cards with Baxter and Williams," another said. "Five more minutes and I'd have been in the sack. And I'd have been shed of this thing." He tapped his life jacket with his water-soaked glove.

"I saw those two Danish gals," a third one remembered aloud. "They seemed pretty calm, all things considered. Don't know whatever happened to them. Maybe they're in the other boat."

"Maybe so," another man replied. He was black, one of Morris Jones's kitchen crew. His waterlogged overcoat sleeve was also drenched in blood from a gash he got somehow in the confusion. The bleeding was under control. *At least I'm alive,* he thought. *If you can bleed, you gotta be alive.*

After a minute, the black man spoke up again. "I saw Jones standing on the ship by the captain. He's long gone by now I reckon."

As the shock began to wear off and the men started coming more to their senses, others took their turns trying to express in a few words what they had seen. Soon the group of twenty or so broke up into numerous little knots of conversation, comparing notes and trying to sort out who they knew was alive, who they knew was dead, and who they didn't know about at all.

Listening to the hum of voices, Lieutenant Burch remembered flashes and fragments of what he had seen. Desperate men in the water with no life jackets and no chance. And all those jackets in bunks and lockers below that had been within arm's reach of sleeping men, and even more jackets stowed in the racks below every bunk. He had seen so many faces bobbing on the surface, bobbing for so long and then not coming up any more. His eyes filled with tears as he sat in silence.

He looked down at Adams. That sergeant was one of the toughest buzzards he knew. Nothing seemed to be wrong with him, but he hadn't said a word since he'd been fished out of the water. Adams's complaining would at least have distracted Burch from what was going on all around him, if only for a minute or two.

"Hey, Adams."

Still there was no answer. Burch surveyed the scene on the boat. The other men were stirring now as they continued to talk. They'd been able to rest for a little while and were starting to think a little ahead, checking the stores of food and water, rigging a canvas shelter to keep out the wind and keep in body heat.

O hear us when we cry to thee
For those in peril on the sea. . . .

Wesley Adams fumbled for the pocket of his overcoat. He felt like he was sitting on something. Or maybe one of his life jacket buckles was twisted. Working his gloved hand down through the large, sodden pocket, he felt something tangled in a fold of the lining. His fingers closed around a round metallic object that he couldn't identify by touch alone. He withdrew his hand and slowly opened his icy fingers. In his palm was an elegantly engraved pocket watch. He stared at it intensely for a moment, watching it sparkle in the darkness. He covered it with the other hand, embracing it between his two palms, fingers of the two hands touching, then held them up to his lips, almost the attitude of a man in prayer. Then he slipped the watch back into his coat pocket.

Noticing a movement out of the corner of his eye, Lieutenant Burch turned his head to see Sergeant Adams moving, stretching, and looking around alertly like he had just awakened from a long sleep.

"Adams!"

Adams looked at the lieutenant this time. And then, to Burch's astonishment, he smiled a broad, warm smile. Wordlessly he began making his way through the boat, seeing that the men were as well protected from the wind as possible, helping the injured adjust their positions, and passing hardtack biscuits and water from one survivor to the next.

Some of the men spoke to him. "Hey, Adams, is that *you* in there?" "That don't act like Adams to me." Soon there was even a little good-natured ribbing: "Hey, Florence Nightingale, how about a cigarette over here?" He seemed not to hear them. Though he offered biscuits and water to everyone else and though there was plenty, he did not partake of either. Finishing his rounds, he found a place on one of the benches and took a seat.

The mist was too heavy for the survivors of the *Dorchester* to see the sun when it came up on February 3. But they did see the sky turning from black to charcoal and then to the soft gray of a winter dawn. As the hours passed, Wesley Adams watched the sky change. He hadn't slept—somehow, in spite of the rigors of the night, he didn't feel sleepy—yet it was not because he was disturbed or frightened. He just had so much to think about.

"We're shipping water!" Lieutenant Burch's voice jolted him from his thoughts.

Halfway up the side a little fountain of seawater was spouting into the boat. It had been damaged during its violent launch, though the weakened plank had held until now.

The most able-bodied of the survivors grabbed collapsible canvas bailing buckets and went to work. While others scooped water out of the boat, Wesley Adams held a pail to catch the water spouting in, then took another and held it in place while he emptied the first. Lieutenant Burch could see that there was no way to patch the leak. They could keep up with it, but could they maintain that pace for as long as it took to be rescued?

Concentrating on his work, Wesley Adams thought again of Chaplain Washington. He had no idea what it was, but there was something that told him the chaplain had not preserved his life last night for him to lose it now. Even as water began to collect in the bottom of the boat, he felt perfectly at peace.

The men worked diligently with every bucket they had, but the leak slowly worsened, and the bailers slowly began to fall behind. As other survivors began to wonder if their death had only been postponed a few hours, one of the men gave a shout.

"A ship! A ship! We're saved!"

Rummaging through the supplies on board, Lieutenant Burch found a flare, tied it to an oar, struck it, and waved it aloft. The men held their breaths as they strained to see whether the vessel was headed toward them. A signal light flashed.

"They see us!" a seaman yelled hoarsely. "They see us! They're coming!"

"If we can keep this tub afloat a few more minutes," Corporal Simmons reminded them.

It was the *Comanche,* searching the site around the *Dorchester*'s last known coordinates. By the time the cutter came within hailing distance, the men in the lifeboat were sitting in water halfway up their shins. As the ship came closer, rope ladders and ratlines were hung over the side. A few men climbed slowly up the lines, but many of them were too numb with cold or too badly injured. Seeing their danger, crew members from the *Comanche* began climbing down. Some clambered into the boat to help, and others hauled injured survivors up using the fireman's carry.

Focused entirely now on getting aboard the cutter, the remaining survivors stopped bailing altogether. In a few moments Adams, Burch, and the body of Sergeant Patterson were all that was left. Two coast guardsmen scrambled down the ratlines to help the two last survivors aboard. Burch and Adams exchanged a glance. "Take care of him," the lieutenant told their rescuers, pointing at the body. "We'll make it all right." The survivors each grabbed a ladder and made the slow climb to the deck. By the time the guardsmen got to the ratline with the body, the gunwale of the lifeboat was only a handspan above the water. When they reached the deck, the boat was gone without a trace.

As Sergeant Adams stepped shakily onto the deck, someone wrapped him in a dry blanket. Someone else handed him a steaming mug of coffee.

"Can you walk?" a guardsman asked. He nodded yes. As he headed slowly toward the doorway, he saw stiff, white bodies being laid out all around him. Military casualties were having their dog-tag numbers recorded; other crewmen wrapped the bodies of civilians in olive drab blankets. The guardsman escorted Adams below, out of the weather. Safely inside at last, somebody cut his wet, icy clothes off him and helped him into dry ones. Within the hour he was served a hot meal and taken to a freshly made bunk. He lay his head on the pillow and closed his eyes. In the minute before sleep, he tapped his left shirt pocket, over his heart. He smiled as he felt the round shape of an old Irish pocket watch, then fell softly into the innocent sleep of a child.

The short midwinter day was over by the time the *Comanche* sailed to within sight of the Greenland coast. It was a sight more than six hundred men never lived to see. The cutter docked at the pier alongside the *Escanaba,* which had also been searching for survivors and recovered another lifeboat from the *Dorchester.* A cluster of men and women—a crowd by Blue West One standards—waited to welcome the cutters. Walking off the ship and down the pier, Wesley Adams smiled and nodded at the onlookers as he passed.

The men were broken up into groups of fifty or so and escorted to their quarters. An army major greeted Adams's group and told them they would have time to rest, then would soon find out who the other survivors were. First they would each have a short individual debriefing to record as much information about the U-boat attack as possible while it was still fresh in everyone's mind.

Adams waited for a while in a large anteroom with the rest of his group as one man after another came and went into the adjacent office. But before his turn came, he got up and walked outside. Something he couldn't explain—he could only feel it—drew him to the beach near where he had come ashore from the *Comanche*. Standing there looking out at the water, he lost all track of time.

Watching Adams through his window, Captain Bill Young, U.S. Army Medical Corps, sat waiting for the next soldier to come in for his debriefing. Two minutes passed, then three. He wondered aloud, "Bet a nickel that's my next case."

Grabbing his uniform overcoat and hat from the rack, Captain Young walked out to where the soldier stood beside a huge rock that thrust its way up out of the sand. As he approached, Sergeant Adams heard him and turned.

"Oh, Captain, I was just . . ."

"At ease, soldier," Young interrupted. "You next up to report to the medical officer?"

"Yes, sir."

"Thought so. I saw you through the window and figured we may as well have our little session out here."

Adams smiled.

"Cigarette?" Captain Young offered the pack.

"No thanks." Adams waved it off.

Young shuffled a cigarette for himself and lit it. The two men stood side by side for a moment on the rocks.

"I've seen my share of combat, soldier, but nothing like what I know you've been through. This is a terrible tragedy. However, it will have no effect whatever on the timing or the success of Operation Thunderbolt. We will carry on." Each of the last four words was individually stressed.

Captain Young continued. "But we do want to find out what happened.

"If any good is to come out of this loss, it will be a better understanding of German strategy and ordnance. We understand the Krauts are experimenting with a new type of torpedo. One of the things we want to try to figure out is whether they used one on the *Dorchester.*

"Sergeant, do you remember anything distinctive about the moments immediately after the torpedo hit? Any unusual sensations, unusual smells, distinctive noises, anything like that?"

Wesley Adams remained motionless and mute.

"Soldier," the captain tried again, in a firmer tone, "tell me what happened. What did you see?"

Adams smiled, and his eyes focused on the questioner. He raised his head and squared his shoulders. "What I saw, sir . . ." he spoke in a clear, confident tone but paused for a moment, turning his eyes back to the sea searching for the right words. "What I saw, sir, was the finest, the greatest thing I have ever seen—or hope to see—this side of heaven."

CHAPTER 23

A WISH

IN THE STARLIGHT

Over the next several days, the routine at Blue West One gradually returned to normal. A new runway was under construction, new housing, and, most important of all, the three-story concrete-block building that would be the headquarters and technical nerve center of Operation Thunderbolt. The work had been underway for weeks before the *Dorchester* tragedy. And now a momentum and a sense of urgency restored the pace of activity with little delay. The people there—men and women, military and civilians—well knew the value of their mission.

Even the survivors, after a few days rest, went through their orientation process and began their duties. To many of them, those duties seemed now to be more important and meaningful than before. It was almost as though they felt required to justify their own survival by doing more and working harder than ever.

Of about 245 men rescued alive on the morning of February 3, several died over the course of the next day or two. A few, including Sergeant Patterson, were buried at sea. The rest were laid to rest in small, windswept cemeteries at Narsarssuak and Ivigtut. In the end, 230 of the original 902 passengers aboard the *Dorchester* survived the attack from U-223. Almost all of them were in the lifeboats picked up by the *Comanche* and the *Escanaba*. Five men rescued by one of the cutters survived, insulated from the cold by the fuel oil on the water. Men who had avoided the oil, fearing it would catch fire around them, died of hypothermia, even though one or two of them lived almost a week on dry land. Too soon they joined their comrades-in-arms in the lonely graveyards at Narsarssuak and Ivigtut.

Four days after the *Dorchester* was lost, Sergeant Wesley Adams took up his duties as a member of Operation Thunderbolt. He was an electrician, and he knew he was a good one. Any less good and he'd have busted out of the army years ago. He was assigned to the electrical installation team working on the headquarters building.

Sergeant Adams began by eagerly studying the blueprints for the first section of work he was responsible for. He unrolled the large rectangular sheets, making note of the words "Top Secret" stamped prominently in the corner of every one, and pored over it with a deeply felt sense of urgency—every day, every hour was crucial to the project the *Dorchester* victims had died to serve. The wiring was detailed and intricate, though at first glance there was nothing especially unusual about it. A closer examination, however, revealed a remarkable degree of redundancy. There were not only backup systems, there were backups to the backups.

Another strange thing was a notation on the materials list. Adams was familiar with every size and type of electrical wiring. But one component in the list puzzled him. The size and properties of one particular wire made sense, but not the cryptic notation out to the side: AEC-OT/scw Ag. After thinking about it for a minute, he went on about his work, promising himself he'd unravel the mystery when the installation of the wiring began.

Two days later he was checking his materials inventory when he came across boxes of electrical cable with the mysterious AEC-OT/scw Ag indication. Curious, he broke the seal on one of them and pulled out the cable end. It looked like any other sort of high-quality cable, except that there was a whitish cast to the core of wire inside the thick black layer of insulation.

Pulling a stripping tool from his pocket, Adams stripped a short piece of the insulation away. Instead of the accustomed reddish glow of copper wire, the metal inside was brilliant white. He turned it over in his fingers and held it close to his eyes. There was only one element on earth that conducted electricity more efficiently than copper.

Adams's jaw dropped. He was holding a wire of pure silver.

★ ★ ★ ★

There was no doubt that this job set new standards for quality and reliability, but even if it had been building somebody's garage, Adams would have thrown everything he had into the effort. Being busy and having a routine was comforting to him. As he worked, his thoughts turned constantly to that night on the *Dorchester* when he should have died and Chaplain Washington died in his place.

At all hours of the day he closed his eyes and saw those eyes behind the glasses, kind, confident, and serene. He felt again the panic when he knew the last life jackets had been handed out, the tension in his body when Washington first thrust the jacket over his head, the thousand needles of the icy water, frantic hands hauling him into the lifeboat, the chaplains on the foundering hull, the sound of their voices carrying clear and strong across the water.

> *Eternal Father, strong to save,*
> *Whose arm hath bound the restless*
> *wave, . . .*

"Sergeant Adams." Hearing his name, he snapped back into the present. It was Henry Scott, a middle-aged, pipe-smoking civilian electrical engineer in charge of the installation Adams was working on. He stood at a large table with three or four other electricians. "We're ready to go over this schedule now. No time to waste."

"Right away, Mr. Scott," Adams answered. The sergeant walked briskly to where the other men stood and was soon immersed in the discussion.

Though he had only known him a short time, Scott thought Adams was an exceptional character to have come through the experience of the past. He seemed to have enough energy and enthusiasm for half a dozen people. And he was as fine and capable an electrician as Scott had ever seen.

People who had known the sergeant on board the *Dorchester* scarcely knew what had happened to him. He was notorious as a first-class pain to everyone who had the misfortune to be around him. Though he didn't get to see Adams much any more, Lieutenant Burch, busy day and night with the electronics experts, noticed him whenever their paths crossed at the work site.

Since the two of them had been through so much together, Burch thought at first that it was his perspective that had changed, not Adams's behavior. One day at lunch he asked Tom Eaves what he thought. Tom was a civilian electronics engineer and a survivor of the *Dorchester* who had gone out of his way more than once to avoid the surly, unpleasant sergeant while on board.

"So you see it too then," Lieutenant Burch was saying. "Here's a guy that wasn't worth shooting two weeks ago, and now Scott tells me he's the best electrician he's ever seen."

"Not only that," Eaves laughed, "he's nice all of a sudden. Not just nice, but ready on the spot. Here's a guy who's obviously gone through life with a big chip on his shoulder, who's always thought the world owed him a living. Now he can't wait to help someone else." Eaves shrugged. "What gives?"

"Beats me," the lieutenant replied, smiling and shaking his head. "It's like he traded in his old life for a new one."

Lying in bed at night waiting for sleep, Wesley Adams thought about his old life, about the anger and the loss he had held inside for so long. He thought about how he felt watching from the bottom of the lifeboat as the four chaplains sank beneath the Atlantic swells until only their joined hands were visible, still clasped together in a victory wreath.

He recalled the moment—looking at the empty sea where the *Dorchester* had gone down—that he understood the joy in the chaplains' sacrifice and how they had given themselves for others as Christ had sacrificed himself for them. He felt he was different inside now—not that he had made any conscious effort to change but that a new order of acting and feeling and looking at the world suddenly made sense.

He constantly replayed the scene in his head when Washington took off his life jacket and handed it to him. There was no hesitation. It was like he had loaned Adams a wrench for a minute knowing he'd get it right back. What in a man could produce such valor and confidence and quiet heroism? How could he not be afraid to die?

Why should a chaplain, a man of God, give up his life for a man he hardly knew? Even when it became obvious the chaplains would die, they could have kept their life jackets and jumped into the water to comfort others. Some men were pulled from the water alive, and the chaplains could have been among them. Wesley was desperate to learn more about what made these men so calm and assured in the face of an unfair, violent, agonizing death.

The larger question before him was, what now? He felt different, and he acted differently, but what did that mean for however many years Wesley Adams would be spared to walk on this earth? There was so much he still struggled with.

For what purpose had God spared him?

Sergeant Adams got out of bed, dressed, and walked outside to the edge of the Blue West One compound. It was a little after midnight, about the same hour he had been jolted awake not many nights before by a German torpedo. Adams nodded to the two sentries on perimeter duty in the distance, then stood still on the cold, rocky ground and looked up.

He had never seen so many stars. They looked like a million pin dots shining above him. Maybe it was because the air was so clean and cold in Greenland. Or maybe it was because he'd never really stopped to look at them before.

The questions roiled inside his heart: What has happened to me? What did it mean when Washington said the jacket was mine and not his? Should I not have taken it? Do people like me really go to heaven? Is Madeline there waiting for me?

He hardly knew how to begin sorting it all out. He wondered whether one of those stars up there was Maddie, with their little Margaret beside her. The questions flooded over him. Was God watching him right now? What was God thinking? What was he expecting? Why did he save a misfit with a bad attitude when so many more worthy men were drowned?

In the quiet, cold stillness with those millions of stars shimmering overhead, Wesley Adams's heart burned with questions. *Why am I alive, Lord? Why me and not John Washington, who devoted his life to serving you? Why not George Fox or Clark Poling, who had wives and children and ministries to live for? Why not Alex Goode, who sacrificed his chance to carry on the legacy of his father?*

They deserved to live, not me. What should I do—what can I do—with my life? How can I make a difference in the world the way Washington would have if he had lived and I had died? Oh, I wish I knew. I wish I knew.

Adams dropped to his knees. He couldn't remember the last time he had knelt, or felt like kneeling. "Lord, I don't know what to do with my life. I don't know how to make up for all the years I laughed at you and the people who believed in you. I don't know where all this is headed. Something's happening—I feel it in my gut.

But I can't let go. Help me. Help me know what to do now. That's all I ask. Amen."

Adams rose and scanned the sky again. He looked out over the rocks ahead of him to the dark sea. One enormous boulder towered above the rest, a looming gray slab someone had nicknamed The Rune, after the Viking obelisks that dotted the countryside. It was one of the first sights he remembered seeing when he came ashore from the *Comanche*.

He reached in his overcoat pocket and pulled out the pocket watch he had discovered while he was still in the lifeboat. It was stopped at 1:18, the moment he jumped into the water. When had Washington slipped it into his pocket? It had to be in the short minute between the time Washington gave away his jacket and Adams jumped from the deck of the *Dorchester*. Adams had stolen it from Washington's quarters. Not because he cared anything about the timepiece, but because Washington did, and taking it was a way to get the chaplain riled.

He opened the cover and looked at the dial. "J. Wells & Co., Ltd.," he read. "Dublin." Part of the writing was obscured by condensation and tiny grains of salt and minerals from the seawater. "I gave it back," Adams said softly, watching the old gold case twinkle in the starlight.

Of course it was damaged by the ocean, and Adams wondered for a moment whether he should find a place to get it fixed when he returned stateside. He wanted to take good care of it. But at the same time, there was something deep and precious about keeping the watch just as it was when Washington gave it to him: 1:18, a moment frozen in time. Besides, he couldn't remember whether it worked before or not. For all Adams knew, it might not have run for fifty years.

"He treasured it. Why did he give it to me?"

Then he had a thought. No one in the world loved Chaplain John Washington as much in that moment as Sergeant Wesley Adams. Adams was sure of that. And what better person could there be for Washington to entrust with his most precious possession?

It would forever be a symbol of their bond: a reminder of a life and legacy passed on without remorse or hesitation and of his chance to transform a life of bitterness and dissatisfaction into a journey toward fulfillment, honor, and faith.

Adams looked up at the stars. "Show me, Lord. Lead me. I'm struggling, and I don't understand, but I know I want to keep going." His feet crunching on the frozen gravel, he turned and walked back toward the lights of the barracks, shoulders square, step firm and full of purpose.

CHAPTER 24

EPIPHANY

The war was over—and two later ones as well. Wesley Adams's full head of hair had turned to a gray thatch. Music drifted now from the old Arctic Hotel across the rocky beach to where he stood in the steady sea breeze. As he looked intently along the shore, the images of the four chaplains appeared closer. They seemed to be moving toward him at a moderate pace, talking and smiling, their movements animated and assured.

"Poppy?" His grandson was beside him again. He had been in the hotel only a minute or two. "Mr. Taylor says you're missing all the fun. He told me to tell you to get your tail in here!" Alex giggled as he finished the sentence.

"Oh yeah?" Adams said, a wide grin crossing his face. "Well, in that case I guess I better." As he talked, he kept his gaze on the image of the chaplains.

"Poppy?"

"Yes, Alex?"

"Who are those men?"

Adams looked down at the boy. Alex was wide-eyed with excitement. Of the four figures that seemed to be walking toward them, the one that reminded Adams of Chaplain Goode waved in their direction. Alex waved back with one hand, and with the other arm gripped Adams tightly around the waist.

Adams pulled the old watch from his pocket and held it in his open palm. Alex took it in both of his hands, feeling the smoothness and the weight of it. The boy looked back up at the four figures, now no more than fifty yards away. He handed the watch back to his grandfather, who returned it to his pocket. As Alex turned, he could see the outline of The Rune not far from where he was standing.

The old soldier and the boy stood there, Alex's arm around his grandfather's waist, and his grandfather's hand resting on his shoulder. The same sea breeze that blew Alex's hair, and that Wesley Adams felt on his face, rippled the chaplains' clothes as they walked.

By now, the four men were continuing up the beach and into the deepening twilight, toward the early evening starts.

"We can go now, Poppy," the boy said simply.

It was a moment before Adams could speak. "Yes, Alex. Yes we can.

"For a man to lay down his life for his friends is the greatest love he can give. And this is the finest thing you and I will ever see, this side of heaven."

Their arms still around each other, Wesley and Alex turned and walked together toward the music and the light.

Day is done, gone the sun,
From the hills, from the lake,
From the sky.
All is well, safely rest,
God is nigh.

Fades the light; And afar
Goeth day, And the stars
Shineth bright,
Fare thee well; Day has gone,
Night is on.

Thanks and praise, For our days,
'Neith the sun, Neath the stars,
'Neath the sky,
As we go, This we know,
God is nigh.

"Taps"
Military Bugle Call

AFTERWORDS

I remember it well. Sunday morning sunlight streamed through the stained glass windows and was transformed into hundreds of colored rays that fell upon the chancel of the sanctuary where the minister was preaching from the pulpit. His face was textured by the many hues as he moved dramatically, telling the story of the four chaplains of the *U.S.A.T. Dorchester.*

". . . and as Fox, Washington, Goode, and Poling urgently scrambled to get the few men left on the *Dorchester* over the edge into the water, they turned and suddenly discovered four men who had no life jackets. Without asking, "Are you Methodist, Jewish, Catholic, or Baptist?" they yanked off their own life jackets and put them on the four who had none.

The words etched a vivid picture in my mind. I knew the story by heart, and probably could have told it myself, though not the way the Rev. Dr. Wales E. Smith held the congregation spellbound with his excellent, powerful, from-the-heart sermons. He loved his congregation without condition, always the good shepherd, seeking out the lost sheep, even in the middle of the night until he or she was found and safe in God's care. Now, he was telling his flock his favorite story. You could unfailingly count on his sermons being very topical, relevant, answering a need, biblically based, meaningful, and having a specific point. Actually, three points. That's the *Yale* way.

Dr. Smith's admiration for the World War II story was very much rooted in his Yale connection. You see, Dr. Smith and Rev. Clark Poling, the Dutch Reformed Church chaplain on the *Dorchester,* were close friends and classmates at Yale Divinity School in New Haven, Connecticut! Rev. Poling was in the second-year class of 1936, and Dr. Smith was a senior and president of the class of 1935. Both men were keen students who learned well from great teachers and preachers, and who encouraged and promoted active fellowship among all their classmates. This openness was at the heart of their strong beliefs, and they practiced this spirit everywhere.

Dr. Smith looked directly into the eyes of his congregation . . . "As rapidly rising frigid waters swirled around their legs, the four chaplains locked their arms tightly around each other and prayed strongly and passionately to God."

The minister's moist eyes were now looking at me, with a deep commitment that only a father can share

340

with his son. "Greater love hath no man than this, that a man lay down his life for his friends." This was my own father speaking directly to my heart and soul: "Tell this story well, Ken, so that it will never be forgotten," he pleaded, "so their sacrifice will be remembered and cherished, forever!"

"I will, Dad. I will!"

—Ken Wales

After December 7, 1941, everyone in the United States would always be able to tell others where they were and what they were doing on that Sunday when Pearl Harbor was bombed.

Our family had just come home from church in El Paso, Texas, and within an hour we were glued to the radio for the latest reports. In many cities newspaper extras were on the streets with newsboys shouting the headlines: "Japanese Bomb Pearl Harbor!" For old and young it was a scary day. Later that evening radio broadcasts confirmed that nine major ships were sunk, Hickham Field was out of commission with most aircraft destroyed or disabled, and martial law was enforced in Honolulu. This surprise attack really knocked out the Pacific fleet in Hawaii, sending a shudder throughout North America.

El Paso was filled with military veterans, proud of the city's history and confident of its role in an hour of crisis. Home of the famous First Cavalry, it was an ideal training center for combat troops located at massive Fort Bliss with a million acres of protected land.

In our city military police seemed to be everywhere. Access to the bases was no longer casual or automatic. Patrols constantly circled the military installation, and scientists were rumored to be testing rockets in New Mexico.

As the war became increasingly worldwide, my family had participants everywhere. My clergy uncles, Dan Poling and Charles S. Poling who served in World War I, enlisted again as chaplains. This time Charles was in England at an air force base, while Dan, now war correspondent as well as chaplain, toured every combat theater from Australia to China to North Africa.

Dan served under direct orders of President Roosevelt, who asked him to pursue high-level meetings with world leaders such as Winston Churchill in Great Britain and Chiang Kai-shek in China. He also had conferences with top military commanders: General Douglas MacArthur, General Dwight D. Eisenhower, and General George S. Patton.

Dan Poling's second son, Clark, entered the chaplaincy in 1942. His life had been filled with leadership and popularity and enormous promise. The notice of his death aboard the *Dorchester* had a terrible impact on our El Paso family.

After his first two years at Hope College, Holland, Michigan, Clark moved to Rutgers University in New Brunswick, New Jersey, just twenty minutes from our home then in Bound Brook. While he spent his junior year in a dormitory, weekends were in Bound Brook, and by his senior year he moved in with us, his upstairs bedroom being next to mine. He became like an older brother to Charles and me.

I had come home from my afternoon *El Paso Herald Post* paper route and found my parents and my brother standing in the dining room. Dad's face was ashen, and Mother's eyes were glistening with tears. Charles was pacing in front of the French doors that opened to the backyard. Dad nodded to me and said, "Clark is missing in action."

"Where?" I asked.

"Somewhere in the North Atlantic," replied my father.

Several weeks later Dan Poling called long distance to tell us that Clark was now "lost in action." He was on the *U.S.A.T. Dorcester.*

When Rabbi Goode was a youngster in Washington, D.C., he walked over to Arlington Cemetery on

Armistice Day, 1921, to pay tribute with thousands of others to the Unknown Soldier, whose tomb was being honored by national leaders and reverent tributes. And on that hillside rest, he would have seen the inscription in Latin above the portal to the amphitheater, which read,

IT IS SWEET AND SEEMLY TO DIE
FOR ONE'S COUNTRY.

Alex Goode was late for supper that night. When his rabbi father asked what happened, he said he had walked to Arlington, not riding his bike or taking the trolley out of respect for the honored dead. Arlington and America and Alex seemed to merge as a single spirit, a living ideal rising within his soul, blending reverence with purpose and dedication. In school he had read Walt Whitman's poem, then committed it to memory.

When lilacs last in the dooryard
 bloom'd,
And the great star early droop'd in the
 western sky in the night,
I mourn'd, and yet shall mourn
 with ever-returning spring.
 —*Leaves of Grass*, 140

Of the four chaplains, Rabbi Goode was the most determined in writing and speaking out against Nazi atrocities. In York, Pennsylvania, he spoke to community groups, service clubs, student organizations, and friends at the YMCA about the imperative of supporting a dynamic democracy and maintaining the vitality of a truly free country. When local groups created Bundles for Britain, he was front and center. He gave radio broadcasts spelling out the German threat and the plight of the Jews and other minority groups on the continent.

However, this prewar period leading up to Pearl Harbor revealed a sharply divided nation, since so many people of every political and religious persuasion were determined to stay out of "Europe's War." Millions opposed President Roosevelt's policy of arming England through eight billion dollars of credit in American banks and lending them fifty destroyers for the Battle of the Atlantic. Critics would call it "Roosevelt's War."

Distinguished and popular Americans like Charles A. Lindbergh, the first pilot to fly across the Atlantic nonstop, led the America First Party by flooding the newspapers and airways with assertions that Hitler and Company were simply reformers trying to tidy up their national boundaries and restore the health of the German economy.

Members of Christian churches heard their respected leaders denounce preparations for war. Many of them had sharp memories of the bloodbath and horror of World War I, and they were not about to see that repeated with their children. At the urging of peace groups, young people signed pacifist pledges not to bear arms or have anything to do with military indoctrination. Other activists within the labor movement and on college campuses believed that

Hitler should be engaged and restrained by nonviolent tactics such as employed by Mahatma Gandhi in India and, much later, by Martin Luther King Jr. in this country.

Not only Colonel Lindbergh but also some of our most famous clergy rejected President Roosevelt's warnings of the German menace as purely propaganda. Harry Emerson Fosdick of Riverside Church in New York City, Charles Clayton Morrison with the influential *Christian Century,* and Norman Thomas, Socialist presidential candidate regarded as the most skilled debater in the land, persuaded millions to stay aloof from all foreign conflicts.

In a Sunday morning bombing, the Japanese changed that debate into determination, unifying America.

★ ★ ★ ★

One unresolved issue would confront the four chaplains as well as all chaplains who ever served in the armed forces of the United States. That controversy began more than a century ago in the form of these questions.

How can a minister serve God and take his salary from the government?

How can the clergy in uniform freely preach the Word of God and not be compromised by the military commander?

How can chaplains maintain the separation of church and state? By taking income and orders has not Caesar become their God?

Many critics of military chaplains resented their uniform, suggesting that local clergy in civilian attire could minister to nearby bases. Others resisted the chaplains' officer rank, the privileges and status that inevitably followed. The alignment of pastors in uniform grouped with flags and troops marching with weapons caused anger and resentment in every war you can mention. Vietnam demonstrations brought a youthful resistance to the draft and conscription with constant criticism of President Lyndon Johnson and the military establishment. The chaplains did not escape this rebuke. Not surprisingly, the post-Vietnam era put the four chaplains' story on a shelf in cold storage.

Throughout the years following, I spoke at Civitan meetings retelling the story of the four chaplains. The American Legion, the Veterans of Foreign Wars, the Fraternal Order of Eagles, and active military chaplains also made the story a part of the theme for their annual conventions and assemblies. The Chapel of Four Chaplains was unwavering in its yearly celebration. Within the mainline media community, Robert Schuller's *Hour of Power* remembered the chaplains every year.

When George Cornell of Associated Press was preparing a column in 1993 for the fiftieth anniversary of the *Dorchester* event, he called me to ask some specific questions regarding the four chaplains.

He quoted again John 15:13, seeing how clearly the chaplains embraced it. When the story appeared, I received calls, letters, and remembrances from all over the country including my classmates from Yale Divinity School. One was a personal call from film producer Ken Wales, who had read Cornell's piece in the *Los Angeles Times*. As we became acquainted, a plan unfolded for a book to be developed and possibly a motion picture. It seemed that a new generation was ready for the story.

—David Poling

ACKNOWLEDGMENTS

Ever since I can remember, I have always loved stories. Stories of every kind filled my imagination and wonderful tales created dreams in my mind, transporting me to far and unreachable places. As a filmmaker, I am keenly aware of the priceless value of the team that is gathered to create a film. It may appear to a quick eye that a book is accomplished by someone who simply jots down a few thoughts—perhaps thousands of thoughts—sends the notes and pages to the printer, and *voila!* a book appears. Not quite. *Sea of Glory* has been a call, a challenge, an obsession, many discoveries, frequent frustration, welcome relief, a marathon of perseverance, and ultimately, exhilaration. But most importantly, it is a true joy and sacred honor to share this powerful and compelling story with you.

The task of researching such a broad canvas as World War II is more than daunting. Where does one begin? What is "the scope"? What about differing "factual" accounts? And what is the deeper meaning of it all? These are but a few of the hazards in dealing with historical topics. But even with all this, and more, it is worth every challenge.

I do believe that God creates special people for extraordinary moments and equips them with unique talent and abilities. I feel blessed that this team contributed so tirelessly and selflessly to what you have read.

I am very grateful to one of the most creative persons I have ever known, John Perry . . . a renaissance man, classical pianist, excellent singer, and dedicated writer. John's superb talent is at the heart and center of this story. He enabled it to be told in the best manner possible. His overflowing cache of remarkable abilities is something to behold.

An editor is often thought of as "someone who takes things out." What perfect joy to have an editor who not only "rearranges words and things" but who is also a master of adding just the right concept or phrase. That treasure is Len Goss. Throughout the long endeavor of birthing this book, Len was steadfast in our friendship, knowing just when to give encouraging validation, and when to hold firm to an honest critique.

The text, order, and design of a book are crucial to the pleasure, ease, and enlightenment of the reading experience, and I wish to thank John Landers for his expertise in fashioning this novel.

Ken Stephens, President of Broadman & Holman, knew the story to be told would be inspiring to so many, and was willing to go "extra miles" to see it happen. Ken has exceptional foresight and wisdom and can perceive what others may miss.

My journey into novel writing has been along a path lighted by a special friend, David Shepherd. David always delivers sage advice after listening carefully to what has been said or proposed. God has given him a great gift of being fair and compassionate.

All the fine editorial work is maximized through the splendid efforts of John Thompson, who directs the marketing. John's rich experience has given innovative plans a fresh approach so the books will reach the largest number of readers possible.

The dazzling *Sea of Glory* dust jacket is a winner, and the excellent work of Paul Mikos and his group, who intuitively caught just the right symmetry, color, and balance for the cover. This is what readers see and respond to at first glance, so please accept my heartfelt appreciation for your creativity.

. . . To Jennifer Willingham, whose innovative marketing ideas are quite extraordinary and effective; Kenny Holcomb, for exciting layout and design; Heather Hulse, Robin Patterson, and Elizabeth Randle, whose publicity work will "tell the world"; Kim Overcash, who truly keeps everything going well; Judi Hayes, copy editor who read and reread every word so carefully; and Janis Whipple, who joined the effort in the final days and helped bring the project through on time.

. . . To Harold King, kind friend and visionary, who brought *Christy* to Broadman & Holman for videos, and who first listened to *Sea of Glory* and caught a vision for a book.

. . . Bucky Rosenbaum, a former book executive at B&H, who did not give up on this project through delays and struggles. He always felt God was in charge.

. . . To Matt Jacobson, who loved "the deep, inspirational nature" of the story and did not rest until the agreement was concluded.

All of the Armed Service Chaplaincies—Army, Navy, Air Force, and Marine Corps—have outstanding leaders. Chaplain (Maj. Gen.) Donald Shea, who recently served five years as Chief of Chaplains, U.S. Army, was most encouraging and helpful in providing assistance in researching Army libraries and files. The current Chief of Chaplains, U.S. Army, Chaplain (Maj. Gen.) Gaylord T. Gunhus continues to provide fine leadership and innovation and to sustain the military tradition.

I am in awe of the superb, dedicated work being accomplished by the U.S. Army Chaplains Center and School at Fort Jackson, Columbia, South Carolina, where clergy of all denominations are being prepared to minister to military personnel and their families. These men and women officers go through the same physical training as other soldiers, are educated in the military traditions and discipline, and are committed to bringing spiritual guidance and comfort to the armed services, whether in times of peace or on the battlefield. Chaplains are particularly vulnerable in arenas of battle since they do not carry weapons and are accompanied by a soldier only where possible.

Chaplain (Col.) George Pejacovich, former Commandant of the Center and School, welcomed our project. Our time together was a highlight of this research.

Renee Klish, former director of the Museum at the Center, and now at the Center for U.S. Military History in Washington, D.C., was invaluable in masterminding the research at both institutions, the Library of Congress, and the National Archives. Renee's historical intuition often led to fascinating discoveries.

I am very grateful to Marcia McManus, director of the Museum, for the official photos of the four chaplains and for other valuable information so graciously shared. Nella Hobson, Director of Public Affairs at the Center, has always found the right answer and offered new ideas with a cheerful spirit.

Capt. Lee Reynolds, Public Affairs Officer at the Center, was unique in his ability to relate facts with the surrounding material to tell a good story. Lee sensed what we were looking for, placed it in perfect context, and located the references. He is also a talented actor.

Stan Brewer became voraciously intrigued by the *Dorchester* event. He searched out every related Web site, doggedly visited naval museums, became obsessed and expert on matters relating to the incident, and initiated use of the *Dorchester* pictures and blueprints.

Throughout the early days of this adventure, I was guided by Lt. Col. Archie Roberts. Archie's kind and compassionate friendships with the survivors of the *Dorchester* and their families brought comfort and reassurance to those who had been through times of peril and distress. His keeping in touch, sharing time with them, and annual reunion breakfasts were highlights of their lives.

The Chapel of Four Chaplains in Philadelphia is a special organization with a solid obligation to see that all people are made aware of this great American example of self-sacrifice. The chapel is the cutting edge in the move toward true brotherhood. The chairman, Dante Mattioni, has given years of dedicated service to lead in the work of the chapel.

I am grateful to the staff of the chapel who have over the years given of their time, energy, and assistance in preparing the material. Kim Pierce, invaluable as Executive Director, is a prime example of the spirit of the organization.

My heart was indeed warmed when I shared a day with Navy Chaplain (Rear Adm.) Aaron Landis (ret.). Rabbi Landis invited me to his town outside Philadelphia where he pastors a well-known synagogue designed by Frank Lloyd Wright. Being with Aaron in this beautiful place of worship was truly a divine moment.

The Immortal Chaplains Foundation, Minneapolis, Minnesota, was founded by David Fox, nephew of *Dorchester* Chaplain George Fox. This organization awards a prize each year to "a person who has shown extraordinary efforts to serve humanity." David has worked diligently to preserve the legacy of the four chaplains on the *Dorchester* and his family's relationship to Chaplain Fox. He has a strong passion for the noble values and principles in the story and is a documentary filmmaker. David, thank you from my heart for your passion for the triumph of goodness.

I owe much to Father John Gaeney, who served for many years with Paulist Productions. John has been a steadfast encourager from the beginning and arranged for me to research valuable archive materials at the Naval Yard in Washington, D.C.

Our nation is blessed to have Dr. Lloyd Ogilvie, an extraordinary minister, serving as Chaplain of the United States Senate. Dr. Ogilvie has long honored the legacy of the four chaplains and knows many of the persons and families associated with them. *Sea of Glory* could not be what it is, or what it will yet become, without his prayerful counsel.

Having known Dr. Ogilvie for many years during his pastorate of Hollywood Presbyterian Church, and listened with rapture to his soul-reaching sermons, I treasure our many times together, especially with our heads bowed in prayer. He is indeed "a man of God."

Quentin Schultze is a professor, technology guru, pioneer of the Internet, fellow amateur radio operator, renaissance man, and friend extraordinaire who always knows exactly when I need a phone call, just to talk. Thank you, Quin and Barbara.

I am indebted to a gifted writer and friend, Dean McClure, whose steadfastness and words of encouragement have often brought me from the depths, only to soar even higher.

Sea of Glory is truly possible because of the love of my mother, Clara Smith, whose rich appreciation of history, arts, music, and writing enabled me to fulfill my dreams. She is indeed my mentor, and her passion for teaching continues to bring letters of testimony from her students whose lives were transformed while in her classroom.

Grateful thanks also to my sister, Joanna McGinn, whose enjoyment of reading is matched only by her dedication to a life of compassionate teaching.

Many good thoughts about life and God's promises have been written about in books by Susan Wales, my wife. The books are evocative, inspiring, and helpful. They invite reflection. And she will write more. I wish her well.

I am very grateful to my coauthor David Poling, whose lifelong dedication as a minister has seen him write books, preach wonderful sermons, and maintain a long line of Polings in the ministry. David's literary insights heightened our work. It is an honor to have labored with him in our efforts to tell this story about four men of God who gave up their lives so that others might live.

It is a great joy to share our vision with you!

—Ken Wales

ACKNOWLEDGMENTS

My initiative in this book owes its start and completion to the support of the Poling family. My wife Ann has been advisor on strategy, reviewer of topics and content, relentless fact checker. Her Reid heritage taught directness and candor. Such qualities were described by Stephen Tennant when he remembered Willa Cather: "She loved faithfulness. It was her preferred climate . . . Loyalty, fine character, solidarity, or honesty—these formed the cornerstones of her spiritual edifice."

Our grown and married young people, John David, Lesley Poling-Kempes, Andrew Paul, and Charles Cupp have trailed the four chaplains with stories from grandparents, uncles and aunts, and cousins, anticipating the appearance of this book. My clergy brothers, Charles Earle Poling and John Clark Poling, have offered serious and unduplicated suggestions and reminders. Charles, our older brother, brings both family history and military experience as a retired navy chaplain himself.

Chaplain Clark V. Poling's married children Clark V. Poling II and Susan Poling Smith; his brother, Daniel K. Poling; his sisters Mary Poling Wood and Treva Poling Roy claim the same spiritual heritage that flourished for him.

Older cousins of my youth belong here: Bob Poling, a Marine language specialist in World War II, and Barbara Wood Tyler, whose mother, Mabel Poling Wood cared so often for young Clark Poling.

Among the survivors, Navy gunner Willie F. Strickland and his daughter Tamara Strickland Boss gave unselfishly of their time.

—David Poling